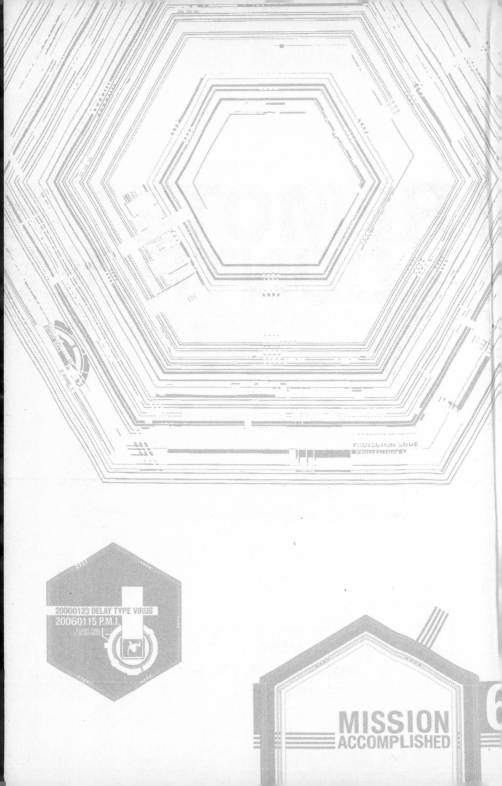

REMOTE CONTROL

Jack Heath

Scholastic Press
New York

PROLOGUE

PROLOGUE

Awake.

The girl's eyes opened. Inky pupils dilated, absorbing the tiniest echoes of light from the fragmented darkness of the room. In the temporary absence of a conscious mind, instinct dug its claws into her brain, and every muscle in her body tensed.

She rolled quickly off the steel table on which she had been lying, and landed with an undignified thump on the gritty concrete floor. The scrabbling of her long nails against the cold, rough surface echoed around the cavernous room.

Darkness.

Cold.

Fear.

She rose to all fours, her eyes straining against the unfamiliar blackness. Her naked skin erupted into goose bumps in the slight draft.

Fragmented memories slashed at her mind, more felt than seen. Pounding footsteps, smashing windows. Dozens of giants scooping her up, examining her with glowing orange eyes. She felt painfully alert, yet weak, as if she had been asleep for many years, or as if she had just been born.

Slowly the room came into dim focus. There was the table she had woken upon, there was the concrete beneath her bare knees, and there were the grimy brick walls. There was a tickling on her back, like the crawling of spindly spiders. She whirled around and grabbed a tuft of her waist-length brown hair in a slender fist. She continued scanning the room, storing visual data in an otherwise empty brain. There was a heavy metal door with

THE CARGO

The truck roared through the warehouse, narrowly avoiding a stack of crates.

The smugglers glanced sharply towards it. After a moment's hesitation, they abandoned their work. Drivers climbed out of trucks and cranes. Loaders pulled their carts to a halt. Guards raised their weapons. And suddenly everyone was running towards the runaway truck, guns first. Hundreds of bullet dents appeared in the door of the cabin. Sparks blossomed off the walls from the shots that missed, and off the aluminum frames of the crates. A halogen lamp fizzed out in the opposite corner of the warehouse.

From his hiding place behind a nearby crane, Agent Six of Hearts couldn't see Kyntak at the wheel of the truck. He hoped he was keeping his head down.

The truck broke through the row of guards and kept going, screaming towards the giant warehouse door. The armed soldiers running after it hung back for a moment, expecting it to swerve.

It didn't.

Boom! The walls shook and the door buckled outward, twisting its slides out of line. Silence fell as the last cartridges hit the floor and the echoes died away. The smugglers crept silently towards the motionless truck, guns steady.

One of them, apparently the group's commander, put his hand on the door handle of the half-crushed cabin. He motioned to the others, who slipped into firing stances and locked their crosshairs on the door. The leader stepped aside, pulling the door wide open.

There was a tense pause as the smugglers realized their quarry was no longer inside the cabin. They edged closer. Then they heard a beeping sound.

There was a shoebox-size lump of plastic on the seat, with a glowing LED display attached with red wires. It read STATUS: ARMED.

"That's five hundred grams of Semtex A," Agent Six called out from behind them as he approached.

They whirled to face him, and a flurry of clicking filled the warehouse as the guns were cocked again. "That means more than four hundred seventy grams of Penthrite," Six continued. "Enough to vaporize everyone in this warehouse."

He waved the detonator in his right hand. A green light blinked ominously on it. "If I release this button, the bomb goes off. If I hit the disarm switch, it doesn't."

The smugglers stared at him in absolute silence. Their guns didn't waver.

"I'll make this simple," Six said, uncomfortably aware of the number of guns trained on him. "Drop your weapons and put your hands on your heads. Deck agents will come in and handcuff you. Then I'll disarm the bomb."

No one moved. "Your alternatives include shooting me and getting blown up," Six continued, "trying to disarm the bomb from inside the truck and getting blown up, or running for the door, realizing it won't open, and then getting blown up."

A few of the smugglers glanced at the door, which did look too twisted to open.

"You have ten seconds," Six said. "Nine."

Still no one moved.

"Eight," Six continued.

As if a telepathic command had been issued, they all lunged forward at once. Six was suddenly faced with a hundred furious smugglers, charging at him like a herd of rhinoceroses.

They've called my bluff, thought Six. *Kyntak's fake bomb obviously wasn't convincing enough. Lucky I have a plan B.*

Run.

The concrete flashed past under his feet as a lone bullet sparked off a crate next to him — he hoped the cargo inside wasn't harmed. He ducked and weaved in and out of the stacks of crates, with the smugglers thundering hot on his heels.

Mid-step, Six dropped backward onto his side and slid under the base of a towering yellow crane. Scrambling to his feet on the other side, he kept running.

Too late, he realized that he was trapped. There were now two trucks parked nose-to-nose in his path. Someone had moved them since he'd last come through here.

The smugglers had elected to go around the crane rather than underneath it. They were coming into view behind him. A bullet pinged off one of the trucks, and Six ducked to avoid the ricochet.

Six drew his Phoenix SK909 and aimed it at the passenger-side window of the truck on the right. He pulled the trigger, and cracks latticed over the shatterproof glass. He took a deep breath, ran, and jumped.

His arms, head, and shoulders penetrated the glass like a fist through rice paper. Before he'd even touched the seats inside he was firing again, shredding the window on the driver's side. In mid-flight, he reached forward and grabbed the window frame for balance, then catapulted his torso through to the other side.

The smugglers didn't attempt to copy his maneuver. They ran past the trucks, looking for another way around. Six paused for a moment to give them time to catch up. This plan wouldn't work if they lost sight of him and decided to find a different exit.

A shot whistled by overhead. *Guess they know where I am,* he thought. He picked up the pace again, keeping his head low.

Ahead was the door marked EXIT. Six burst through it and kept running, finding himself in a perfectly straight hallway about forty meters long and three meters wide, with no doors or windows except for the door he'd entered through and a similar one at the opposite end. The walls were concrete, the floor was linoleum. A sign on the wall to his left read FIRE EXIT→.

All according to plan, Six thought. He kept running.

Behind him he heard the first of the smugglers hit the door, and it burst open again, swinging wildly on its hinges and slamming into the wall.

The wall crumbled slightly in the impact, revealing that it was plaster, not concrete. But the smugglers streaming through the doorway didn't notice. All they saw was the boy up ahead, dashing towards the door at the other end of the corridor.

They charged. Some leveled their guns again.

Six was nearly at the end of the corridor now. He saw the plaster around the doorway splinter in a hail of bullets, exposing the steel underneath. He lunged forward and grabbed the door handle, wrenched the door open, and dived through, slamming it shut behind him.

The first of the smugglers reached the door, pulled it open, and tried to run through — but he crashed into a metal wall. Falling over backward and clutching his broken nose, he saw that the door didn't lead outside at all. It didn't lead anywhere. A steel barrier had slid across the door frame, blocking off the exit. The smuggler cried out as the others trampled him when they too charged into the solid doorway. Soon he was buried under a pile of people.

The last smuggler had just run through the door leading into the corridor when something slammed shut behind him. He whirled around and saw that the door itself hadn't closed, but the door frame was no longer empty. A slab of metal, identical to the one at the other end, was blocking the exit.

Outside the corridor, Kyntak looked at Six. "May I do the honors?" he asked.

"Go ahead," Six said.

A voice boomed through the corridor from an unseen PA system.

"The doors and walls are steel, bonded with tungsten. I doubt you'll do much damage with your bare hands or your weapons."

The smugglers looked around, searching for the source of the voice.

"You are all under arrest for possession of contraband."

There was a pause.

"Ha-ha."

Kyntak parked the truck with the trapped criminals inside next to the crumpled front door of the warehouse, while Six pried open some of the crates.

The first one had five children in it, all between seven and ten years old. The multiple needle marks in their arms suggested that they could have been in this drug-induced sleep for some time, and Six could see their bones through their skin. They probably hadn't been fed in days.

He looked away, feeling sick. It wasn't the sight of these kids as much as the knowledge that he'd find the same thing in every crate he opened. This warehouse held hundreds of children, stuffed inside packing crates like food or furniture.

Child-smuggling was happening more and more these days — presumably some new sector of ChaoSonic was buying up big. The giant corporation had all sorts of uses for children, from black-market adoptions to slave labor, but Six had a feeling he knew what had caused this sudden boom. Eight months ago, he had broken into the headquarters of the Lab, ChaoSonic's primary biological weapons research division, to rescue captured Deck agents. He and Kyntak had destroyed the facility and plucked the Lab's latest human weapon from the flames: a genetically engineered baby girl — their sister. The collapse of the Lab had crippled ChaoSonic's bioweapons work for a while, but Six knew that they would find another division to fill the vacuum. And now someone was purchasing thousands of children. Six figured that the increased demand was caused by the need for test subjects.

Saving these kids would slow ChaoSonic down, he knew. But it wouldn't stop them.

Six had opened all the crates. She wasn't here. It had been six months since soldiers had invaded Kyntak's house and abducted the baby girl, and each day made it less likely that they would find her. By now she was probably either dead or a prisoner of whoever had devised the abduction.

"No sign of Nai?" Kyntak asked as he approached, carrying a large yellow box.

"No," Six replied.

Kyntak clapped a hand on Six's shoulder. "There are plenty more places to look. We'll find her."

Six didn't respond. The fact that there were plenty more places to look didn't reassure him. The City was 7.5 million square kilometers, and Nai could be anywhere in it. He began walking back to the truck as Kyntak opened the box, exposing fruit bars, chocolate biscuits, and water bottles, which he distributed to the dazed children emerging from the crates.

"When will the shelter vans arrive?" he asked.

"About twenty minutes," Six called over his shoulder. There was a small organization operating under ChaoSonic's radar which found homes for orphaned or abandoned children — he had called them already. They would provide housing for the kids until homes could be found for them.

"Job well done," Kyntak said as he walked back towards the truck. "I should promote myself."

"The other agents don't know you're one of the Jokers," Six pointed out. "It'd be suspicious. And all you did was drive a truck into a door and park another one in front of an exit."

"All you did was run." Kyntak opened the passenger door. "All you *ever* do is run."

The yelling and cursing of smugglers from inside the artificial corridor interrupted them. Kyntak picked up the microphone.

"This is your captain speaking," he said. "We'll be cruising at an altitude of one meter and having a brief stopover at a roadside merchant so I can have a sandwich before we reach our eventual destination — prison.

"You will be traveling in a twenty-four-wheel ChaoSonic

Roamer truck — it is thirty-eight meters long with a three-meter cabin, three meters wide, and two meters high plus one-meter wheels. It weighs about seventeen metric tons. As we have around a hundred passengers today, excluding myself and my lovely crew . . ."

He winked cheekily at Six.

"Copilot," Six hissed.

"I calculate that you each get just over one square meter of floor space for your journey. Have a pleasant trip."

The yelling and cursing increased in volume.

THE CATALYST

Six stepped into the lobby of the Deck, crossing the glittering floor under the artificial stars. Kyntak had driven the truck around to the Visitor's Center — a concrete ramp down to a tunnel which led to a labyrinth of cells under the Deck.

The foyer was humming with activity. Men and women were comparing notes on suspects and organizations, and even those who were alone were talking on mobile phones. The Hearts agents all acknowledged Six with silent glances. When he'd rescued them from the Lab, he'd been forced to reveal his origins — they now knew that he was a super-soldier, genetically engineered by ChaoSonic in Project Falcon.

Some still approached Six with gushing gratitude for saving their lives. He never knew how to respond to that; there were only so many times he could say "you're welcome" or "anytime" before he felt awkward and lapsed into silence. Others treated Six with quiet resentment, maybe because he'd never told them what he was, or perhaps because he was a better agent than they could ever be. But most of the glances directed at him across the lobby were halfway between respect and fear. Respect because he was stronger, faster, and smarter than them; fear for the same reasons.

Six had liked it better when all the other agents had dismissed him as a jerk. The worst he'd had to suffer then was their basic courtesy. Now all the Hearts knew his secret. And he was fast becoming a symbol of the ongoing fight against ChaoSonic's stranglehold on the City.

Six supposed that many of the other Deck agents would feel honored by such a reputation, but he didn't like it at all. In his experience, the more people who knew about him, the more who wanted to kill him. ChaoSonic was a double threat to Six; they would study him and experiment on him for being one of the Lab's creations, and they would execute him for being a Deck agent. But the danger which scared Six the most was the one closest to him — the Spades.

The Deck was divided into four sections: the Hearts, who did the fieldwork; the Diamonds, who managed research and design; the Clubs, who trained new recruits; and the Spades, who

monitored the rest of the Deck, watching it for signs of corruption. Six knew that the Spades wouldn't take kindly to him if they ever learned of his origins. He would be seen as nothing more than a weapon of ChaoSonic, and would probably be "shuffled" — locked up in the Deck's cells alongside the hundreds of Code-breakers he had caught. The King of Hearts would probably suffer the same fate. He had been protecting Six for sixteen years.

The irony wasn't lost on Six. He and his colleagues at the Deck had dedicated years of their lives to resurrecting the world of pre-Takeover times, protecting its values and enforcing its laws. But while the present-day City seemed to have no place for him, in the lost world of pre-Takeover times, things would be far worse. He would be considered a scientific monstrosity.

But he didn't think he was in any immediate danger. ChaoSonic didn't know who he was, or where he was — Kyntak had wiped the Lab computers clean eight months ago, erasing their records of Six's DNA and the hidden location of the Deck. Methryn Crexe, the director of the Lab, was safely shuffled so ChaoSonic couldn't get to him. While ChaoSonic probably suspected Deck involvement in the collapse of the Lab, they would never know for sure. And excluding monitoring of e-mails and phone calls, the Spades relied mainly on the two Jokers for their intel, so Six was relatively safe. Neither Kyntak nor Grysat, the other Joker, would turn him in.

As usual, Grysat was sitting behind the reception desk, fiddling with his cuffs as he watched the agents come and go.

"How'd the mission go, Six?" he asked cheerfully.

"Well, thank you." Six looked at his watch. It was 07:49:13. "Buzz me in, please."

Grysat complied.

The elevator doors slid open, revealing polished mirrors gleaming in the incandescent lighting. Agent Two was standing in it, leaning on the aluminum handrail.

Six had been rude to Agent Two from the day he joined the Deck to the day Two was kidnapped by the Lab. Six had been rude to everybody. It was nothing personal. But Two had never held it against him.

"Hey, Six," he said. "Successful mission?"

"One hundred and four arrested," Six said, "no casualties, and a few hundred thousand in the Potential Funds Intake." The elevator doors swished shut.

"Pretty standard, then," Two said, deadpan.

"Substandard. Kyntak sang all the way home."

Two laughed. "Is he any good?"

"Either his DNA isn't perfect after all, or he's living proof that musicianship isn't genetic."

"Does that mean you're just as bad?"

Six shrugged. "I have the sense not to try."

Ping. The doors slid open on the fifth floor.

Out of efficiency rather than urgency, Six sprinted along the empty corridors until he reached his office. He disarmed the door, entered, armed it behind him, and sat down in front of the laptop on his desk. He hit the power switch.

His office was tidy, clean, and minimal. Besides the computer and desk, the only objects were his spare coat, hanging on a hook behind the door, and a painting on the wall. The painting had been a gift from the Queen of Hearts. He suspected she'd given it to him as an experiment, just to see if he would discard it. He hadn't.

The mission report template opened automatically on the screen. He began to type:

MISSION REPORT: 8066-7145-9899

AGENT NUMBER: 06-4 (Six of Hearts)

LOCATION: Warehouse for storage and transfer of human cargo on Highway 03649

BRIEF: Enter facility, arrest suspects, recover hostages for adoption

AGENT IN CHARGE: 06-4 (Six of Hearts)

MISSION DESCRIPTION: Entered through roof (0542 hours). Established validity of suspicions by confirming presence of hostages (0600 hours). Led suspects to holding vehicle (0608 hours). Left scene (0614 hours).

Looks pretty simple on paper, Six thought. Lucky there was so much equipment to be sold and so many arrests, or this would practically be a blemish on his record.

GENERAL CASUALTIES/INJURIES: None

DAMAGE TO AREA: Warehouse door damaged. Corridor and stairwell at rear demolished

ESTIMATED COST: 18,000 standard credits

DAMAGE TO PERSONAL PROPERTY: N/A

ESTIMATED COST: N/A

NUMBER OF KNOWN SIGHTINGS: 104. All offenders in custody.

ESTIMATED POTENTIAL FUNDS INTAKE: 760,000 standard credits

Save. Proofread. Print. Shut down.

Disarm. Exit. Arm.

"Not bad, Six," the King of Hearts said, green eyes twinkling. "Not too bad at all."

Lucky I do this for the money as opposed to praise from my boss, thought Six. *No matter how successful the mission, he always says much the same thing.*

King saw the look in Six's eyes. "Sorry," he said, scratching his clean-shaven scalp. "I try to be enthusiastic, but you've desensitized me with three years of amazing work."

"I could use a raise," Six said.

"You barely spend any of the millions of credits you have," King said. "You *could* use a raise, but you wouldn't."

Six raised an eyebrow. He hadn't known that his minimal lifestyle had been watched so carefully.

"So," King began. He stared at Six, waiting for an answer to the unasked question. Six held his gaze.

"She wasn't there?" King asked finally.

Six shook his head.

There was a pause.

"There's still hope," King said.

"For an eight-month-old child? In the City?"

"You were younger than that when I found you crawling the streets," King pointed out.

"Exactly." Six stared at King's desk. "By now someone must have her. And I doubt they'll be as upstanding as you."

King conceded the point with a grim nod. "But to mount an assault like the one on Kyntak's house, you'd need resources. Lots of money, manpower, and information. There aren't many people in the City with the capabilities. And those who have them can't stay hidden."

"I think there's a new part of ChaoSonic," Six said. "Someone filling the hole the Lab left in biological research. Adults react more slowly to drugs and viruses than children do, unless you've got some of Tridya's product to accelerate growth. And using animals doesn't reliably predict a result in humans."

Chelsea Tridya was a freelance scientist who had been kidnapped by the Lab. She'd invented a drug that was able to control the rate of aging by manipulating the gene known as P53 — something which no one had previously been able to do without causing tumors in the subjects. She had intended to use it to help people lead longer lives, postponing the early death that came from breathing the City's polluted air. But the Lab had had other plans. They wanted a drug to make people age faster so they could grow clones of Six to maturity in days instead of years. They had planned to build a superhuman army.

Six had rescued Chelsea, and she was now working under the Deck's protection. But the Lab's supply of her drug had never been found. If there was an upside to the fact that children were being sourced for experimentation, it was that ChaoSonic probably didn't have the missing supplies.

"And you think Nai was taken by whoever has taken the Lab's place?" King asked.

Six said nothing. He hadn't thought so at first, because the abduction had happened only two months after the Lab was liquidated. There hadn't been much time for a new division to take its place. But now it seemed the most likely scenario. Nai was a flesh-and-blood weapon, the Lab's most advanced, and final, super-soldier. So whatever new division had sprung up to take its place, they would have a keen interest in her. And they would have ChaoSonic's cash, intel, and muscle.

"Still no mention of her from our spies inside ChaoSonic," King said. "So if they have her, they haven't gotten what they want from her yet. Therefore she's still alive." He put Six's mission report in a desk drawer. "There's still hope."

King's terminal buzzed. "It's Queen," he said as he slipped the headphones on and pushed ACCEPT.

Six stared into space. He had escaped from the Lab as a baby, albeit because Methryn Crexe had let him. Crexe, the executive in charge of the Lab, had wanted Six, Kyntak, and Sevadonn, the three clones, to grow up with different personalities. That way he could see which one made the best soldier, and duplicate his upbringing with the next batch. Six had wanted Nai to have a normal childhood, but she'd only had two months of freedom before she'd been taken. Even if he found her, who knew what mental and physical damage might . . .

King's face had grown ashen. He looked Six in the eye. "I'll send Six right away," he said grimly into the mouthpiece. "Get all the agents you can for backup."

He replaced the headphones in the terminal. "There's been an explosion in the cells. Methryn Crexe has escaped," he said.

*　　*　　*

The cell-block door marked 81-B slid open with a hydraulic hiss as Six approached. A cloud of dust avalanced out, blinding him for a moment as if he'd stepped outside into the fog. He could taste brick and mortar in the air, and smell the tangy scent of twisted steel.

He walked into the dust cloud, and the door slid shut behind him.

The noise inside was piercing. Some of the criminals howled abuse at Six as he walked past, kicking and shaking the bars of their cells. Others begged him for information, demanding to know what all the noise had been. A few cried out that they hadn't committed the acts for which they had been shuffled.

The latter were the easiest to ignore. Six didn't make mistakes, and he had faith in his fellow agents.

It was obvious which cell had been Methryn Crexe's — it had no ceiling. It was as if a Dumpster-size fist had punched through the roof and snatched up Crexe, then vanished into thin air.

Six walked through the open cell door. He could see the remnants of the cell above, missing its floor *and* ceiling, and, above that, the opaque grey sky.

A woman's body was lying in the dust, surrounded by a puddle of dried blood — the former occupant of the cell above, Six presumed. He knelt down beside her. Shot in the head. Probably killed instantly.

Six looked up again, trying to picture the scene. *It's a miracle she survived the demolition of the ceiling,* he thought. They must have expected her to die in the blast, but she was sheltered somehow, so they had to shoot her.

But how could she have survived a massive explosion like this? How did Crexe survive it?

A large disc of concrete in the corner caught Six's eye. He squinted through the smoke and the fog seeping in from above. The disc was perfectly circular.

There was another one just like it, lying on the floor to one side. Six hadn't seen them immediately in the rubble.

What are the chances of an explosion creating two identical concrete discs? he wondered. *The odds against it must be huge.*

Six looked down at the body again. *So,* he thought. They drilled a round hole in the ceiling first, shot the woman, drilled an identical hole through the floor, rescued Crexe, and then blew up both cells to destroy the evidence.

What evidence? Crexe is gone; the woman's dead. What am I missing?

Six looked harder at the puddle of dried blood around the woman.

He rolled the body over. Her blank eyes stared up at the foggy sky. The bullet hole was in the underside of her chin, and the exit wound was a small hole near her crown.

With a wound like that, Six thought, her heart should have stopped beating before she even hit the ground. So why was there such a large puddle of blood?

Because it isn't her blood. It couldn't be.

Six started to picture the incident from scratch. The rescue team drilled a hole in the ceiling. The round block of concrete fell, alerting the woman. She attacked the first one to climb down . . . with a broken-off piece of concrete, perhaps, or even just her bare hands. The intruder shot her during the struggle, from close range — hence the bullet wound under her chin, rather than in her face, as it would be if the shot had been taken from a distance. But she'd wounded her attacker, and he was bleeding. Perhaps his gun discharged during the struggle, and he was hit. Perhaps he died, Six thought, and later the others put him in their getaway vehicle. There was a lot of blood.

No, wait. The blood was on the floor of Crexe's cell, not hers. So the attacker was still alive, and still bleeding when they drilled a new hole, climbed down into Crexe's cell, and grabbed him.

It was even possible that they'd placed the woman's body on top of the blood puddle so it appeared to be her blood and was never examined more closely.

Once they had Crexe, someone up above must have lowered the rope. They grabbed it and were lifted out, explosives were set (some kind of powerful directional bombs, Six thought, though not claymores, because there would be ball bearings on the floor), and they drove away.

This explains how they did it so quickly, Six thought. The explosion happened after the rescue, not before. And there were probably at least four perpetrators: two to break in (one to drill and one to shoot), one to lift the intruders and Crexe out, and one to drive the car. There may have been an extra person to set up the explosives, but one of the others could have done it without too much trouble — probably the driller.

The important thing is, Six thought, looking at the body on the floor, *that this blood belongs to one of the attackers. It can be traced.*

Six scraped some of the stained crimson dust into a small plastic case and left the cell block.

Door 81-B slid closed behind him.

RUNNING BLIND

Six knocked on the door of Kyntak's office.

"Go away, I'm busy," came a voice from inside.

Six pushed open the door. Kyntak had his feet up on his desk and was throwing peanuts into the wastepaper basket.

"You don't look busy," said Six.

"No," Kyntak admitted, "but an initial warning is usually enough to get rid of people who want to harass me with trivialities."

"Having an office has gone to your head," Six observed. He kicked a crumpled potato-chip packet away from his foot, and it rejoined the others in a corner. The clock on the wall said 9:15:00.

"That sounds like insubordination to me, Agent Six of Hearts," Kyntak warned. "State your business or get out of here."

"You heard about Methryn Crexe."

"Yeah — I thought you were taking care of it. Need a hand?"

"I've given a blood sample of one of the intruders to Ace of Diamonds; she's going to analyze it and pass it over to King of Diamonds, who'll compare it to those in the ChaoSonic database and get the address of the suspect. When we have that, King of Hearts'll send in a team — and I'll be doing recon." He paused. "But there are too many variables for my peace of mind — I'd appreciate you watching my back."

Kyntak smiled. "Only if you'll watch mine."

"Deal," Six said. "I'll let you know when we have the address."

His phone buzzed in his pocket.

"Let's go," said Kyntak.

"Sorry," Jack said as he zipped up the back of Six's combat suit, "but I won't have much time to chat with you today."

"That's a shame," Six replied flatly.

Jack was probably the most talkative person he knew — he seemed to be able to ramble for hours without caring if his victim was listening. Six tried not to be too rude to him; Jack had suffered more of his blunt coldness than anyone else at the Deck. But Six didn't know how to apologize for years of poor social skills. So he just tried his best to keep his mouth shut. And Jack seemed capable of handling the conversation on his own.

"I've got seven other agents to suit up, you see," Jack continued, picking up equipment from a nearby table. "Busy busy busy. Lucky none of you need makeovers or I'd be here all day. And time's a factor, as I understand it. Is it true that someone managed to break out of one of the cells? I always thought it couldn't be done!"

"So did I," Six growled. "They had outside help. Lots of it."

"Well, if anyone can bring in the culprits, it's you. Good luck, Six. Here's your radio earpiece, your PDA, Owl 5525, and your ski mask."

Six clipped the radio and the gun onto his belt and pulled the ski mask over his head.

"Oh, and the grenades," Jack added, picking them up from his desk. "They're OT-78s, so they explode on impact after the pin is pulled rather than on a timer. Don't rely on rebound, don't squeeze them too hard, and don't drop them once they're armed."

Six pocketed the four grenades.

"Ready?" Jack asked.

Six nodded. And left without a word.

"The blood recovered from the cell belonged to a man named Vidar Dehayt," King said to the eight agents standing before him. "Our only information on him comes from his confidential ChaoSonic file. He worked in security for the Lab last year. And you all know what that means."

They did. King was telling them that this may have something to do with the history of Six, or Kyntak. Tread carefully.

"By necessity, this is a top secret case," King said. "Need to know, classified, etcetera. So you report to no one but the following people: me, Queen, Six, or Kyntak. Except in the event of an emergency, you are not to share details of this case with anyone outside the Hearts department, and if you'll take my advice, you won't discuss them with one another either. If you need assistance from another suit, contact me or Queen first. Clear?"

"*Yes, sir!*" the agents said in unison.

"Good. According to the ChaoSonic database, Dehayt lives in a semi-abandoned apartment block about thirty klicks west of here. The method used to rescue Crexe suggests that he is dangerous and will be armed. While your first mission priority is to recapture Methryn Crexe before he does any harm, it's probable that he won't be on-site. So it's also important to bring Dehayt in. We need him alive to find out what's going on.

"Each floor will be searched by Six and Kyntak first. If the floor is clear, they'll call the rest of you up. If not, they'll come back down with a recon report. You can then use their info and the maps in your PDAs to make a game plan and move in. Standard protocol applies — if shots are fired, move in immediately.

"We're running blind in this case. We don't know who arranged for the rescue of Crexe, or what he plans to do on the outside. You're all highly skilled agents, but this mission is an intelligence nightmare. So until Crexe and Dehayt are arrested, don't let your guard down. Any questions?"

There were none.

"All right," King said. "Good luck. Let's load up the trucks."

MISSION TWO
11:31:17

THE APARTMENT BLOCK

Agent Six rode in the vehicle with Kyntak, Two, and Nine. Agent Two was driving. The grimy, crumbling City rolled past the windows of the cabin and the omnipresent fog leaked in through the floor.

Pedestrians had started wearing gas masks and goggles — not so much for their safety, Six knew, but as part of a new fashion trend. He'd seen women wearing various types of masks on the covers of several magazines lately, and that was usually a good indicator of what would become fashionable in the next few weeks.

"So," Two said. "What's our current theory?"

"I think that Methryn Crexe has been pulled back into operation by ChaoSonic," Kyntak said. "They don't really know a lot about what happened at the Lab. They never got a chance to debrief Crexe before we shuffled him. Retuni Lerke was the one who knew the most about the experiments they'd been doing, but they never found him and neither did we. So if they really wanted information about Project Falcon, how else could they get it besides freeing Crexe?"

Six shivered. He'd been hoping that ChaoSonic had dismissed Project Falcon as a failure. If that wasn't the case, he and Kyntak could be in even greater danger than he'd imagined.

"But if ChaoSonic has worked out where the Deck is, why haven't they attacked it?" Nine said. "There are heaps of shuffled ChaoSonic operatives in the cells. Why rescue Crexe and none of the others?"

"And why use a low-life, ex-Lab security guard to do it?" Two added.

The truck screeched to a halt as a black sedan roared past in front of it. The blaring of horns followed it into the grey void, and the truck rumbled forward again. Two barely blinked. Traffic was rough everywhere in the City. To a trained Deck agent, a few sudden stops and swerves were nothing. Despite the crisis Six could feel building around him, he was touched by a hint of satisfaction as he watched Two drive. He wasn't close to any of the other team members, and maybe he would always feel isolated, but they were well trained and reliable, like a parachute that he could feel on his back no matter how fast he was falling.

"What if it's a diversion?" Nine said suddenly. "We've got our eight best agents on this mission, including you two!" He gestured at Six and Kyntak. "If there was a perfect time to attack the Deck, wouldn't it be now?"

Six snapped back to reality and held his radio up to his mouth.

"This is Six of Hearts. Come in, King."

"Copy that, Six, this is King. What's up?"

"It's been suggested that the rescue operation was staged to draw us away, leaving the Deck undefended. I'm just checking that you've implemented all security measures. Over."

"We're walled in tight," Six's radio crackled. *"The Spades and Clubs aren't on-site, obviously, but Queen, Jack, all the Diamonds, and I are sealed in the Audiovisual Surveillance room. Ace, Three, and*

Seven are patrolling outside. We're keeping our eyes on the screens, and everything seems okay. Over."

"I suddenly have a very bad feeling about this," said Six.

"At least you have feelings," Kyntak said. "That's an improvement."

"We can take care of ourselves, Six. Keep us posted."

"Copy that." Six clipped the radio back onto his belt. "I doubt ChaoSonic has found the Deck — we'd know by now if they had. Any other theories?"

"Debtors?" Nine suggested. "Maybe Crexe owed someone."

"Friends or relatives who wanted him back, maybe," Two said with a shrug. "Not everything is motivated by money."

The apartment block had come into view — a blackened slab of concrete, crumbling at the joints, rising into the fog. The charred walls were peppered with windows, mostly grimy, broken, or boarded up. Six couldn't see any doors.

Moments later he discovered why. The cabin of the truck sank forward until it was rolling down a concrete ramp into a parking lot underneath the building. There was no door, no boom gate, no security of any kind. A scattering of cheap neon bulbs on the low ceiling struggled to pierce the fog which poured down the ramp. The silence was smothering, as if the place had been empty for years and every last echo of life had faded to nothing.

Agent Two parked the truck in one of the bays. Six watched through the window as the second truck parked beside it.

"This is Agent Five; we are good to go."

Two glanced at Nine, who nodded. "This is Agent Two," he said. "We're ready."

Kyntak looked at Six. As the reconnaissance part of the team, they would be separated from the rest of the group. Their independent confirmation was needed before dealing.

Six held Kyntak's gaze nervously. He was still uneasy. They didn't have sufficient information to do this mission. They didn't know what the risks were.

But what choice did they have? Methryn Crexe was on the loose. He was being used for something by someone — someone with the resources and motivation to break in to a high-security cell block to get him out.

This is our only lead, Six thought. *So this is our only choice.*

He nodded to Kyntak.

"This is Kyntak," Kyntak said cheerfully into the radio. "Six and I are ready to deal." He grinned at Six. "Let's get this party started."

Six looked at his watch. It was 11:52:50.

The doors to both trucks opened simultaneously. The agents swarmed out, guns at the ready, their rubber-soled shoes carrying them across the filthy parking lot floor without so much as a scuffle.

Six was to take the north stairwell; Kyntak, the west. The rest of the team was to wait by the south stairwell, ready to move up to the first floor when Six and Kyntak gave them the all-clear, or when they were needed as backup. Six was glad King had given those instructions. The Hearts agents were tough, but he and Kyntak were tougher, and he didn't want to put anyone in unnecessary danger.

Before peeling off towards the west stairs, Kyntak clapped Six lightly on the back. "Good luck."

Six nodded and ran for the north stairs. Behind him, the other agents melted into the shadows, splitting off towards darkened corners of the parking lot.

Six read the grease-stained sign on the door through the flickering neon light. FIRE DOOR — DO NOT PREVENT CLOSING. He eased it open gently.

34

The hinges didn't creak as much as scrape — years of rust being scratched away as the door moved. Six peered through the gap. There was no movement on the other side.

He pushed the door the rest of the way open very quickly to minimize the noise. The stairwell was tiled in white, but was stained grey, yellow, and brown at the corners. The steps were dark aluminum and nearly as rusted as the door. There was a lightbulb above his head, but it was off, and there was no apparent switch.

The chamber was empty. Given the state of this stairwell and the door he had entered through, Six guessed that no one had been in this part of the building for years. He eased the door shut behind him.

He peered up the stairs, gun in hand. No movement.

Six climbed the steps two at a time. He felt slight vibrations under his feet and sensed that if he didn't tread gently enough, every step would boom through the stairwell. He kept his feet close to the wall, where the stairs were structurally strongest and where his footfalls would make the least noise. The longer he and the other agents remained undetected, the better their chances of success. He didn't want Dehayt, Crexe, and whoever else lay hidden in this building to have time to prepare a counterattack.

The first landing was empty. Six saw nothing unusual above, just a tunnel of darkness between the rusted flights of stairs.

He heard a deep, quiet groan, a shifting metallic ache as one might hear on the inside of a submarine.

The noise faded away into the darkness. Six held still for a moment longer, but no other sounds followed.

This is a very old building, he thought. A noise like that could be made by weather conditions outside, causing the structure to shift slightly, or by someone moving somewhere within its walls.

But Six had no way of knowing whether that someone might be his friend or foe.

"Are you on the first floor yet, Six?" crackled Kyntak through the earpiece.

"Just reached the landing," Six whispered. "Why?"

"I've found signs of a struggle. A recent one. Tables overturned and cartridges on the floor, but no dust settled on them yet. And no bodies. There's a pile of cheap mobile phones in one of the rooms."

Six frowned. "How many?" he asked.

"Eleven," Kyntak said. *"Any ideas?"*

"Just a second." Six changed frequencies. "King, do you copy?"

"I read you, Six. What's happening?"

"Kyntak's found a pile of phones. How many other drifters were living in this building that we know of, besides Vidar Dehayt?"

"Ten or eleven. How many phones?"

"Yeah, it matches." Six balled his hands into fists. "Someone didn't want to be seen, so they disposed of all the previous occupants."

All mobile phones broadcast a passive signal, traceable within a few meters. Professional attack teams always left the phones of their victims behind so no one could use that signal to find the bodies. A pile of phones probably meant that all the residents of the building were dead.

He switched frequencies again. "Kyntak, be careful."

"Now, where's the fun in that?" Kyntak's cheer sounded slightly forced. *"Let me know if you find anything. Over and out."*

The door to the first floor was immediately in front of him, but Six was distracted by a silver box bolted to the wall. It was about the size of an ice-cream container, with a small antenna out to the side, and a few control dials on the front. It had caught Six's eye because it looked newer than the rest of the building; the omnipresent grime and dust had yet to settle on its gleaming surface.

Six touched the chrome hinges thoughtfully. It looked like a signal relay — the ground-based equivalent of a communications satellite. Data from a mobile phone could be sent via a relay instead of a tower, provided the sender and recipient were within its operational radius. The advantage was that the signal couldn't be intercepted except by someone within that radius. Relays were often installed at secret bases of operations.

But this building doesn't look like someone's base, Six thought. *It looks abandoned. So who installed the relay, and why?*

He turned back to the door. After they had scoured the building for other clues, he would examine the box more thoroughly. If need be, he could take it back to the Deck for analysis. But right now, he had other things to do.

He hefted his pistol and eased the stairwell door open a crack. He listened. Nothing.

He swung it all the way open. The corridor was empty — the grinding of the door hinges echoed and bounced away into the distance. The wind blew through shattered windows.

There were more neon bulbs on the ceiling, but none appeared to have power. Broken glass crunched underneath Six's shoes.

There were entrances to apartments on his right. Most had no doors, just empty door frames with half-attached hinges. Six peered into each room as he crept past, but saw only broken furniture and dirt. He suspected the building was used as a squat by homeless people.

The economics of the City were fragile. ChaoSonic needed to sell goods and services to the public to keep making money. But because the giant corporation owned almost everything, its only customers were its own employees. No one else had any funds. Six had heard it called the CFC, or cash flow cycle. ChaoSonic officials paid their employees, who paid *their* employees, and so on. Money filtered down through the ranks of the company until everyone with a ChaoSonic job had some. Then they all bought ChaoSonic meals and ChaoSonic clothes. They paid the rent on their ChaoSonic apartments and put ChaoSonic fuel in their ChaoSonic cars. The money all found its way back to ChaoSonic officials.

But like all companies, ChaoSonic demanded growth and profit. To save money, it replaced its workers with software, machines, and even slaves. To survive, the suddenly penniless former employees now had to steal ChaoSonic goods instead of buying them. This decreased ChaoSonic revenue, leading to more

job losses.

Six didn't know if there was a name for that cycle. But he knew where the jobless people ended up. They could be found all over the City, living in rags, sleeping on concrete.

Six could see an empty paint can in one of the rooms, scorch marks on the floor under it. Someone had obviously tried to make a hot meal.

The shredded mattress and sticks of firewood could have been undisturbed for weeks or years. The only sign of recent occupation was the lack of current occupation. Places like this never stayed empty for long.

Kyntak rounded the corner ahead of Six. "Nothing," he said.

Six nodded. "This way too. Call up the agents."

Kyntak tapped his earpiece. "This is Kyntak. The first floor is clear. Move up — we're going to the second."

"Copy that," Two said in Six's ear.

Kyntak headed back towards the west stairwell. "See you in a minute." The fog swallowed him up.

Six turned back to the north.

The stairwell didn't get any cleaner with altitude. Six hoped that the steps were still capable of supporting his weight.

The second landing was in a similar state of disrepair to the first. If this floor yielded no evidence of Methryn Crexe or Vidar Dehayt, they would have to check the roof and then leave.

Six was getting worried. The blood of Vidar Dehayt on the floor of Methryn Crexe's cell was their only lead in this case — and beyond searching Dehayt's last known place of residence for clues, there wasn't much they could do.

Did Crexe or Dehayt know they would be coming? Six wondered. Was murdering the neighbors of accomplices just a precaution because they knew Dehayt's blood had been left behind at the crime scene? Or was it standard operating procedure for these people, whoever they were?

He cracked open another rusty door. He was on the second floor.

It looked the same as the previous floor, but better lit. Daylight and fog leaked through small holes that seemed to cover the whole ceiling.

Dust billowed silently around Six's feet and he felt a sneeze building up in his sinuses.

He held his nose, suppressing it, then moved on.

As on the lower floor, few of the apartments had doors, and those that did had broken locks. A mattress leaning against one wall of the corridor indicated that someone had been moving in or out — but there was no sign of them now.

There was an apartment with an undamaged door on Six's right. He gripped his gun tightly and reached out to touch the greasy handle.

A hand snaked out from behind him and clamped over his mouth, while another ripped his pistol from his fingers.

Six tried to struggle, but he was held from behind in a crushing bear hug. He was completely powerless.

He kicked backward, aiming for the legs of his assailant. He missed and was hoisted into the air, facing the ceiling. The hand pulled his head backward.

"Shhhhh . . ."

Six stopped moving. It seemed pointless. He was being held by someone much stronger than him, but someone who apparently didn't want him dead.

"I thought you would know a trap when you saw one," a voice whispered behind his ear. "I thought by now you'd been tricked enough times to know when you were being manipulated."

The voice was female. Six couldn't determine the age of the speaker while she was whispering.

"Apparently," she continued, "I was wrong."

Six couldn't reply. The woman's hand was still firmly clamped over his lips, like a car parked on his face. Six's first thought was that she might be a machine. The only sentient being who'd ever overpowered him, besides his superhuman brothers, was Harry, his robot. But the hand was as warm and yielding as flesh.

"He wants you to shoot before you think. To decide on instinct, so he will have the upper hand. It seems like a game, but it's not. He's trying to put you off balance because he knows that's the easiest way to beat you. He aims to *deceive*."

Who? Six thought. Vidar Dehayt? Methryn Crexe? He tried to speak through the palm of his captor. She responded by pulling harder against his face.

"All hell is about to break loose," she continued, "but you can survive it, if you're careful. He knows you. He knows the assumptions you'll make. So *assume nothing*.

"I'd tell you to go home. But I know you wouldn't listen. So don't go in the front door. Go back to the apartment you just passed, go inside, and enter the closet. There's a hole leading to this apartment.

"Don't trust your instincts today, Six. Think before you act."

The hand left Six's mouth, and he fell to the floor. Landing feetfirst, he whirled around to see . . .

. . . an empty corridor, gritty and gloomy, with pale dust stirred from the floor by a faint breeze.

After searching the immediate area and finding no trace of the mystery woman, Six decided to take her advice. Alarmed as he was by the fact that he seemed to have been overpowered by a ghost, he realized that if she'd wanted to hurt or kill him, she would have done so when she had the chance. If she'd wanted to exploit him somehow, she would have given more specific and suspicious advice than "think before you act" and "don't go in the front door."

The last possibility was that she was trying to help him, for whatever reason — and Six lost nothing by changing his search route slightly.

He went inside the apartment she had suggested. It was unremarkable — glass and grit on the floor, wallpaper yellowing at the edges, a boarded-up window on one wall, and a single light-bulb above his head. There was a dirty sledgehammer lying in the corner, surrounded by brick dust. Perhaps someone had planned some renovations that never took place.

The closet door was leaning against its frame rather than attached to it. The closet was empty except for one crinkled shirt, with a large coffee stain, on a coat hanger. Six slid it gently aside and saw that there was indeed a hole — about one meter square and presumably made with the sledgehammer — leading to the next apartment.

And through it, he saw the face of Methryn Crexe.

The former Lab boss was sitting on a rickety wooden chair, facing the door to the apartment, with a Hawk 9-millimeter pistol in his hand. Crexe hadn't seen Six yet. His eyes stared straight ahead at the door. His gun hand was perfectly still.

Was this what the mystery woman had been trying to warn him about? Six thought. *He wants you to shoot before you think*, she had said. *It seems like a game, but it's not.*

Why would Crexe want Six to shoot him? And why lie in wait in a room of this ancient apartment building? Crexe would probably know that Six abhorred killing, and that he was hesitant to use lethal force, even in self-defense. But would he stake his own life upon that?

He wants you to shoot, she'd said. None of this made sense.

Six thought he heard a distant rattling sound. He took his eyes off Methryn Crexe for a moment to look over his shoulder, but the apartment was still empty.

Could be Kyntak, he thought. *Could be the other agents on the floor below. Could be just the wind, or the building shifting.*

Crexe didn't seem to have heard the noise. His knuckles were white around the grip of the Hawk.

Six leaned forward very slowly and put one leg through the hole in the closet, keeping his Owl trained on Crexe the whole time. His foot touched the dirty concrete without a sound. He slipped his torso through the hole into Crexe's apartment.

Six lifted his other leg through the hole, and stood in a defensive crouch, his gun aimed at Crexe's temple.

"Don't move a single muscle," he hissed.

Crexe was still.

"Drop the gun, and put your hands behind your head," Six said. "Slowly."

Crexe ignored him completely. His gaze didn't falter.

Six lunged and grabbed the Hawk out of Crexe's hand. He met no resistance. Crexe's empty hand fell into his lap. His skin was ice-cold.

Agent Six pressed two fingers against Methryn Crexe's throat, searching for a pulse. There was none.

Crexe's narrow, focused eyes turned from the door to the ceiling as he pitched sideways off his chair, his delicate balance disrupted by Six's touch. He landed with a thud on the concrete floor.

He wants you to shoot before you think, the woman had said. *He aims to deceive.*

So "he" was not Methryn Crexe, Six thought. *And if I'd entered through the front door, I would've seen Methryn Crexe pointing a gun at me.*

I probably would have shot him.

So "he" wanted Six to think that he'd killed Methryn Crexe? *He's trying to put you off balance*, she had said. To unnerve him, confuse him?

"Six, where are you?" It was Kyntak. *"My half of the floor is clear."*

"Copy that," Six said. "The rest of the team can move up. I've found Crexe — he's dead. I'm in the room with the closed door. Come and meet me."

Six's earpiece crackled. *"This is Agent Two; we're on our way."*

If someone was trying to confuse or unnerve me, Six thought, *they've succeeded. Methryn Crexe escapes from the Deck. Blood at the scene leads us to an abandoned apartment block. All the occupants have vanished, leaving only a pile of phones and Methryn Crexe's corpse behind, arranged in such a way as to try to force me into a one-sided gunfight . . . and in the middle of it all, a strong, fast, seemingly* invisible *woman gives me a warning that is too cryptic to be useful.*

This is too weird for ChaoSonic. It must be something else.

What if I had fired? Six thought. Crexe's body would've

been damaged — perhaps there was a clue which could've been destroyed by the shot. But why leave the body here for them to find if it had evidence on it?

He thought of the mystery woman's words. *All hell is about to break loose, but you can survive it, if you're careful.*

What else would have happened if he had shot Crexe? The noise would have carried — and the other agents would have heard it. They would have raced up here to the second floor to back him up . . .

Kyntak and Agents Two, Four, Five, Eight, Nine, and Ten would *all* have been on this floor, where they were headed right now anyway . . .

There was a scuffle, close. Six whirled around, but the room was empty. Crexe stared blankly up at him.

"Two," Six hissed into his radio. "Wait! Are you on the second floor yet?"

"Just arrived. Why?"

"I think —" Six broke off. He was looking up at the ceiling, at the small holes that riddled it.

In one of them, just for a moment, he had seen an eye staring at him.

"We have hostiles," Six yelled. "There are hostiles on the roof!"

And then the ceiling exploded into millions of tiny concrete chunks.

PINNED DOWN

The gunfire shrieked through the air as Six dived for cover. The ceiling was gone, just *gone*, leaving the sky exposed. Fog flooded down to fill the room. Six felt as though he'd been hiding in a box and someone had lifted up the lid.

The attackers were dressed in black fatigues, with gleaming gas masks and Kevlar combat vests. They were armed to the teeth, hefting Eagle OI779 automatic rifles fitted with laser sights and Raptor sidearms. PGC387 stun grenades and long diamond-edged Feather knives hung from their belts, along with devices that looked curiously like TV remotes in synthetic rubber holsters.

Six landed with a thud, elbow first, as bullets tore over his head and ripped the wall behind him to shreds. A pair of armored combat boots landed beside him. He grabbed them and pulled.

There was a growl of surprise as the man lost his balance. He landed on his back, and Six punched him in the head.

The man kept struggling, his skull protected by the gas mask. Six ripped it off, sending shards of plastic buckles flying, and jabbed a gland in the assailant's throat. He slumped to the floor immediately.

There were five attackers in the room now, but Six noticed that the gunfire didn't seem to be directed at him. It was aimed at the walls, shredding plaster and cracking bricks, leaving holes like the ones Six had noticed in the now-demolished ceiling. They seemed intent on making a lot of noise and creating panic, but the force used didn't seem to have lethal intent.

Or maybe it did. One of the attackers in the room had spotted Six on the ground next to the unconscious man and was leveling his Eagle.

"Surprise," Six said as he pulled the pin out of one of the PGCs on the unconscious man's belt.

In the moments before the explosion, he scrambled to his feet and dived for the bullet-riddled door, shutting his eyes tightly.

Crack!

The white light was dazzling even through his eyelids. The sound of the grenade bursting mingled with the crunching of the door as Six plunged headfirst through it.

The stun grenade didn't disorient the soldiers for long — the goggles in their gas masks protected them from much of the impact. But they were still blinded for a moment, and when that moment was over, Six was gone.

Outside in the corridor, Six took a quick look around — and his jaw dropped.

It wasn't just the ceiling to Crexe's room that had been demolished. The attackers had blown the roof off the entire building. And out here in the corridor, there were more than thirty men storming out of the fog, firing bullets into the walls and scanning the corridor with goggled eyes.

Nine's voice echoed through Six's head. *What if it's a diversion? We've got our eight best agents here on this. If there was a perfect time to attack the Deck, wouldn't it be now?*

Perhaps it wasn't a diversion intended to leave the Deck unprotected; instead, it was a trap for the best agents. Lure them here, then exterminate them — crippling the Deck.

But why do that with a platoon of soldiers? Why the elaborate trap with Dehayt's blood and Crexe's body? Why not just blow up the building once the agents were inside?

Boom!

As if on cue, the floor shook beneath Six's feet, and he staggered against a bullet-peppered wall. For a moment he thought the building *was* being blown up; but no, the foundation stood. The shock wave had come from nearby, but destroying the building clearly wasn't the aim.

Six pointed his Owl at the crowd of attackers. *Whoever they are*, he thought, *whatever their motives may be, they've underestimated me. We'll see who cripples whom.*

Six opened fire, emptying the entire eighteen-shot clip into the crowd. Nine of the soldiers were hit in both knees — but not a single one fell.

The armor seemed to cover their entire bodies. All Six's shots had done was attract their attention.

Thirty soldiers turned as one to face him, and leveled their rifles.

Maybe I should have used a grenade, thought Six.

He turned and ran.

Bullets chattered over his head and slammed into the roof-less walls, cracking the plaster and spilling brick dust into the corridor. The fog smothered everything, like a cold, grey blanket.

The soldiers were dim shapes and shadows behind him — but the bullets were still very solid.

Six dived to one side, into a doorless apartment. He crouched behind the wall and tapped his earpiece.

"This is Agent Six," he hissed. "Two, do you copy?"

"I read you, Six," came the reply. *"What's your status?"*

"I'm hiding. Don't worry about me, I'm safe. Where are you?"

Six kept his voice low. He could hear the troops moving about in the corridor outside — getting closer, he thought.

"The whole team is pinned down in one of the apartments. The enemy knows we're here, and they don't seem scared of our bullets. I reckon we've got maybe a minute before they move in. After that, we're dead."

Six clenched his fists. *This has been well planned,* he thought. *We're lucky to still be alive now. Almost too lucky.*

"Two," he hissed. "Get back to the south stairwell. Don't use the corridors — climb over the walls between the apartments. Get two agents to lay down a suppressing fire through the doorway while you're doing it. Tell them to throw a grenade before pulling back. I'll meet you at the stairs. Do you copy?"

"Copy that, Six. Wish us luck."

The gunfire outside seemed to be getting nearer. A lone bullet punched a hole in the wall above Six's head. He ducked lower. "Kyntak! Where are you?"

"I'm in one of the apartments with a bunch of sleeping soldiers," Kyntak's voice crackled. *"They're not so tough. The backs of their necks aren't armored, so you can knock 'em out that way."*

"The other agents are headed for the stairs," Six said. "I suggest you follow suit."

"Retreat? Are you crazy? How're we gonna find out who they are?"

"Getting the agents out safely is more important, Kyntak. Understood?"

"Got it. Good luck."

Six changed the frequency. "King, do you copy?"

"I read you, Six. What's going on?"

"No time to explain. We're retreating, but when the hostiles leave, I want to know where they go. Can you hack into a satellite above us?"

"Downloading the pictures now. What the —"

The radio crackled and died. *Flat battery?* Six thought. Not likely. The hostiles had to be jamming their communications.

Outside in the corridor he heard the boom of a grenade. The Deck agents were headed for the stairwell. Time to go. Six sprinted out the door into the foggy corridor.

The other agents emerged from the apartment nearest the stairwell as he arrived. He couldn't see Kyntak anywhere. But Kyntak was superhuman. He wasn't in as much danger as the other agents. Six knew they couldn't wait for him. The stairs were the only way down, and that was where the soldiers would expect them to go. They all ran towards the stairwell door.

It was a clever plan, Six thought. A double trap. Crexe was the bait for Six, and Six was the bait for the other agents. They hid on the roof, and demolished the ceiling once they were sure all the agents were on the top floor. Thanks to the mystery woman, it didn't go quite as planned: Six didn't fire his gun to make his colleagues come running. But it turned out the same way. They were up here, outgunned and outnumbered.

But coming at us from above might be their undoing, Six thought. They'd left the stairs unguarded. They were putting too much faith in their strategy, which depended upon killing all the agents immediately. No one was stopping them from retreating downward. An image of the soldiers firing into the walls and floor sprung into Six's mind. *They don't seem to be* trying *to kill us*, he thought. *It feels like we're being toyed with.*

But all this was of secondary importance. What mattered was getting out of there — and even though their communications had been jammed, Six had managed to get a request for satellite monitoring through to King. They could puzzle over the motives of the mystery troops later.

They had reached the door to the stairwell. Though they couldn't see far behind them through the fog, falling like grey snow from the sky above, they had to assume that the hostiles were on their way. Six pulled open the door . . .

. . . and gasped as he fell into open space. The stairs were *gone*. He caught himself on the door handle and pulled back, bumping into the agents behind him. The walls of the stairwell were charred and burned, and besides a pile of twisted aluminum debris about twenty meters below, there was no evidence that there had ever been stairs. The well looked more like an elevator shaft — without the elevator.

Six remembered the silver box he had found attached to the wall, which he'd thought was a relay. Yes, it was designed to receive signals, but not so it could pass them on. It had been a bomb.

The explosion he'd heard a few minutes ago had been the demolition of the stairs. The hostiles had been cleverer than he'd thought. They had cut off the escape route in advance.

There was no other way down. They were all trapped on the second floor, with no roof above their heads.

And now Six heard the whirling of helicopter blades.

NO WAY DOWN

We must look like rats in a maze, Six thought. Eight Deck agents hiding from thirty hostile troops in a roofless apartment block.

"What are we going to do?" hissed Nine. "There's no way down! That helicopter's going to shoot us to pieces!"

Six stared up into the fog. The silhouette of a big Twin-600 helicopter was forming above them. As it got closer Six saw a gunner leaning out of the side, scanning the corridors below. He was holding a bulky Pelican GN860 — a super–machine gun capable of pumping out huge slugs at a rate of 900,000 per minute.

Okay, focus! Six thought. *What do they want?*

They want to kill us, he answered himself. But if that was the case, why hadn't they? They could have blown up the building. They could have left the soldiers out of it completely and mown the agents down from the helicopter. There were a million methods for killing people more efficiently than this.

So they're not trying to kill us. Not all *of us. They need something from us. But what? How can I form a strategy when I don't know what they want?*

New thought. What *didn't* they want? They didn't want Methryn Crexe alive. Six frowned. What else had they done?

They've blown up the stairs. Six's eyes widened. *So whatever it is they want from us, they can't get it if we're on the floor below.*

But there's no way down!

Think. Just because there are no stairs and no elevator, does that mean there's no way down?

He peered back into the stairwell. The stairs and landings were gone, and there were no hand or footholds in the walls. But the doors were still intact. If someone opened the one directly below them from the other side, they could drop down and grab hold of the doorway.

Six whirled around to face the others.

"Wait here," he said. "Stay low. Don't give away your position by firing, unless they see you and shoot first. I'm going to create a distraction, draw them away. Then I'll come back for you." He checked his watch. 12:09:48.

"Six, the stairwell is a dead end," Agent Five objected. "We're sitting ducks here."

"We trust you, Six," Two said, ignoring Five. "Go."

Six sprinted into the fog without another word.

Three soldiers loomed out of the mist in the corridor in front of him, but Six didn't slow down. He ran into a crouch-jump, hurling himself a meter and a half into the air, then slammed shoulder-first into the skull of one of the soldiers.

Before the unlucky commando had even hit the ground, Six had executed a perfect landing and was back on his feet — with the other two troops on either side of him, leveling their weapons.

Six whirled around and leaned back, swinging his foot out from under him as he did so. In a wild sweeping kick, he smashed into the knees of the commando on one side and, lifting his leg higher as he spun, the head of the other.

Both soldiers fell, one with a dislocated knee and the other with a bruised skull. Six crouched down and pressed his fingers swiftly under the jaw of the first, forcing him into a deep sleep.

Six didn't have time for a thorough examination, but he could see from the equipment of the soldiers that they weren't ChaoSonic troops — they never carried knives — and the TV remotes were a bizarre twist.

The helicopter thundered overhead. Six could see shadows moving in the fog as more troops approached. Once they saw him, they would soon see the other agents by the stairwell. It was time for his diversion.

Six unclipped an OT-78 grenade from his belt. In one smooth motion he pulled the pin with his thumb, swung to face the chopper, and hurled the grenade into the air.

A red light blinked on it as it spun lazily towards the helicopter.

The gunner wasted a fraction of a second staring at it. Then he dropped the Pelican and dived out of the hold. A climbing rope unraveled behind him as he plummeted earthward.

The grenade clipped the tail of the chopper.

Boom!

The rear end of the helicopter disintegrated in a ball of white-hot energy. The main rotor splintered, sending shards of the blades flying in all directions. The chassis pitched sideways, engine screaming, and one of the landing skis fell off. With a hiss, the ejector seat shot forward out of the cockpit and a large black parachute bloomed immediately behind it.

Six took cover as the skeletal frame dived towards the floor of the corridor. The nearby soldiers shouted as they did the same.

Clang! The cockpit and chassis slammed into a corridor wall, shattering it into dust and debris. Six felt the floor shudder with the impact.

He was on his feet before the echoes had died away. He braced himself for an explosion, but none came. The fuel tank hadn't ignited. He could still hear the chattering of helicopter blades, so he had a sinking feeling that there was more air support coming. But at least . . .

There was a loud crack, and a strong black net wrapped itself around Six. He stumbled and fell, palms first, onto the concrete. Turning his head, he saw the gunner from the helicopter drop a launcher to the floor, and draw an AM-92 tranquilizer pistol.

It was incredible that the soldier was still walking, let alone launching nets. But Six stifled his astonishment and began tearing at the rope with his fingers. It wouldn't break. It was some kind of synthetic nylon fiber that cut and burned his skin.

There was movement in the fog. The commandos were clambering back to their feet, and the gunner was approaching.

Tearing the net didn't seem to be an option. Six tried to stand up, but all six corners of the net were weighted with ball bearings. They swung in as he stood, banging painfully against his ankles and tightening the net around his legs. He lost his balance and fell back down onto the concrete.

I can't let them neutralize me, Six thought, *or the others are as good as dead.* He wriggled forward across the floor, the ball bearings rolling noisily as they dragged behind him. He stretched out his hand, wincing as the nylon ropes tightened over him, and grabbed the foot of one of the three soldiers he had already knocked out.

He pulled the soldier back towards him by the ankle, not

daring to waste time looking to see how close the gunner was. He reached out, releasing a clasp on the soldier's belt, and the diamond-edged Feather knife fell to the floor.

The gunner raised the tranq gun. Took aim.

Six swished the knife outward in a straight line, and the net zipped open like a body bag. He dived through the gap, just as a tranquilizer dart snapped out of the pistol and slammed into the floor.

One of the soldiers made a dive for him. Six smacked his elbow down into his neck and slipped out of his grip. With the remains of the net still tangled around one hand, he dashed into the foggy corridors once again, heading for the outer wall.

Okay, he thought as he ran, *that's one helicopter and at least four soldiers down. What's left?*

Another helicopter and at least twenty-five more soldiers, he surmised. It wasn't looking good. Retreat was definitely still their best option. He had to get the others off the second floor. He sprinted down the foggy corridor, heading towards the apartment containing Crexe's body. When he was about seven meters from the door, three commandos burst through it, turning to face him.

Six dived into a rolling position and swung his arms out like clubs as he hit the floor. One commando was knocked over as Six's shoulder collided with his knee, and the other two were taken out by Six's whirling arms.

Blunt, Six reflected, *but efficient.*

He ran past the door they had come through and turned into the room with the shattered closet wall. He hoisted the sledgehammer from the floor onto his shoulder and, with a mighty swing, drove it right through the boarded-up window.

The wood splintered easily, leaving a meterwide hole through which Six could see the dim outlines of the streets and buildings of the City below. Clutching the sledgehammer in one hand and the knife and net in the other, Six dived into the void.

It took him less than a second to establish that the remaining Twin was not on this side of the building. *Good*, he thought. *It's about time I had some luck.*

He began to plummet towards the distant ground, but a meter below the window, he stabbed his knife into the wall. The plaster cracked with the force of the blow, and the knife was driven in almost to the hilt. Six gripped on to the handle firmly, and he stopped falling.

He checked his watch: 12:12:33. Almost three minutes had passed since he'd seen the others — he had to hurry. Taking down the helicopter had ensured that the soldiers were focused on finding him, but he wasn't sure how long that would last.

Dangling from one hand high above the ground, with the sledgehammer clamped between his knees, Six used his free hand to untangle the net. Except for the slit he had made with the knife, the nylon cords were intact. He attached one corner to the handle of the Feather with a clove hitch and lifted the sledgehammer again.

Six had abseiled many times before, although usually with the proper equipment — a climbing rope, a harness, a carabiner, gloves, and a pickax. Doing it with only a net and a knife while carrying a sledgehammer was like trying to play Beethoven on a piano lacking half its strings.

But there was no time to improvise anything better. He could still hear the chattering of gunfire and the pounding of helicopter blades. Resting his feet against the wall to stop his body from swinging in the breeze, he looked around for a first-floor window to climb through.

And he found it. Like most of the windows in the building, it was boarded up, but Six was sure he could break through the barrier with the sledge. He lowered himself until he was holding the bottom of the net. Then he rappelled towards the window, walking horizontally across the wall of the building with the net in one hand.

He could *just* reach; if he held the bottom of the net at arm's length in his left hand, and stretched out with his right as far as he could, he could touch the boards sealing the window. He looked back at the knife in the wall with the net wrapped around it. It still looked stable.

Taking a deep breath, he hefted the sledgehammer and swung it.

Crack! The wooden boards splintered on impact, leaving an opening wide enough to climb through. Six put the sledge between his knees and reached for the sill.

Thump! His knee banged against the frame as he fell through the window, and he tumbled to the floor in a cloud of dust.

Immediately he rolled out of the room into the first-floor corridor and ducked behind the wall, out of sight of the window. His instincts proved correct. Like a giant black bird, the helicopter loomed in the window and the opposite wall boiled with bullet holes as the Twin's gunner opened fire with the GN-860.

But as long as the helicopter was hovering beside the building and peering in the first-floor windows, the Deck agents on the roofless second floor were safe. Six clambered to his feet and began to run towards the hollowed-out stairwell, shaking the dust off his fatigues as he went.

*   *   *

He glanced at his watch. 12:16:21 — almost seven minutes had gone by since he had seen the agents. He hoped they were still safe.

The stairwell door had been jammed shut by the explosion, but the hinges seemed intact. Six took aim about fifteen centimeters above the handle, where the lock should be, and gave the door a hefty kick.

The door swung outward with a crash, showering plaster into the stairwell. Chunks fell to the basement level, cracking against the mound of debris which had once been the staircase, almost invisible in the darkness.

Six pressed a hand against the door frame, testing its strength. It seemed capable of holding his weight. Gripping it with one hand, he leaned out into the well and switched on his radio.

59

"Assault team, do you copy?" he whispered.

Only static came back.

"Kyntak, can you hear me?" he tried.

Still nothing. Six was about to try again when Agent Nine poked his head out of the door on the floor above, silhouetted in the foggy light. He looked down at Six.

"Whoa," he said. "How'd you get down there?"

"It wasn't easy. The rest of you will have to come this way. Just drop and I'll catch you."

Nine nodded nervously. "Okay. Ready?"

"Yes. Go."

Nine stepped through the doorway into the well, and Six caught him with one arm and swung him into the first-floor corridor. Nine landed in a catlike stance, rattled but safe.

Six looked up. "Who's next?"

It took less than two minutes to ferry agents Four, Five, Eight, and Ten to the first floor. The sounds of gunfire still raged on upstairs — Six hoped that this was just because the attacking soldiers were using it as a scare tactic.

He leaned out through the doorway again, but no one seemed to be coming down.

He took a swift head count. "Where's Two?" he demanded. "And Kyntak?"

"I haven't seen Kyntak since we left the van," Nine said. "But Two was with us at the door."

Six peered out again and looked up. There was no movement above.

He glanced at his watch again — 12:19:30. The longer the other agents stayed, the more danger they were in. He wouldn't leave Kyntak and Two behind, but he couldn't risk the lives of the others.

"Go," he said. "Now. The floor is structurally weakest in the center of each apartment — use your grenades to break through it, and get back to the trucks in the basement. Head for the Deck. I'll find Kyntak and Two."

The agents nodded and headed down the corridor, following Agent Five. They were soon out of sight around a corner.

The stairwell door was still open. Six put his foot on the handle and climbed up onto the top of the door. It rocked on its hinges, but being thick and heavy, its inertia was too strong for the movement to dislodge him.

He ducked instinctively as another blast of gunfire came from the floor above, closer this time. Keeping one hand on the door, he drew his Owl pistol from his belt and aimed it at the upper doorway.

When a figure flew out into the stairwell, Six almost fired. But then he recognized the Deck-issue fatigues, identical to his own. Two, he thought, or Kyntak.

The figure fell towards him limply, arms hanging from slackened shoulders, knees bent at ninety degrees, gloved fingers letting an Eagle automatic slip away from them.

He's unconscious! Six thought. Letting go of his Owl, he leaned out into the center of the well, reaching for the arm of the falling agent.

But as the figure spun slowly in the air to face him, Six found himself looking into the still, lifeless eyes of Agent Two — and the bullet wound between them.

The body slipped through Six's clutching hand and disappeared into the darkness below.

Six lost his balance and toppled off the door. He grabbed the handle on his way down and hung there, reality seeming to fade as the color washed out of it. He felt dizzy and light-headed.

He looked down. Two was dead.

The first thing Six felt was relief that it hadn't been Kyntak. The second thing he felt was shame for feeling this.

The third thing was self-loathing, disgust for failing to protect Two, letting him die — a man whose last words to Six had been, "We trust you, Six. Go."

And for witnessing the murder of a friend and feeling guilt instead of grief.

But it was Six's first thought that brought him back to reality. Kyntak. It was too late to help Two, but Kyntak was still up there. *And if I hang on to this door handle much longer*, he thought, staring into the void, *Kyntak could die too.*

If he isn't dead already.

Like a flash, Six was on the move. He scrambled back up to the top of the door, took aim at the doorway above, and jumped.

There was a soldier standing in the corridor. His face revealed nothing behind the mask and goggles, but as he saw Six appear through the doorway, he raised his weapon.

This is the one, Six thought. *The soldier who killed Two.*

Six had no gun, but it didn't matter. He preferred it that way. He charged silently towards the soldier just as he got his weapon up and opened fire.

Six ran up the wall on his left-hand side, keeping his head at the same altitude but his torso out of the way of the barrage of bullets. The soldier didn't have time to readjust his aim before Six punched him in the face.

The soldier's mask cracked and he fell to the floor, dropping his weapon — but he wasn't too dazed to kick Six in the knee. Six spun his leg, bending with the impact so no bones were broken, then stepped forward and pinned down the soldier's arm with his other foot as the man reached for the fallen gun.

The soldier aimed a punch at Six's hip with his free fist. Six blocked it, caught the man's forearm, and held it against the ground with one hand. He used the other to reach under the man's mask and grab his throat.

He found the windpipe and squeezed.

The soldier's legs began kicking wildly, trying to throw Six off. Six squeezed tighter. He could feel his victim's adrenaline-powered pulse through the jugular vein, racing at 150 beats per minute.

Don't kill him, Six reminded himself. *You're not a murderer.*

The soldier tried to lift his arms up from the floor, in vain. His pulse climbed to 170 as he realized he was at Six's mercy.

Six squeezed tighter. *No*, he thought. *Killing this man won't bring Two back.* But he didn't seem to be able to control his hands.

180.

190.

The scrabbling of the soldier's legs was getting slower, weaker. His arms were resisting Six's pressure with less and less force. Like a spider sprayed with pesticide, his panicked motions were subsiding. His heart rate began falling fast, slipping back to 150, then 100.

If you kill him, Six thought, *you are worse than him. He may have shot Two in self-defense.*

Eighty.

Sixty-five.

And every second you spend here, Six told himself, *Kyntak is in more danger.*

He unclenched his hand. The soldier slumped to the floor, bruised, unconscious — but alive. Six fell backward. He stared at his gloved hands for a moment, flexing the fingers to unstiffen them. *Look what I almost did*, he thought. The human body could sometimes survive as much as four minutes of strangulation, and Six was confident that he had done no permanent damage. But he was alarmed. His subconscious had taken over. He was a being of reason. He saw the futility of killing the soldier for what he had done to Two, but a deeply buried part of Six's mind had wanted to do it anyway, a raw aggression which circumstances had activated.

Murder is like a virus, he thought. *Infectious. The more you see it, the closer it comes to you, the more likely you are to succumb to it.*

Six peered into the fog. The floor was thick with the bodies of soldiers, all out cold. Most were lying where they had fallen, it seemed — but all had been disarmed. This looked like Kyntak's work.

Six could hear the thundering of helicopter blades again. He reached towards the unconscious soldier. The Eagle lay beside him. Six picked it up and checked the magazine as the Twin descended out of the fog above him.

There was a whistling noise, and then a tranquilizer dart thudded into Six's neck. He gasped in pain, which lasted only a second before a pleasant numbness began to spread through his veins.

The gunner launched another net at him. Six tried to get out from under it, but the muscles in his legs seemed to melt away. The world tilted towards him and he staggered into the wall.

The side of his head collided with the plaster, which cracked, but Six felt no pain as stars exploded before his eyes. The net covering him wobbled, as if he were looking at it from underwater. Six fell to his knees.

The Twin descended farther, apparently looking for somewhere to set down. The gunner was fiddling with his harness and climbing through the door. Suddenly Six realized that the soldiers hadn't come to wipe out the Deck. It was about him. The bait had been for him. They'd come to take him away.

The logical part of his brain overcame the desire to sleep, and Six tried to tear the net off. But he only fell over. His arms hit the ground, and suddenly felt as if they were made of iron. His head landed on his elbow.

"Yeaaaaaarrgh!" Screeching like an eagle, Kyntak suddenly sprinted out of the grey air towards Six and the helicopter, not through the corridor, but along the top of one of the walls. He raced by above Six without even glancing at him, and then jumped into the air, legs together and arms outstretched . . .

. . . and flew headfirst through the hold door of the helicopter, crashing into the gunner. They both tumbled out of sight into the hold. The Twin reared back, as if it had been hit by a cannonball instead of a teenager. Then the pilot pulled it up, engines whining, and it vanished into the mist above.

The sound of whirling blades faded from the air. The gunfire had stopped. Soon only a cold, dead silence filled Six's ears. It was as if Kyntak and the helicopter had never existed.

And then he saw, and felt, nothing.

THE MESSAGE

Awake.

The world swam into bright, painful focus. *Eyes*, Six thought. *Green eyes.*

"Good morning, sunshine," Ace of Diamonds said, tucking her blond hair behind her ear as she leaned over him. "Are you in pain?"

Six stretched his limbs. They were stiff, but not sore. "No."

"Glad to hear it," Ace said. She walked briskly over to a bench and rummaged through her instruments. "You were injected with a heavy dose of Syncal-4, a benzodiazepine derivative. Think of it as flurazepam's bigger, meaner cousin. It creates a deep, refreshing sleep in small doses, but I'd estimate they hit you with about 35 cc, enough sedative to put most people in a coma. Not you, though. Out for less than two hours, and now you're as good as new." She shook her head. "Unbelievable."

When Kyntak had carried Six back to the Deck after his ordeal at the Lab, Ace had been the doctor on call. Six was suffering from horrific injuries — injuries that would have a killed a human. So Kyntak had reluctantly told Ace the full story. Because she knew Six was a superhuman, she had been his preferred doctor ever since. She quietly tailored her treatments to his unusual needs. Six was glad of her presence — while she wasn't much older than Six, her skill in all fields of medical science was matched only by her passion for the Deck's cause.

"Am I at the Deck?" he asked.

Ace nodded. "The basement of the hospital wing."

The morgue, Six thought. *Why have they put me down here?*

"It's a busy day for me," she said, picking up Six's chart. "Two bodies and a patient. There's no info on how superhumans react to Syncal, so I thought I'd take you down here and do the autopsies while I monitored your condition."

Six rolled his head to one side. Methryn Crexe was lying on a chrome table only meters away in an open black body bag. His dark, narrow eyes, which had once sparkled with avarice and suspicion, were shut forever.

There was another body on a table farther away. He presumed it was Two; he didn't want to look. He shut his eyes.

"I dug out the dart they hit you with," Ace was saying. She held it up. "Weirdest thing I ever saw — less like a dart than an automatic syringe. The tube has two airtight compartments, one for the Syncal, the other containing a pod filled with compressed nitrogen. The needle had a trigger hooked into it, so when it broke your skin a valve opened on the pod, letting the nitrogen expand into the container. The expanding gas put pressure on the other container, forcing Syncal into the needle."

Six kept his eyes shut. "Why go to so much trouble?"

"Because a normal dart would just have leaked some sedative into your system. This baby actually pumped you full of it." Six could hear her scribbling on his chart. "As I said, they put enough into you to stun a decent-size horse."

The events of the day were slowly returning to Six. Methryn Crexe, rescued, murdered. Two, shot dead. Kyntak, missing.

It makes no sense, he thought.

He opened his eyes. "Have you done the autopsies?"

Ace nodded. "Agent Two of Hearts was shot in the head with a 9-millimeter round. Plenty of bruising to the back, left arm, and left leg, mostly postmortem. The rigor mortis shows that he's been dead for more than two and a half hours, but I'm sure you knew that. I'm sorry." She paused. "Crexe is a little weirder. Let me show you why."

Six swung his legs off the table and tried to stand up. His legs felt like jelly, and he fell backward against the edge of the table.

Ace gripped his arm. "Careful. Remember, they hit you with a huge dose."

He regained his balance and shook Ace's hand off his arm.

She turned to the table with Crexe's body.

"Killed by a shot to the head. Another 9-millimeter, but not the same gun. The lividity shows that his body was carried somewhere immediately after death. The blood drained into his extremities before congealing in the capillaries. My guess is that he was dead before he left his cell."

Six frowned. Why would they kill Crexe before abducting him? "There must be something they didn't want us to know," he said. "Something he could have told us."

"But why take the body?" Ace asked. "Why not leave him where he fell?"

"They wanted him as bait — to lead Deck agents to the apartment building." Six rubbed his eyes with the palm of his hand.

"There's something else." Ace adjusted the body bag. "He has a tattoo."

Six gasped. Imprinted across Crexe's chest was . . .

" . . . a web address?"

"Http://cww.1500hours/23June.ps," said Ace.

Hyper Text Transfer Protocol, Six translated in his head, *City Wide Web, dot 3 o'clock, slash 23 June, dot Private Server.*

Today was June 23. Six looked at his watch. 14:55:03.

"I can do some tests on his skin," Ace was saying, "but beyond the type of ink and when it was inscribed, there won't be a lot I can tell you."

"Do them anyway," Six said. "I need all the information I can get."

"Gotcha," Ace said. "In that case, head to King of Hearts's office; he's about to check out the website. He'll be glad to see you're okay. And it's nearly three o'clock."

Six nodded. "Stay alert. Today would not be a good day to mess up."

"I'll take that as concern for my well-being," Ace said, raising an eyebrow.

Six touched King's door handle and heard the buzzer sound inside. The door opened. King was sitting behind his desk, squinting at an LCD through red-rimmed eyes. Six couldn't see the screen. The computer looked new; the matte-finish casing was still smooth from the factory and no dust had settled on the CPU.

Six shivered a little when he saw the burst blood vessels in King's eyes. It looked like he'd been staring at the screen for so long he'd forgotten how to blink.

"I'm glad you're okay," King said, glancing at him briefly.

Six sat down. His health was irrelevant. It was Kyntak's whereabouts that concerned him.

"Have you heard from Kyntak?" he asked.

King shook his head. "The agents are still searching. But as far as we can tell, he's vanished off the face of the earth. Except for the unconscious ones, the rest of the soldiers who ambushed you have disappeared as well!"

"What about the satellite pictures?"

"Someone jammed the server soon after I lost contact with you. The Diamonds say it's a dead end."

"So what's on the screen?" Six asked.

King spun the LCD on its stand so it faced him. Six recognized the ChaoNet web browser and saw that King had already typed in the address from Crexe's tattoo. The web page was a simple black backdrop with large white numbers in the center. It read **00:03:19**, and flicked over to **00:03:18** as Six watched. Then **00:03:17**.

Hours, minutes, seconds, Six thought. A countdown.

"You've disabled cookies?" he asked.

"Yes. This is a new PC, taken from the most recent shipment for Diamonds. It has nothing on it besides ChaoOffice and the browser. Grysat rigged up the best firewall he could, not that it should matter, given that the PC isn't connected to the Deck network." He pinched the bridge of his nose between thumb and forefinger. "The server will still have registered us as a hit on their stats, so they know that someone's watching. But besides sending other computers to the same site as a smoke screen, which would be a security risk, there's nothing we can do about that."

"What happens when the countdown is up?"

King's eyes didn't waver from the screen. "Your guess is as good as mine."

"We've got a dead agent," Six said, "a dead fugitive, an AWOL Joker, and no answers. What can we do in three minutes?"

"The Clubs are retrieving the unconscious soldiers from the apartment building," King said. "We'll learn something from them once we get them shuffled and they wake up."

"How long will that take?"

"An hour, perhaps."

Six looked at the screen again. **00:02:41**.

"What if it's a bomb?" he demanded. "Here? Inside the Deck?"

"Then why would they give us a countdown?" King said. "And a body with a web address on it?"

Six remembered the mystery woman's words. *It seems like a game, but it's not. He's trying to put you off balance because he knows that's the easiest way to beat you. He aims to* deceive.

"Forget why," Six said. "Evacuate the building, right now."

"I have Diamond bomb squads sweeping the building as a precaution," King said. "All nonessential personnel have been moved to the underground shelter."

"What about Ace of Diamonds?" Six demanded. "She's still running tests on the bodies!"

"There's no bomb, Six." King looked at him properly for the first time, and Six was again frightened by the hemorrhaged veins in his eyes. "If there were, they wouldn't have warned us."

"If there's even the slightest chance —" Six persisted.

"Then what? We should all evacuate, and have no one watching this screen when it hits zero?"

"As opposed to getting ourselves killed to satisfy your curiosity?"

"We met a formidable new enemy today, Six," King said. "Not the Lab, not even ChaoSonic. Someone worse. In a matter of hours, they broke into our cells as if the walls were made of paper, wiped the floor with a team of our best Hearts, and left the toughest agent I've got sleeping on the floor of some prehistoric apartment building." He glared at Six, and Six's gut wrenched. *Is King angry at me?* he wondered.

"If you want to run," King said quietly, "then that's fine. Take Ace with you. But this website is the only lead we have, and I'm not prepared to leave the City to their mercy just yet. I'm not leaving this computer."

00:01:03. Six's heart was beating a little faster. "We could set up something to record it. You don't have to wait here."

"It's being recorded internally — Grysat set that up. But the website could have a copyright filter that blocks the recording — and traditional DVCs are too easily monitored." He forced a smile. "After all you've been through, a few numbers on a screen are making you jittery?"

Six hung his head slightly. "I've had a rough day," he admitted.

00:00:30.

The numbers clicked down. Every instinct screamed at Six to run, to climb out the window and jump, or at least to brace himself in the doorway or under the desk. But King had never steered him wrong before.

00:00:20.

But if it wasn't a bomb, Six thought, what could it be? Why else would they have been given the web address? Perhaps it was a bomb — just not here. A shiver ran up his spine.

00:00:10.

Perhaps ten seconds from now, somewhere in the City, a building was going to shatter like glass, turning the thousands of people inside to dust.

00:00:04.

00:00:03.

00:00:02.

00:00:01.

00:00:00.

Six jumped. He'd been able to picture the explosion so vividly in his head that the anticlimax was more surprising than a colossal fireball would have been.

The numbers faded from the screen. The website was now completely black.

"Are you thinking what I'm thinking?" King asked.

Six nodded grimly. "A bomb went off somewhere else."

"I'll get the Diamonds to check the —"

A flash from the screen interrupted him — the grainy flicker of exposure levels adjusting themselves. A hiss was emitted from the sound membrane over the LCD. They both stared at it, and their eyes widened in alarm.

An image had appeared. A man was sitting on a chair in front of a blank brick wall. His shaved head hung forward. Someone was standing behind him. The picture was too dark to see the person's face, but from the posture and figure Six guessed it was a female.

The woman put her hand on the man's scalp and pulled his head backward, exposing his face to the light.

Six gasped. It was Kyntak. Eyes shut, face bruised, but unquestionably him.

"I now have in my possession," the woman on the screen said, "Agent Six of Hearts."

ULTIMATUM

"By the end of today, I will be a hundred million credits richer," the woman continued. "I could sell Six to ChaoSonic, who I'm sure would be thrilled to have him returned, or I could perform my own tests upon him until I have collected a hundred million credits worth of data."

Six was searching Kyntak's face for signs of life. He found none.

"But there is a third alternative. If you deposit that same amount into a nominated account before six o'clock this evening, then Six will be returned to you unharmed."

Six remembered the net cutting his skin. *A ransom*, he thought. *That's what this is all about.*

"Once the deposit has been verified, Six will be at the corner of 452nd Street and the Seawall at seven o'clock. If the money is not deposited, Six disappears forever."

She leaned forward. "You've seen what I can do. Don't test me."

The screen cut to a string of letters and numbers — a bank account, Six realized.

There was a long silence. Then King exploded into a stream of curses, many of which Six had never heard before. He slammed his fist down on the desk, his teeth grinding together and veins popping out on his forehead.

"That doesn't help us," Six said.

"It helps me," King said, breathing heavily. He wiped some sweat off his brow.

"Why do they think Kyntak is me?" Six asked.

"You're identical twins," King said. "You're the same age, you have the same DNA, and the same superhuman abilities. The only reason the rest of us can tell you apart is that he's always smiling and you're always in a black coat."

"How did they get a sample of our DNA?" Six demanded. "Kyntak and I wiped the Lab computers!"

"I don't know. But they have one. Even so, they could tell he's superhuman just by analyzing a blood sample."

"It wasn't about Crexe at all," Six realized. "They knew he was the one thing they could take from us that would make me come running."

"They just didn't know you had a brother who'd go with you," King said. "I assume he did some stunt that proved he was superhuman?"

Six remembered Kyntak jumping off the wall into the hold of the helicopter. "Yeah, he did."

"Okay." King rubbed his eyes. "I'll call Queen, get her to dig into the reserves and scrape together a hundred million credits."

"What?" Six stared at King. "You're going to pay up?"

"We may have to. Otherwise —"

"No." Six sprang up and started pacing around the room. "We can examine the video, search through the usual suspects, and see what leads we can dig up. They obviously planned this a long time in advance, so there'll be a reason they picked 452nd

Street as the drop-off point. If I go there, I'm bound to work out something. They may already have stakeouts, and I could grab them." He stopped walking and glared at King. "They're not going to get away with this."

King was silent for a few seconds. "What's more important to you, Six? Bringing them to justice or getting Kyntak back?"

"Getting Kyntak back," Six said without hesitation. "But even if we pay, there's no guarantee that —"

King cut him off with a wave of his hand. "I know. The money is there because we may need to give it to them and take it back later. But we won't let them keep it." He hit PRINT and the bank account details scrolled out of the printer. "I just wanted to check you were still on my side."

"Always," Six said.

"Good. Call Ace of Diamonds. Let's see what we can get off this video."

By 15:30, they didn't know much more. They'd watched the recording dozens of times. Seeing Kyntak's bruised face again and again made Six feel cold in his stomach.

The brick wall behind the woman was moderately weathered clay, held together with quicklime mortar. There were millions like it in the City. That was probably why it had been chosen.

Ace said the chair Kyntak was sitting in looked like pure lead, and it had been soldered together rather than screwed. He was chained to it despite the fact that he was clearly unconscious when he was filmed. *A bad sign*, Six thought. *They're being over-cautious; therefore, they know what we're capable of.*

Kyntak's Deck fatigues had been removed — he was wearing a bright orange undershirt and shorts. That seemed unusual, but it didn't get them anywhere.

But they had learned one thing. When they zoomed right in, they saw that Kyntak's jugular vein pulsed with a steady rhythm. He was alive.

Six ground his teeth together. "We have three and a half hours," he said. "And we know nothing."

"The soldiers from the apartment building should be back any minute now," King said. "We'll learn plenty from them."

That was their best shot, Six knew. But his subconscious screamed out for action. He was wasting precious seconds *waiting*. There must be something he could do, instead of just standing still in front of a screen . . .

"Cut to the end," he said suddenly. "Where she leans forward."

Ace clicked, and the picture shifted. The woman was leaning over Kyntak, hands on his shoulders. Her face was closer to the light, but still too dark to identify.

"Now take a snapshot," Six said. He didn't need to elaborate. Ace was already fiddling with the brightness/contrast and hue/saturation settings. She clicked PROCESS.

And suddenly the woman's face was clear, staring at them out of the screen. Narrow lips, a nose that had once been broken, and fishlike crimson eyes. Black hair framed a narrow face.

Red eyes? Six thought. *Could be contacts, surgery, gene therapy — or just computer graphics. But not an accident.*

"Can we check her facial focal points against our database?" King asked Ace. "And hack into the ChaoSonic one if we don't have a match?"

"Sorry," Ace said. "The picture is stretched — that's why her face looks so narrow — and I don't know what ratio was used. That'll mess up the stats of the program; she could be any of a million people."

"These people have histories, though," King said, with a meaningful glance at Six. "Whoever she is, she's experienced, smart, probably rich, and distinctive in both style and appearance. This isn't her first job. There are people who will know her."

Ace gaped. "You're going to go door-to-door in the cell blocks, showing inmates a picture and asking for a name?"

"No need," Six said, hitting PRINT. "We have a contact she's already worked with."

"How can you know that for sure?"

Six was already on his way out the door. "Our contact has worked with everyone."

The sun had passed its peak behind the burnt sky, and shadows were starting to creep back along the oily concrete as Six eased his

car to a halt.

The house was bigger than he'd expected. When he'd last checked the surveillance records, the owner had been living in a one-room apartment near the City steelworks. By contrast, her current residence had turrets: narrow spines of grey synthetic wood rising out of a dark concrete hut which admittedly seemed too small to support them.

That's Earle Shuji, Six thought. *Regardless of practicality, she always has to live in style.*

Six had met Shuji eight months earlier on an undercover mission. She had been kidnapping engineers and soldiers to help her produce robots. The engineers had designed and programmed the bots, and the soldiers had tested them by fighting for their lives. The soldiers were all dead by the time Six arrived, but he had rescued the engineers and shut down her operation. And he had taken home one of her robots, Harry, who had proven himself useful a few times since.

But less than forty-eight hours after shuffling her, Six had set Shuji free in return for information — information that had helped him save the lives of his colleagues. He hadn't seen her since, but the Deck had been watching her carefully. Apparently she'd found an honest job — as honest as they came in the City, anyway. Under a new name, she was working as a consultant for ChaoSonic in their shoe-design sector, abandoning her extensive knowledge of robotics and biomechanics.

There was a bullnecked guard by the door, dressed in immaculate pre-Takeover clothes — a clean-pressed charcoal suit, with polished leather loafers and opaque dark glasses.

Six had expected Shuji's security to be inside, not guarding the door. He was going to have to change his plan.

He looked at his watch. 16:03:58: less than three hours until the deadline. No time for an elaborate plan. He just needed to get inside.

Six had parked the car on the opposite side of the street, about thirty meters farther along from Shuji's house, so it would be out of her surveillance range. He locked it and examined the house next door to Shuji's.

There was a square protrusion running up the front wall, which led to a chimney behind the guttering of the slightly sloped roof. *Too easy*, Six thought.

He glanced around the empty street to check that no one was watching him. He could hear the distant sound of traffic on the highway.

Six sprinted towards the house and jumped before hitting the wall. After landing momentarily on the sideboards he sprang out again, ricocheted off the chimney, and swung one-handed from the gutter to the roof.

He crouched there, pausing for a second to watch and listen. The front door was opening below him. Someone was investigating the noise.

He ran across the roof, jumped when he hit the edge, and flew across the divide between the neighbor's house and Shuji's, before thumping into one of the turrets and grabbing the window so he didn't fall.

He examined the latch on the window. It looked unlocked, but rusted and probably stiff. He gave the frame a hefty shove, and paint around the hinges cracked and crumbled as the window swung inward. He slipped through into the darkness.

Six found himself on an oak-paneled spiral staircase, leading up to a distant attic door. There was a picture hanging in a simple chrome frame on the wall. A handsome man in his thirties smiled out at Six from the black-and-white photo.

Six turned around and started to shut the window, but froze when he saw a green laser slash across the glass. *An alarm system*, he thought. *Why didn't I trigger it when I broke in?*

His answer came in the form of a punch to the lower back, which knocked him forward against the stairs. *I did* trip it, he thought. *It's a silent alarm.*

The bullnecked security guard had a taser in one hand, which he now aimed at Six. Six jumped, and the electric barb sparked harmlessly off the stairs. The guard lunged forward in a crash tackle as Six was about to land, but Six slammed one foot against the banister and pirouetted in midair, kicking the taser out of the guard's hand, then rebounding off the wall and landing behind his opponent.

The guard tried to turn around, but he was too slow. Six

caught the taser before it hit the ground and blasted him in the back of the neck.

The guard thrashed backward into Six's bear hug, and Six jammed his thumbs up beneath the big man's jaw. The guard went limp instantly.

Six crept the rest of the way down the stairs.

He found Shuji in her lounge room, sitting on a pristine white couch with her feet up on the cushions beside her, watching a cream-colored television. She no longer had the ponytail or business suit that Six remembered. Her hair was short, dyed red, and scruffed up carefully at the back. Her clothes resembled a silk jogging suit.

"I don't suppose running would do me any good," she said without looking at Six.

"A waste of time for both of us," he agreed.

"We had a deal."

"We still do." Six glanced around. "Nice house."

"I have a good job," she responded, "and just as my suffering won't undo my crimes, my indulgences do nothing to worsen them." She switched off the television and looked him in the eye. "Are you here to recapture me?"

Six shook his head. "I want information."

She sighed. "You could have just e-mailed. I wouldn't have needed workplace comp for Dwayne, whom I assume is lying unconscious upstairs?"

"I was in a hurry," Six said. He pulled the picture of the red-eyed woman out of his pocket. He handed it over. "Who is this?"

Shuji took the photograph, and glanced at it. Her eyes widened and she dropped it as if it were on fire. "Where did you get this?"

"You know her?" Six asked. *There's still hope*, he thought. He looked at his watch. 16:16:05. "She kidnapped an agent; I need to find her."

Shuji seemed to shrink into the couch. Six saw goose bumps rise on her arms. "You're in way over your head," she said.

"I don't have time for this," Six said icily. "Tell me who she is."

"It's not who *she* is that's important," Shuji said. "It's who she works for." She glanced around the room uneasily, as if her words alone could bring forth enemies from the shadows. *"Vanish."*

THE CELL

"No way," Six said. "I'm not leaving without —"

"It wasn't an instruction," Shuji hissed. "It's his name — the only one anyone knows. He's called Vanish because he's so good at disappearing, even when you think you've got him completely cornered."

"Who is he?" Six asked. "And what does he want with a Deck agent?"

"I assume there was a ransom," Shuji replied. "If money is what he asked for, that's what he wants; and believe me, if that's what he wants, that's exactly what he'll get."

"There are easier ways to get rich," Six growled. "And he could've asked for a lot more than he did. The kidnapping alone must have cost him a fortune."

"He used to be a scientist," Shuji said. "A nanotechnology expert, or so the story goes, and he still has a thirst for data. He doesn't want to get rich the same way as everyone else, or any of the ways he already knows he can. He wants to *learn*."

"I need details," Six said.

Shuji shrugged. "I've never met him. Everything I know is hearsay."

"How do you know she works for him?" Six asked, picking up the photograph.

"She came as a potential buyer for my bots last year," Shuji said. "The day before you showed up, actually. I checked her out and discovered she worked for Vanish. I figured he was interested in saving money by replacing his private army with bots."

A private army, Six thought. *That would explain this morning's disaster.* "Did she turn you down, or the other way around?"

"She said she couldn't negotiate on her employer's behalf. She took the specs and stats and said she'd get back to me."

"But the Deck shuffled you first," Six said.

Shuji nodded and scraped her feet nervously across the sofa cushions. *She's not telling me everything*, Six thought. "Is there any way to track them down?"

Shuji shook her head. "You can't find him — that's his defining characteristic. ChaoSonic's been searching as far back as their private records go. He has hundreds of secret employees, and almost all of them have worked for ChaoSonic. ChaoSonic doesn't take kindly to that."

"How old is he?" Six asked. Shuji could probably have accessed ChaoSonic records as far back as fifty years. Surely Vanish couldn't have been in the business that long.

"No one knows," Shuji said. "No one knows anything about him for sure, except that he's rich, a lot of people work for him, and everyone else is either scared or oblivious. But there are stories —"

"I'm not interested in stories," Six said. "I'm interested in keeping my friend alive."

"Then pay the money," Shuji said. "No one gets the better of Vanish."

Alarm bells rang inside Six's head. What if this was a setup? What if the woman in the video had *expected* him to go to Shuji and had already coerced her into telling him to pay up?

"What about the woman?" Six asked. "Can I find her?"

"Her name is Niskev Pacye," Shuji said, looking at her feet. "There'll be an address she uses for deliveries on my old company mainframe, if you still have it."

"Why did she give you that when she hadn't agreed to buy the bots?"

"I research all my contacts thoroughly," · Shuji said. "I couldn't find a home address for Pacye, but a drop-off point is better than nothing. I needn't have worried about her, though. It was you who turned out to be a fed." She looked at him. "You're going to get yourself killed, Six."

"I'm sure you'd be really upset," Six said sarcastically, pocketing the photograph.

"You're the only reason I'm not in a cell right now," Shuji reminded him. "Even though I have an honest job, I'm sure the other agents would gladly lock me up again."

"Your information saved their lives."

"*You* saved their lives," Shuji corrected. "I was just lucky I had the intel to offer. And besides, Methryn Crexe saved your life, and you still locked him up."

Methryn Crexe. Even after death, his name still haunted Six. Eight months ago, Six had been caught in an explosion. There had been little between him and death. Methryn Crexe had grown a clone of him, matured it with Chelsea Tridya's aging formula, then harvested organs and limbs from it and transplanted them onto Six to save his life. But Six felt little gratitude; the explosion had been Crexe's fault. He was surprised Shuji knew about it. She must still have a network of some kind.

It was 16:29:28. Six headed for the door.

"Six," Shuji said. "Do you still have that prototype bot?"

Six froze. "Everything in the factory was dismantled and sold as spare parts."

"Harry wasn't in the warehouse," Shuji said. "And you wouldn't destroy him. Not when he could be so useful to you."

Six turned around. "You're insane. If you think I'll let you anywhere near —"

Shuji shook her head. "That's not it. I wanted to warn you — all my test prototypes had a self-destruct mechanism — there's thirteen hundred grams of C-4 set to go off if the exoskeleton is pierced." She made eye contact. "I installed it so no one could look at the inner workings and steal my design."

Six frowned. "Why are you telling me this?"

"Because if you tried to open Harry, his CPU would explode, and if you happened to be in the way of his exhaust valve, you'd be fried. And I don't want you to die. So shut down all his systems first by saying 'cerfitipus talotus.'"

"Thanks," Six said. He was unsettled by Shuji. She seemed forthcoming with information, warnings, and advice, without needing bribes or threats. But was that because she'd been compromised, or had she genuinely turned her life around?

"Whose picture is that on your stairs?" he asked, remembering the man he'd seen on his way in. The Deck hadn't been able to find any family before arresting her. "Your husband? Your brother?"

"It came with the frame," she said.

"Why do you have it?" he asked.

"To remind me," she said, "that someday there might be someone I can put in there. If I work hard."

Six raised an eyebrow. This was not the arrogant, confident

Earle Shuji he remembered. "Will you tell him you're a mass murderer?"

"That's none of your business."

"I spared you your punishment. I'm involved."

"No one can spare me my punishment," she said in a whisper. "And it has nothing to do with you."

Awake.

Kyntak opened his eyes to a bright light. *I must be dead*, he thought. *This isn't so bad.* He tried to sit up.

Pain slashed into every nerve in his body, and he gritted his teeth to stifle a scream as he fell back to his original position. *Okay, I take that back*, he said to himself. *It is bad. What happened? Where am I?*

He could remember one of the soldiers punching him in the face; he still had the wobbly tooth to prove it. He could remember jabbing the soldier in his solar plexus, and knocking him over, and then hearing gunshots nearby, and going to investigate — and soon after that, seeing some goon about to jump onto Six from a helicopter, crash-tackling him, and then . . . and then . . .

. . . and then nothing, he thought. Someone must have hit him with a tranq, and now he was captured. But he was alive. Whatever they wanted from him, they hadn't gotten it yet, and until they did, he was safe. So where was he?

He rolled his head to the side, trying to ignore the aching of his neck and the pounding pressure in his brain as he did so. Mirrored walls, polished to a pristine gleam. *Great*, he thought, *that narrows it down. Which places have shiny walls? How about every single ChaoSonic institution in the City?*

There didn't seem to be a door. *How did I get in here?* he wondered. *Maybe there's a trapdoor in the floor.*

His arms were stretched out to either side as if he had been crucified, and as he stared up at the mirrored ceiling, he saw that his feet were almost half a meter apart. He had been clamped to a white table by his wrists, knees, and ankles. There was something he couldn't see restraining his neck. It was looser than the other clamps, but tight enough so he couldn't lift his head completely off the cushioned pad beneath it. He was wearing a garish orange undershirt and matching shorts, and they'd shaved his head. He shuddered. *I look ridiculous*, he thought.

There were two needle marks in his right arm, each puncturing the radial artery. *Not enough to shoot me with a tranq*, Kyntak thought, *they have to pump me full of drugs as well. And who are "they," anyway?*

There was a sudden hissing noise from above, like the burning of a fuse. Kyntak's gaze snapped towards the source. At first he saw nothing, but as his eyes focused he could see that a narrow clear, plastic tube ran along the seam between the walls and the ceiling. It ended in one corner with a kind of rubber nozzle, which sealed itself as he watched. The hissing noise ceased. The cell lapsed into icy silence.

Okay, Kyntak thought, *what do I know? They have good-quality manpower and equipment, therefore money. But they've been hiding, operating under the radar, so they're not ChaoSonic.*

Vigilante? He didn't think so. If there was a vigilante group better funded and bigger than the Deck, he would've heard of it before now.

So, a private company. One that liked rescuing shuffled criminals, shooting Deck agents, and imprisoning people in rooms that hissed. *Man*, he thought. *This is turning out to be one lousy day.*

"Good afternoon, Agent Six."

Kyntak flinched. The voice seemed deafening after the silence. There were now two men in the corners of the room beyond his feet, which surprised him. He still couldn't see a door. One man wore the same fatigues as the soldiers from the apartment block. He cradled a Hawk 9-millimeter.

The other man wore a loose white T-shirt and grey jeans. He had a pleasant, roundish face, with stubbly brown hair and wide-spaced grey-green eyes, which stared inquisitively at Kyntak. There was a faded scar stretched across his forehead, just below the hairline. A rugby player's neck led to a bulky, broad-shouldered torso, but his hands were narrow and delicate. He looked as though he was in his midtwenties.

He thinks I'm Six, Kyntak realized. *Great.* "My reputation precedes me?" he asked.

The man smiled broadly. "Of course. But even as we speak, I am learning more."

Kyntak closed his eyes and groaned inwardly. *Abducted by a crazy Six of Hearts fan in a case of mistaken identity*, he thought. *Six will never let me hear the end of this.*

There was a pause. What do you say, Kyntak wondered, to your kidnapper? *What are you doing to do with me?* maybe, or the slightly less weak-sounding abbreviation: *What do you want with me?* But neither of those felt right.

When he had been Six's captor in a cell last year, the first thing Six had said was, "I'm not buying this," before proceeding to mock the quality of his surroundings. *That's fine for an arrogant snob like him*, Kyntak thought, *but it doesn't suit me.*

"Can I help you?" he asked finally. It was meant to sound levelheaded, even threatening; but he thought he sounded more like a shop assistant approaching a hesitant customer.

"I expect so," the man said. "At the moment, I only want to learn."

"Loosen my chains," Kyntak offered, "and I'll teach you jujitsu."

The man's smile vanished. "I'm serious."

Kyntak laughed. "So am I."

"First impressions," the man said. "You're either hiding your fear behind a façade of good humor, or you're not afraid. If you're not afraid, you're either crazy or stupid. If you *are* afraid and you're hiding it with jokes, then that makes you either self-conscious or impulsive." He walked slowly around the table, keeping a half-meter distance from its edge. "You know, I've studied your history and it seems to rule out stupid. Impulsive is unlikely too."

He bared his teeth in a curious smile. "So, are you self-conscious? Everyone who knows you is either an admirer or an enemy, so that would be a reasonable cause. On the other hand, it's been a long sixteen years for you — pain, confusion, constant peril. No one could blame you for being crazy."

"Give me some boots," Kyntak said. "I'd like to shake in them."

"This," the man said, "will be an interesting two hours."

Kyntak knew he was being baited, but he couldn't resist. "What happens in two hours?"

"Ah, you *are* impulsive," the man said. "In two hours, I'll know all I need to know."

LOCKDOWN

"I'm headed back to the Deck now," Six said as he turned a corner. Fluorescent lamps were flickering on throughout the streets as the fog darkened around the car. The roads and paths were becoming more crowded; people of all ages were driving, walking, jogging, and cycling in and out of the gloom.

Because the lamps lit the City better than the feeble daylight, most of the citizens chose to emerge from their houses at nighttime. The suffocating fog kept the temperature much the same, and because the City was in the Southern Hemisphere, the summer solstice was only five hours longer than the winter one — perfect conditions for the nocturnal.

Six had the feeling that ChaoSonic would standardize the weather completely if they could — make a permanent grey middle ground between day and night, tone the wind down to a dull breeze, and set the temperature to an eternal nineteen degrees Celsius. Consumers reacted more predictably in unchanging environments. But he took some comfort from the knowledge that ChaoSonic didn't have that power. No one did. Regardless of what happened down here in the City — skies soiled, bombs dropped, people murdered — the world just kept on turning, obliviously spinning its infinite loops around the sun.

Maybe life's greatest condolence, he thought, *is how little difference any of us makes to the big picture. And maybe our greatest strength is that we never stop trying.*

"We've only got an hour and fifty minutes left until the deadline," King was saying in his headset. "What's your ETA?"

"About ten minutes," Six replied. "What's the situation with the money?"

"I'll conference the call to Grysat; he'll explain that."

There was a short pause, then Grysat's voice came on the line. "Can you hear me, Six?"

"I read you," Six said. He swerved to overtake a motorcycle; the driver pulled back, sensibly. "What's the plan?"

"I've rounded up a hundred million credits," Grysat began. "It's ready to be transferred to the account in the ransom demand at the click of a mouse."

"Have you rigged it so it can be traced?" Six asked. "They'll check for that."

"Each digital credit has time-activated beacon software on it, which is armed only after it's been moved twice. So when we move it into the kidnappers' account, they'll scan it, but they shouldn't see anything because it hasn't been armed. When they move it again to hide it from us, that's the trigger. That's when every single credit of the money will send out the name and password of the account it's in."

"Will they be able to stop it?"

"It's likely they won't even notice," Grysat said. "The burst of data takes seven microseconds, so even if it sets off their security alarms, the damage will be done long before they work out what has happened. And once it's armed, the beacon can't be disarmed, so even if they know it's there, they can't do anything about it. Worst-case scenario, they scan it thoroughly a second time and see the armed beacon, and then they try to launder the money digitally. But laundering a hundred million credits in less than twelve hours is difficult, and even if they succeed, when the beacon is activated we'll have the names and passwords of all the accounts the money ends up in."

"So we could get it back," Six said, "and follow a digital trail to the kidnappers?"

"Exactly. Relax, Six. The money is taken care of. You just focus on getting Kyntak."

"I'm setting up a team to stake out the drop-off point," King said, taking over. "They'll be in their civvies, fully briefed, and ready to leave in thirty minutes."

So they'll be there and in place about an hour before the drop-off, Six thought. *It'll have to do.* "How many?"

"Five Hearts, three Clubs. Enough to watch every entrance to the street corner."

"Six? I have more information for you." The new voice on the line was Ace of Diamonds.

"I'm listening," said Six.

"The unconscious soldiers have all been brought back to the Deck."

"Are they responding to interrogation?"

"I can't wake them up."

Six frowned. "Any of them?"

"They're still unconscious. All fourteen of them."

"But how?" said Six.

"Someone must have shot them with tranquilizer darts. There are trace amounts of Syncal-4 in their bloodstreams — nothing like the amount they pumped into you, but enough to keep them sleeping for another half hour at least. I can't find any needle marks, but it could be another strange kind of dart."

Six frowned. "None of the Deck agents were armed with tranquilizers."

"It's the best explanation I have," Ace said.

Six thought about the woman who'd grabbed him from behind, and her cryptic warning. Could she have shot some of the soldiers with a tranq gun? Or perhaps Kyntak had picked one up and used it.

"I'll come down and take a look after I see King." Six swung his car into the parking garage.

The line clicked dead.

It isn't right, Retuni Lerke thought. *My sons, taken from me so many times. None to raise as my own.*

The fire had hurt most. In one blazing sweep, Six, Kyntak, and Sevadonn had been released into the City to do as they pleased. He had not been given the chance to bring them up like a good father should — and they had been too young to shoulder their own responsibilities without a wise guiding hand.

They're still too young, he thought. *Sixteen? They've grown up quickly, but they shouldn't have had to. What sixteen-year-old is ready to be responsible for all his actions?*

No wonder they had turned out so wrong.

He knew Crexe was dead — and he was glad. The fire had been Crexe's intervention, and it had torn all their lives apart. Years later, Crexe had crippled the old man's fourth son, mere hours after growing him. Lerke's glorious genome. Used to make a mere organ donor. And then Crexe had killed Sevadonn, the child Lerke had been closest to. The use of Crexe's corpse as bait had seemed a fitting end.

Lerke coughed, and scuffed his feet angrily against the carpet. His elation had been temporary. Crexe had been the lesser of two evils, or at least the more foolish. Vanish was smarter. He had already captured Kyntak. Kyntak was the old man's least favorite son, but the loss of a child still hurt. What kind of father stops caring for his children, even once they fail him?

Without help, Six would certainly fall. He was headed down a dark path. Vanish would get the better of him, and then Lerke would be left with no sons at all. Four years of design, sixteen years of observation, all wasted — Project Falcon terminated at last and nothing to show for it. Lerke had sent Nai to act as Six's guardian angel, but he was far from sure she would be protection enough.

And she couldn't be Lerke's living legacy, not in the same way that Six or Kyntak could. He had made her strong of body and mind, and she was growing up to become something very special. But she didn't have the same telomeres — Lerke had been watched too closely as he designed her to include them. He certainly hadn't been prepared to reveal his genetic invention to Crexe. Lerke had never even wanted a daughter; Crexe had been the one who insisted that the next generation should be female, and had demanded all sorts of other specifications. Lerke had fought it every step of the way, but it had been futile.

With Sevadonn dead, the nameless one crippled, and Kyntak captured by Vanish and therefore doomed, only Six could be a living testament to Lerke's genius. And if he, too, were to die at Vanish's hands, Lerke's heart would break.

He could have no more children. Designing them was hard, raising them was harder, and he lacked the energy to make more, even if he had the resources. Six was his final chance to leave a lasting impression on the City, make Retuni Lerke a name that people would remember. But Six was in a deadly situation he didn't understand.

Like any parent, Lerke was torn. *Do I show faith in the abilities of my son*, he wondered, *or step in to protect him? Can I really let him face Vanish, and lose? Is there anything I can do to prevent it?*

There was a way, he realized. He could stop Six from trying to rescue Kyntak. And then he could concentrate on keeping Nai safe, without having to worry about Six. It was risky — but less risky than letting him stay on his current path. Choose your battles, and you'll win most of them.

The decision was made. The old man picked up the telephone.

Six pushed the button for King's floor. The elevator doors slid closed.

His phone buzzed in his pocket. He flipped it open and put it to his ear. "Yes?"

"I want you to go to the drop-off point right now." It was King. "Stop what you're doing, and go."

Six frowned. "I'm almost at your office. Has something happened?"

"Trust me," King said. "It's important. If you don't hurry . . . you might not make the rendezvous."

His voice sounded measured, hesitant. Six got the feeling that he was choosing his words carefully. "Is someone in the room with you?" he asked. "Say, 'Okay, call me when you get there' for yes."

"Not yet."

The elevator doors slid open. Six hesitated before going through them. Not yet? "King, what's going on? Is this —"

"Just do what I tell you," King interrupted. "Go to the drop-off point. That's an order." He ended the call.

Six put his hand over the laser to stop the doors from closing. He stood uncertainly on the threshold. *If I go to the drop-off point now*, he thought, *there'll be no other agents backing me up. Why would King send me there so soon?*

He sounded on edge, Six thought. Was that because of the imminent deadline, or because someone had compromised him? If there'd been someone in the room, he would have said so. Was someone listening in on the line?

The phone lines in the Deck were protected by the same firewall as the computer networks, and should be almost impossible to hack into unless you were actually inside the building. *But the kidnappers have amazing manpower as far as infantry goes*, Six thought. *Maybe their computer hackers are equally good.*

Insufficient information to act upon, Six thought. He looked at his watch: 17:22:02. He'd go to see King in person, and if he was okay and sent him straight to the rendezvous, he'd have only wasted a minute or two.

He let the doors close behind him and started jogging towards King's office. Then he stopped.

There were two figures coming out of the stairwell at the far end of the corridor, both wearing black suits and anti-flash goggles. They were carrying pistols.

One waited at the stairwell door, gun lowered. The other headed towards King's office.

Something clicked in Six's head. The monitoring of telephone conversations would be easier if you were already behind the firewall, and had a surveillance team inside the building.

He looked closely at their uniforms. Each had a silver circle on the shoulder with a black shape in the center. The Spades, he realized. But why were they here, in the red building?

Stop what you're doing, and go. If you don't hurry . . . you might not make the rendezvous.

They're looking for me, he realized. *Someone has tipped them off about Project Falcon, and now they've come for me!*

His first instinct was to run to King's office to protect him. If the Spades knew about Six, they'd probably know that King had been covering for him, and King would be in danger. But logic stopped him. There was no way out of King's office other than the front door, so they'd both be sitting ducks.

King had said to get out of the building — and he hadn't used Six's name when he called. That suggested he thought the Spades couldn't implicate him yet — and so it would be best for Six to follow his instructions.

Six turned back towards the elevator. There were two similarly dressed agents at the stairwell at the other end of the corridor. One was guarding the door, the other was headed his way.

Six pushed the button and waited for the doors to open. His heart was pounding in his chest as he felt the Spades agent draw nearer. They were sure to have seen him by now, so his fate depended on their orders. Apprehend and arrest King? If so, they would go to King's office and leave Six alone. Locate and apprehend Agent Six of Hearts? Then they would attack him in a matter of seconds.

The elevator doors slid open. Six walked in as casually and calmly as he could, and pushed the button for the ground floor.

He waited for the doors to shut. Footsteps were drawing closer from either side — the agent who had been headed towards

King's office evidently hadn't gone in. Both Spades were coming towards the elevator. Six jabbed the button for the ground floor again, even though he knew that wouldn't make the doors close any quicker.

The footsteps were very near now.

Six sank into a close-quarters boxing stance: knees slightly bent, most body weight resting on his back leg, one forearm extended to guard his torso and his other fist hovering next to his cheek. A punch, no matter how strong or well placed, was inadequate next to an accurate bullet, but it seemed to be his only option. The setting was on his side — the enclosed space of the elevator leveled the playing field a little — optimum range for most pistols in combat was between two and eight meters, and the elevator was less than two meters square.

The quiet footsteps stopped. Six sensed that the two agents were standing on either side of the elevator. He squeezed his fists tighter.

The doors began to slide shut. There was a grunt of dismay from one of the Spades, who tried to stop them with his free hand. His fingers didn't find the laser in time, and he pulled his hand back before it could be crushed between the doors.

Six took a deep breath. There would be more Spades waiting for him in the lobby. He needed a plan of action.

He had nothing he could use to disguise himself. He was still in the civvies he had worn to Shuji's house — a long black coat, dark blue jeans, and grey running shoes. He couldn't pass himself off as another agent.

He could fight his way out, but where would that lead? The lobby could be full of people — Hearts and Diamonds. If Six tried to fight a squad of Spades in the presence of so many of his colleagues, some of them would almost certainly be hurt or killed.

Enclosed gunfights always had collateral damage. Procedure dictated that once an agent was implicated in Code-breaking behavior, he was not allowed to leave Deck custody until he was proven innocent; all other considerations were secondary, including the life of the agent in question and that of any bystander caught in the cross fire. And it wasn't as if the other agents could just leave for their own safety when the Spades showed up, because standard protocol was to put the Deck into lockdown status as soon as an agent became a suspect. No one could enter or leave.

And then Six realized why the elevator hadn't started moving towards the lobby yet. Lockdown status also means that all the elevators were frozen in place and could only be moved between floors with the approval of the Queen of Spades.

He jammed his thumb against the DOOR CLOSE button to stop the doors from sliding open when the elevator's computer registered that it couldn't leave the floor. Presumably the button could be remotely overridden by the Queen of Spades too, but with the two Spades waiting for him on the other side of the doors, he needed all the time he could get.

"Why aren't the doors opening?" one of the Spades outside the elevator whispered into his collar mike.

"The system says the manual override has been engaged," his earpiece crackled. *"The suspect must still have his finger on the CLOSE button. Give us five seconds to reconfigure access."*

The Spade signaled to his counterpart on the other side by pointing his index finger at the doors, holding his fist in the air, and tugging it down as if pulling a train whistle. *I'll go first — you stay back and prepare for cover fire.*

The other agent nodded in comprehension.

"Got it," the earpiece said. *"You're good to go."*

The doors pinged and slid open. The agent swung into the elevator, gun barrel first. "Freeze!" he roared.

The elevator was empty. The Spade retreated back into the corridor immediately, wary that Agent Six of Hearts might have somehow slipped behind or beneath him. But the corridor was deserted.

"What the . . ." The other agent stared. The aluminum handrail had been bent at ninety degrees and twisted on its joints so it depressed the DOOR CLOSE button. But other than that, there was no evidence that anyone had even been in the elevator. The boy they had seen enter less than a minute earlier had vanished into thin air.

Six listened at the lid of the maintenance trapdoor, concealed in the darkness of the elevator shaft. He knew that while he hadn't left behind any evidence of his escape route, it wouldn't be long before the Spades eliminated all the other options and figured it out. But he knew their protocols. They would check the corridor again before deciding they'd lost him. It was always embarrassing to call in a lost visual, so they'd want to be sure he hadn't somehow crept past them first.

And while he had to move, and soon, it wouldn't be smart to do it right now. Not with one of them inside the elevator, listening for the revealing scuffle that would put them back on his trail.

Six heard the clumping of boots as the Spade left the elevator. "Suspect is not inside," he confessed after a moment. "We've lost him."

Now! Six pushed himself off the elevator's roof and slapped his palm around a pipe welded horizontally to the shaft wall.

Hauling his body up to stand on it, he sprang off the wall and swung around the elevator cables before landing froglike on a supporting beam above.

Unfortunately, he thought as he bounced up into the darkness, *I'm on the wrong side of the elevator. I need to be below it, climbing down, not above it, climbing up. I need to escape from the building, and I can only do that from the ground floor. The choppers on the roof will be well guarded or decommissioned.*

Six was horrified that the Deck, the one place in the City he'd thought was safe, had finally turned against him. When soldiers from the Lab had broken in and abducted all the agents, that had been different — it was an attack by external forces, and it had been happening to everyone but him. Now it was the reverse; the Deck was still functioning, but he had been excluded.

He tried to put the fear and confusion out of his head and focus on his current goals. His watch read 17:33:17 — he had less than an hour and a half until the drop-off. That meant getting out of the Deck, getting the bugged money into the kidnappers' account, and then making it to the rendezvous point and hoping they were willing to give Kyntak back.

But even now, Six thought, the Spades would probably be working out where he was. They'd seal off all the elevator doors except the ones at the top, and send some Spades down the shaft to corner him or flush him back out the way he came. He had two options: force open the first door he found and escape onto that floor, or race them to the top to see if he could reach the maintenance tunnel under the roof.

But, Six realized, neither of those options was guaranteed to work. They knew how he thought, just like he knew how they thought. Even if they didn't all necessarily work under the same roof all the time, they followed the same Code and operated in the same way. They'd seen the schematics of this building, so they knew about the maintenance tunnel and they'd have the individual layouts of every floor. Whichever way he tried to escape, they'd be prepared for it and they'd be on him well before he could figure out an escape route.

Okay, Six thought. *I know their strategies, and they know mine. But do they know how well I understand theirs? Just running won't be enough, but maybe I can trick them.*

He stopped at the first door he found — the floor above King's. It's where they'd expect him to escape the shaft, because his ultimate goal was to reach the ground. He wrenched a piece of narrow pipe off the shaft wall. It came free with a grinding squeal, showering him with cold water. Jamming the point between the elevator doors, he braced his feet against a support beam and pulled. After some initial resistance, the doors slid wide open, flooding the inside of the elevator shaft with light.

Six didn't climb through the opening. He knew that in the Spade command center, the QS had just watched an alert light flicker, telling her that the doors on Floor 12 had been forced open. They'd scour Floor 12 and stop searching the elevator shaft.

He let his improvised lever fall into the shaft. Hopefully it would clatter against the ceiling of the elevator and trick the agents on King's floor into thinking he was still on the roof of the elevator. Confusion would be created. Some agents would think he was on Floor 11, some would guess Floor 12, and no one would be checking the maintenance tunnel.

It was time to leave. Six resumed his upward climb.

While Six had never been inside the elevator shafts of the Deck before, the tunnel wasn't hard to find. He'd spent hours examining the schematics of this building when it was first constructed, preparing for a situation like this. He knew the length of every corridor, the width of every tunnel, and the size of every room. On paper, his opponents should know as much as he did — they had access to the same information and more — but normal human memories were unreliable and, unlike Six, the Spades hadn't been here every day for the past three years.

And whether you're in a five-star hotel, Six reflected, *a prehistoric apartment block, or the headquarters of a vigilante agency, the inside of an elevator shaft always looks pretty much the same.*

The lid of the maintenance tunnel was marked with a yellow triangle of aluminum, featuring a picture of a stick figure crawling between two horizontal lines. Six slid his fingers into the seam between the lid and the wall and pulled until the seal broke. The lid swung open on a hinge at the bottom, and Six caught it with one hand to stop it from clanging noisily against the shaft wall.

The tunnel was circular, with a diameter of almost one meter. Not enough to stand in — barely enough room to crawl on all fours. Six slipped into the tunnel and pulled the lid shut behind him, letting the suffocating darkness swallow him up.

The shuffling of his hands along the warm metal floor seemed deafening in the enclosed space. His breath filled his ears, rumbling like the snores of a sleeping tiger. He knew that the sounds he was making seemed loud because they were bouncing back at him off the walls but he was still unsettled — he couldn't hear anything else. There could be Spades waiting at the other end of the tunnel, or crawling behind him, gaining ground with every second . . .

Six stopped himself from thinking about that. The chances that they'd be onto him already were minimal, and imagining them behind him would make him breathe more loudly.

This is why humans have been afraid of the dark for so long, he thought. *It makes your imagination so much more convincing. Reality and nightmares in stereo.*

Six grunted in pain as his fingers banged against something on the floor, then he slammed his hand over his mouth in panic at the sound he'd made.

There was no sign that the noise had caused anything other than a dim echo. The tunnel was as quiet as a tomb. Reassured, Six began to cautiously touch the object he had struck.

It was a square trench, only a few centimeters deep, with a floor made from the same metal as the shaft. Six's knuckles had hit the opposite side of it. He felt around the surface of the trench floor. There was a rectangular piece of metal at the edge . . . a hinge. This was a hatch, an opening to a room below.

Six was confused. The schematics he'd read stated that there was no exit from this shaft until more than halfway along its length, and there was no way he'd gone that far already. He'd crawled about 350 paces, and each pace of crawling was about forty centimeters, so he was approximately 140 meters from the elevator shaft.

What room would be on the other side of this hatch? Six wondered. He'd passed the Floor 11 bathrooms, the offices of Diamond agents Five to Ten . . .

This hatch must have been installed after the schematics were made, he thought. Therefore the Spades wouldn't know it was here. The magnitude of Six's good fortune hit him. No matter how quickly they worked out that he'd escaped into this tunnel, they wouldn't post guards in the room below him, because they didn't know that it was an option. They'd have to send agents into the tunnel after him to find it.

Six opened the hatch. It was dark below. He dropped down and landed on a tiled floor. He listened. There was no scuffling, no breathing — no indication that the dark room contained anyone but him. He rose to his feet, stretched his arms out forward, and walked. The room was small — two seconds later he could sense a wall in his path. He touched it with his fingers — shelves. A storeroom? He walked parallel to the wall until he found a door.

Where there's a door, he thought, *there's a light switch*. He ran his fingers over the surface of the wall until he found it — a cold plastic ridge surrounded by the polished ceramic. He switched the lights on.

As the room was illuminated in a sudden harsh glare, Six realized that he couldn't have picked a better place to drop into. He was surrounded by rows and rows of shelves, packed with firearms, gadgets, and disguises.

He was next door to Jack's office.

He was in the armory.

MISSION THREE
17:49:04

OUT OF REACH

Six quickly sealed the hatch with a miniature welding torch he'd found on the armory's shelves. When the QS sent her agents into the tunnel to look for him, he didn't want his escape route to be obvious, and if the hatch was permanently sealed, not only would that make him hard to follow, but it would be a plausible explanation for its absence from the schematics. It would be impossible to tell in the darkness how recently the soldering had taken place, provided the metal had had time to cool. They wouldn't follow until they'd exhausted every other alternative. And Six hoped to be long gone by then.

Of course, he thought as he put the welding torch back on the shelves, the QS wasn't stupid. She'd still have guards on every exit to the building, the elevators would still be frozen, and there'd still be sentries on the stairwell doors.

Escaping was going to be tricky. But the more he stretched her resources, the safer he would be.

Looking at the shelves, Six felt shivers run up his spine. The selection of potentially useful gizmos was enormous. There were bombs disguised as cameras, cameras disguised as phones, and phones disguised as pens. There were parachutes ranging from small BASE-jumping webs to huge airplane traction canvases. There were racks upon racks of Hawks and Eagles, and even an oversize Condor super–machine gun in the corner.

Six knew he couldn't carry it all, so he compromised. He took one tranq gun and a small AM-77, which he slipped into a hip holster. He took a lump of Detasheet plastic explosive, bent it into a half cylinder, and strapped it to his forearm. He found a detonator for it and put it in his pocket, along with a beacon, a locator, and a pair of earplugs. He put a small glider-type parachute in a thin backpack and found a lock-release gun underneath it, which he took as well.

Mixed in with the guns, Six saw a katana — an eighty-centimeter samurai sword. He picked it up and felt its weight. It was short for its type, but long enough to do the job. He unsheathed it; it was slightly curved, and single-edged. He placed his hands on the rubber-lined grip as far apart as possible and tried a few practice swings. The blade cut silently through the air of the armory.

Quiet, but intimidating, and easier to use with nonlethal force than a gun, particularly given the single-edged blade. *Done deal*, Six thought as he sheathed it under the parachute backpack, ready for an over-the-shoulder draw.

As a last thought, he grabbed an Eagle automatic as well. He wouldn't use it on ground troops, but automatic weapons were good for dealing with hostile vehicles.

Six switched off the lights and slowly opened the door into Jack's office. It seemed empty, the only sound the humming of the computer. The door leading to the corridor was closed.

He crossed the room and listened at the door. Nothing. He opened it, turned into the corridor outside, and walked straight into Jack, who stumbled backward.

"Excuse me!" Jack spluttered, before looking at Six's face. "Oh my god, Six! It's you!" He glanced nervously over his shoulder. "The Spades are looking everywhere for you. They're searching the building!"

"Do you —" Six began, but Jack cut him off.

"Don't talk, just listen," he said. "There are dozens of Spades in the foyer. You can't get out that way. That leaves the choppers on the roof, which will be guarded, and the basement access into the sewers. That's your best shot at getting out. The west stairwell on this floor is guarded. Maybe try the south.

"They'll be monitoring your phone. Not only can they listen in to any calls you make or receive, but they can trace your location through your SIM card." He tossed Six a phone — a silver DigiCall ultra. "Take mine, throw yours away or destroy it. The Queen of Hearts went off to stake out some suspicious warehouse a couple of hours ago. She was outside when the lockdown came into place, so call her. Maybe she can help you."

Six pocketed the phone. He should have thought of that. His phone was probably a blinking light on a Spade computer screen somewhere.

"I don't know what's going on here, Six," Jack said. "But I know that you're on our side. So go. Run."

Six needed no further encouragement. He sprinted away down the corridor towards the south stairwell.

Unlike Jack, Six didn't think that the QS would have forgotten the basement as a possible escape route. She would have guards down there too. And even if she didn't, he was currently on the top floor — Floor 14. How was he supposed to get all the way down to the basement with every elevator frozen and guards at most stairwell doors?

But Jack was probably right about everything else. The foyer was not an option; nor was the roof. The building was sealed up tight. He looked at his watch: 17:55:02. His usual tactic would be to hide until his opponents were forced to assume that he'd escaped somehow and let down their guard. But that would take longer than an hour.

Six stopped running and leaned against an emergency fire hose wheel, pushing his palms to the sides of his head. There was always a way — always. After all he'd been through today, he wasn't prepared to give up, not even when his own organization had turned against him.

A cleaning robot buzzed past him on the floor, polishing the linoleum with furry treads. Six bent down and unzipped its dust bag, dropping his mobile inside. *The Spades can chase a robot for a while*, he thought.

He opened his eyes. A plan was forming in his head. The only windows in the Deck were near stairwells, so he'd need to take out some of the stairwell guards. He'd need something that weighed slightly less than he did, and he'd have to rig up a pulley. But it was possible.

Six was sure that the QS would have ordered her agents to do a radio sound-off regularly — that was standard operating procedure whenever quarantining a building, because it was imperative to know as soon as the integrity had been breached. He should deal with the stairwell guards as late in his preparations as possible, so the Spades weren't warned of his location too soon.

Six spun the fire hose wheel and caught the steel nozzle as it fell. Thick, tough hose spooled out onto the floor, coiling like a beige, leathery snake. The Deck was about sixty meters high. The Floor 14 windows were about five meters from the roof. He would need fifty-five meters of hose. Six walked backward down the hallway, holding the fire hose nozzle until he was fifty-seven meters away from the wheel — that would give him some extra slack to tie the knots with. Leaving the nozzle on the floor of the corridor, Six jogged back to the wheel and drew his katana. The blade sang as he swung it. He slashed through the hose where it met the wheel, and the end flopped to the floor. Six now had fifty-seven meters of fire hose to work with, which he coiled and hung over his shoulder.

He tried the door to the nearest office — it belonged to the Queen of Hearts. Locked, as he had expected. Deck agents weren't in the habit of leaving their offices unlocked, even before Lab soldiers had broken in and abducted everybody.

"Sorry, Queen," he muttered. He leaned back, took aim, and kicked the door in.

No alarms sounded, and no soldiers came running. Six entered the office, looking for something that was the right weight.

Six was heavy for his height — seventy-three kilograms. Adding two kilograms for the katana, another two for the AM-77, three for the Eagle, one for the parachute, one for the Detasheet and one for his clothes, he was currently a little more than eighty-three kilograms. *And two kilograms for the lock-release gun*, he thought.

He wanted something just under eighty-five kilograms to act as his counterweight. Too light and he would fall too fast. Too heavy and he wouldn't fall at all, or he'd be dragged upward.

Queen's PC would be too light, Six thought as he scanned the room, not to mention fragile. Her desk was about the right weight, but too bulky. The smaller his counterweight, the better.

He hesitated as he looked at her filing cabinet. Eighty centimeters high, sixty deep, fifty wide — not too big to use. He put his hands on either side of it and lifted. About eighty-two kilograms, he estimated. He kicked one of the legs of the desk, breaking it off at the top. He picked it up and snapped it in half over his knee, then opened the bottom drawer of the cabinet and stuffed the pieces inside. Eighty-four kilograms — perfect.

Now he needed some way to attach the fire hose to the cabinet. There was no handle, nor any bar of structural significance that could be substituted for one. He was going to have to punch some holes in it.

Queen had left her coat hanging on the back of her chair — a knee-length grey cloak with a black grid pattern. Six folded it up and wrapped it around the muzzle of his Eagle, switching the safety to semiautomatic.

He pressed the gun against the center of one of the filing cabinet's sides, and listened carefully. No noise from outside — it was probably safe. He pulled the trigger.

Queen's jacket muffled the shot, which punctured the metal shell with a dull *thunk*, zipped through the papers in the drawer, and drilled through the other side. Six sat perfectly still for a few seconds. No noise from the corridor.

Six peered through the hole he'd made. Excellent — he could see out the other side. He jammed the barrel of the Eagle into the opening and pushed the gun from side to side to widen the hole. Then he twisted the fire hose into a tight tube, forced the cut end into the hole, and pulled it out the other side of the cabinet. He locked the bottom drawer so it wouldn't fall open, grabbed the hose on either side of the cabinet, and pulled. Nothing broke — neither the sides of the filing cabinet nor the fire hose, and the cabinet lifted into the air. Six put it back down and pulled the hose the rest of the way through, stopping only when the nozzle clanked against the hole — it was too large to fit through.

Six tossed Queen's bullet-torn coat back onto her chair and carried the cabinet out into the corridor, shutting the door behind him. *A pulley is easy,* he realized — *I'll just wrap the hose around the guardrail in the stairwell. Now it's time to get over there.*

He took the cabinet as far as the corner in the corridor, then put it down again. *I can't fight a Spade while carrying a filing cabinet,* he thought.

He peered around the corner. The corridor was a cul-de-sac, with the stairwell doors on the left wall and the window on the right. There was only one Spade in sight. She was standing by the window, facing Six but watching the stairwell door. *I must have them confused by now,* Six thought. *They'll have checked the elevator, Floor 12, and maybe even the maintenance tunnel, and they have no idea where I am. That's why she's watching the stairwell door. She thinks I'm just as likely to come up from behind her as down the corridor.*

He quietly drew his AM-77 and aimed it at the Spade. The dart would knock her out quickest if it hit her in the jugular vein — the sedative would be secreted almost directly into her brain. However, aiming for that spot would risk puncturing her trachea and seriously wounding her. Instead, Six lined the muzzle up with her left thigh, where the femoral artery was.

Crack! He pulled the trigger, and the anesthetic dart zipped along the length of the corridor. But the guard was already moving, drawing her weapon, and the dart broke as it slammed into the wall.

No one reacts that quickly, Six thought as he charged into the corridor towards her. *She must have known I was here. She was just waiting for me to make the first move.*

Six drew his katana from its sheath as he ran. The Spade already had her gun up. "Freeze," she roared.

Six jumped into a half flip, landed feetfirst on the ceiling, and kept running. The Spade stepped back and tried to readjust her aim, but Six was almost above her, and he jumped again, soaring back down towards the floor, blade first.

The Spade dived aside, as Six had expected, but her gun hand was the last part to move. Her Hawk 9-millimeter was slicked in half by the blade, and the shock of the impact knocked the stock out of her grip. She reached for a combat knife with her other hand, but Six was already on his feet, and the katana was at her throat.

"Don't," he said. Her hand had frozen, fingers resting lightly on the handle of her knife.

"Who do you work for?" she demanded.

"We're on the same side," he replied. Her question seemed unusual. If the Spades knew he was a ChaoSonic weapon, wouldn't they assume he worked for them?

"If you had nothing to hide," the Spade said, "you'd surrender."

"When this is over," he said, "I will. And I'll want a written apology from the Queen of Spades. Take your knife out. Slowly."

She did.

"Drop it," Six said. "In front of you."

The knife clattered to the floor. "Kick it away," he continued. "Right back down the corridor."

"I'm willing to die for what I believe in," she said. It sounded like a warning.

"I don't care," Six said truthfully. "You're going to call in and say everything's fine. You just heard a rattle in the air-conditioning."

"You're on the top floor," she said. "You'll never get past all the guards between here and the ground."

"That's not your concern," Six said. "You —"

He hesitated. Something in the woman's voice wasn't right — it sounded staged. He saw that her earpiece was not in her ear. He looked down. It was in her gloved hand, and the TRANSMIT button was depressed.

He drew his AM-77 and shot her in the thigh. She cried out and staggered to the side, reaching down to touch the injury, but already her fingers were limp.

"Sorry," Six muttered.

With his free hand he grabbed the woman's arm and caught her as she fell, then put her on the floor in the recovery position. He was already running back towards the filing cabinet by the time her eyes were shut.

Six assumed he had only minutes before more Spades showed up. They knew that he'd taken out the guard on a Floor 14 stairwell door, and this would now be the first place they would come looking.

Six opened the double doors to the stairwell and pressed them against the magnetic discs in the walls so they stayed open. He looped the fire hose around the guardrail on the stairs twice, knotted the free end into his belt, and placed the filing cabinet about a meter from the rail. He kicked the window opposite the doors until its hinges snapped, and then pried it out of the frame, leaning it against the wall next to the unconscious Spade.

The plan was to climb into the window frame and tug on the hose until it ran out of slack, dragging the filing cabinet under the guardrail and causing it to fall into the stairwell. Fire hoses were always frictionless so they could unspool quickly, so his pulley should work smoothly. When it reached the bottom, Six could simply jump out the window. The cabinet would slow his descent to a safe level as it was lifted through the hollow in the center of the stairwell. He could untie the hose when he was close enough to the ground to fall safely, and then he'd get as far away from the Deck as he could.

Six still had his parachute on his back, of course — and he would have much preferred to use it. But BASE-jumping from a window was often fatal. The parachute usually became caught on the building and didn't open properly, leaving the jumper to fall to his or her death. Six would need more momentum than he could build up by just leaping out the window. The pulley-assisted abseil was by far the safest option.

Six paused in his preparations and listened. He thought he'd heard a scuffle — the sound of a carelessly placed shoe in the corridor behind him. He peered into the fluorescent light.

Nothing. It was empty, and he couldn't detect any further noises from beyond the corner. He climbed into the window frame and prepared to pull on the hose, sending the filing cabinet down into the stairwell.

"Agent Six of Hearts!"

The voice had been artificially amplified. Six's first thought was that it was being channeled through the Deck's PA system. But it was coming from outside the building. He leaned out into the void and looked down. Fog and darkness. He looked up and fell back through the window in surprise, landing with a thud on the floor of the corridor. A fighter jet had taken off from the roof of the Deck, and was descending towards the window. Six could feel the heat from the blazing thrusters as they burned fuel to keep the plane in the air.

A halogen spotlight snapped on, blinding him, and he ducked below the frame of the window.

"*Agent Six of Hearts,*" the loudspeaker boomed again. "*You have ten seconds to stand down. I repeat: You have ten seconds to stand down.*"

Six heard the clattering of boots and the clicking of safety catches being adjusted. He turned and saw that there were Spades rounding the corner of the corridor, guns raised.

"*You have nine seconds —*" the voice began. But Six heard no more; he was already racing down the stairs.

He heard the chattering of gunfire as the walls of the stairwell raced past in a blur. The guardrail hummed and pinged as bullets sparked off it, and chunks of brick and plaster plummeted through the hollow in the center like dusty raindrops. Six gave up trying to put his feet on the stairs — he just jumped from one landing to the next, his right hand sliding down the rail to keep himself from falling into the well or crashing into the walls. The fire hose twisted in the air above him; he was lucky that he hadn't knocked the cabinet into the stairwell yet, or it would be slowing his descent. The Spades were crashing down the stairs a few flights above him, but he was widening the gap every second. One person could go down stairs more quickly than twelve at the same time.

The gunfire had stopped — they could no longer see him. But Six knew that this was only temporary. There would still be guards on the other side of every stairwell door, plus the ones in the lobby, and now that the QS knew where he was she would know where to concentrate all her forces. *Perhaps I can still make it to the sewers*, he thought. *But I'd have to leave the stairwell somehow and get across to —*

He skidded to a halt on one of the landings. A desk had been put in his path, lying on its side, with fire doors propped up against it — a crude roadblock, designed to stop him from going any farther down. He was on the third floor, only fifteen meters from the ground, so he prepared to jump into the stairwell and free-fall the rest of the way, but then he remembered that he was still tied to the fire hose, and therefore the filing cabinet on Floor 11. He reached to untie the knot . . .

"Freeze!" Once again, he heard the sound of guns being cocked. Lots of them.

Six looked to his right, into the corridor extending from the landing. He didn't bother doing a head count. The number of Spades pointing guns at him exceeded thirty. Too many to fight. Too many bullets to dodge.

"Hands where I can see them," the leader said. A badge on her shoulder read *Queen of Spades*. She tapped her earpiece with her free hand. "All units to Floor 3. Air support, return to base. We have the suspect."

Six let go of the hose, leaving the knot tied. "You're making a mistake," he said as he put his hands up.

"If I were, you wouldn't have tried to run," the QS said icily.

All you did was run. His brother's voice echoed through Six's head. *All you ever do is run.*

I'm sorry I let you down, Kyntak, he thought. Part of him was relieved that he wouldn't have to risk his life. Now that he had been captured, he might spend the rest of his days in a cell, safe and alone. But he was immediately horrified that such thoughts had entered his head. He had failed, and now Kyntak was as good as dead. Even if Vanish didn't dissect him, ChaoSonic would.

"Take out the sword slowly," the QS said, "drop it, and kick it over here."

The katana glided smoothly across the linoleum, and the QS stopped it with her boot.

"Now the pistol," she said, gesturing at the AM-77. "With your right hand — keep your left in the air."

Six took out the tranq and dropped it. It clattered to the floor.

Seventy-nine kilograms, said a voice in his head. *Without the katana and the pistol, you only weigh seventy-nine kilograms.*

"Now the Eagle," the QS said. "You know the drill."

Six pulled the Eagle automatic off his back and dropped it to the floor. Now seventy-six kilograms.

"You'll regret this," Six said as he kicked the rifle across the floor.

"Are you threatening me?" the QS hissed. "Not a smart move. Now the other gun on your belt."

"It's a lock-release gun," Six said. "It's harmless."

"You think I'd send you to your cell with a lock-release gun? Take it off."

The gun clattered to the floor. Now seventy-four kilograms. The Spades behind the QS watched Six impassively, weapons still raised.

"What's that around your arm?"

"Detasheet," Six said.

"Plastic explosives?" She raised her eyebrows. "Planning on some sabotage, Agent Six?"

"I can't take it off one-handed," Six said.

"The detonator, then," the QS said. "Turn out your pockets."

The detonator and the locator bounced onto the floor. A little less than seventy-four kilograms. He kept Jack's mobile phone concealed in the palm of his hand and slipped it discreetly back into his pocket.

"You're violating the Code," Six said, walking slowly towards her. The fire hose tightened behind him. "I have done nothing wrong."

She stepped backward. "Stop right there. What's that behind you?"

"A hose," Six said. "I was going to use it to climb out the window."

One of the agents snorted, and the QS raised her eyebrows. "Untie it," she said, "and drop it."

Six reached slowly behind his back and started to untie the knot, keeping a firm grip on the end of the hose. He tugged, and felt that the slack had almost run out.

"I'm very disappointed in you, Six," the QS said as he worked. "You had an outstanding track record."

"I'm disappointed in you too," Six said. "You normally get your man."

He pulled the hose with all his might, and jumped backward.

The filing cabinet — now almost ten kilograms heavier than Six — was pulled into the stairwell and fell. Even as the Spades opened fire, Six was dragged backward and sucked up into the stairwell, a human counterweight for the cabinet. He held the hose tightly with both hands and shot upward past flight after flight of stairs.

The Spades reached the landing, and some started racing up the stairs in pursuit, but Six was rising faster than they could climb. A few others stayed on the landing and fired up at him, spitting bullets wildly into the stairwell. Six dodged by shoving off guardrails on his way up and rebounding from wall to wall, adding to his upward momentum with every push. When he was almost halfway up, the filing cabinet appeared out of the darkness above. He punched it as it swept past him, breaking the lock on the bottom drawer and spilling hundreds of papers and files into the well. The gunfire stopped abruptly as a blizzard of flying paper concealed Six from view.

Six looked up again, squinting against the air rushing past his face. In only a couple of seconds he would reach the top floor, where the hose went over the rail for his improvised pulley. He gave one last shove off a rail, increasing his speed so much that the last few flights of stairs were a blur as they shot past him, and curled his body into a ball. He squeezed his eyes shut. Vision would only confuse him for the next few seconds, and this trick was difficult enough already.

When he hit the rail that was acting as the pulley, his guts lurched as the momentum dragged him over the top with a snap. He let go of the hose. Flying horizontally now, still curled up like a cannonball, he rocketed through the double doors, crossed the corridor with the sleeping Spade, and shot out of the window he'd opened earlier.

Six opened his eyes. Grey fog rained down from the night sky all around. The Deck was already vanishing into it behind him. He spread his arms as if they were wings, keeping his legs straight and his feet together as he flew into the darkness.

The fighter jet seemed to have obeyed the order to return to base. Six was finally beyond the reach of the Spades. Satisfied that there was no aircraft nearby, and aware that he was falling faster and faster, he pulled the cord on his parachute. The chute exploded into shape above him, snapping his torso backward as his falling speed was cut ten kilometers per hour.

Six reached upward and found the control handles hanging above him. Unlike a hang glider, a parachute couldn't have a control bar because it had to be folded into a backpack. But this chute had handles that performed a similar function. Six pulled the right-hand one, and the chute swept into a seventy-degree turn above him. He looked at his watch: 18:19:49. Time to head to the rendezvous point.

He pulled the parachute into a swoop and flew into the night.

NIGHTLIFE

Hiss.

Kyntak awoke, startled — first by the noise, second by the pain in his arm, and third by the realization that he had been sleeping. *How many hostages fall asleep after only a few hours of capture?* he asked himself. *Why am I so tired? How long have I been here?*

The hissing stopped after thirty seconds, as before. The room became silent once more.

Kyntak prodded his wobbly tooth gingerly with his tongue. *How am I going to get out of here?*

The door slid open and this time Kyntak saw it happen. It was so seamless that it looked less like a door opening than the entire wall sliding a meter to the left. Kyntak figured that this was probably exactly what had happened.

"It's a good system, if you have the space," the man said as he entered. The guard had been replaced by a woman with vivid red eyes. She was wearing what looked like hospital scrubs; Kyntak wondered if she was the on-site medic. She was pointing a Hawk 9-millimeter at the floor. "It can only be opened from the outside, and it can withstand three hundred fifty kilograms of pressure on any square meter of it from in here." The man stood in the corner. "No one's getting out that way."

"Is there a dumbwaiter?" Kyntak asked. "Not for escaping in, of course; I'm hungry."

"Really?" the man asked. The curiosity in his eyes looked as hungry as Kyntak felt. "How long has it been since you've eaten?"

"Uh, I had breakfast at four-thirty," Kyntak said. "AM."

"How long can you usually go without eating?" the man asked. "And how large is a typical meal in kilojoules?"

The woman had approached the table, and was pointing the gun at Kyntak with a two-handed grip, keeping it safely out of reach above his hand. "Why is she doing that?" Kyntak demanded. "You think I need to be threatened for info on my eating habits?"

A syringe had appeared in the man's hand. "Just a precaution," he said, removing the plastic cover. "Stay still; I'm going to draw some of your blood."

They'd done that a few times already, Kyntak thought, judging by all the puncture marks in his arm. Was there some way they could tell he wasn't Six? Their blood samples should be the same.

"Are you feeding a vampire in the cell next to mine?" he asked.

"We're keeping you weak by draining your blood," the man said as he pushed the needle into Kyntak's arm. "Enough to keep you tired and hungry, but not enough to put you into hypovolemic shock. That's why your arm hurts. It means you won't have the energy to try to escape. Do you feel cold?"

Hiss.

"Most supervillains would be happy with just the ultra-strength roller-door, and maybe a stupid nickname," Kyntak said. "Speaking of which, who are you?"

The man kept watching the needle. "They call me Vanish," he said.

Kyntak blinked. "Seriously?"

Vanish nodded.

"Wow, scary." Kyntak strained against the clamps on his wrists. "Why are the clamps made of copper? You're too cheap for steel?"

"Copper is an excellent conductor. I can fry you at the touch of a button. Also, while it's more than strong enough to hold you, it's more ductile than the walls, the floor, and the ceiling, all of which are thick glass. Even if you managed to get off the table, you couldn't use the clamps to break the walls.

"Your records show uncommon ingenuity. I felt that just the door wasn't enough for a hundred percent certainty. Hence the oxygen burst once every two minutes through the valve above your head, instead of an air duct. And hence the blood draining." He smiled his curious smile. "I take no pleasure in making you uncomfortable. But you won't be here for much longer."

The syringe was nearly full. Kyntak's head was starting to ache and his vision was sparkling — symptoms of blood loss, he knew. "How much money did you ask for? I just want to know what I'm worth."

"To them, you seem to be worth a hundred million credits," Vanish said. "But to me, you're priceless."

"If you hadn't already stolen all of my blood, I'd blush," Kyntak said.

"You'll feel better if you sleep," Vanish said, glancing at his watch. "I have a ransom to collect."

The wall slid smoothly aside, and Vanish and the woman left. Kyntak tried to keep his eyelids open, but the light from the walls seemed to be becoming brighter, and he had to squint against it. The sound of his brain straining for blood was roaring in his ears, and there was a throbbing behind his eyeballs.

Six, he thought as reality faded away to make room for uneasy dreams. *Where are you?*

People gawked from a safe distance as Six swung in to land. It had taken him a while to find a street wide enough so that the parachute wouldn't become tangled on the buildings on either side and long enough for him to take a slow descent and a run down after landing, but not so large that there was much traffic. On the road he'd finally chosen, the streetlamps were the only illumination for the asphalt and the pedestrians; there were no headlights to be seen.

Six pulled both handles to keep the canopy level. The chute cast a curved shadow onto the street as it dipped below the lamps, a shadow which shrank and darkened as he neared the surface.

He hit the ground running, at first with only cursory taps against the road and then with the force of a sprint as the parachute sank farther and he was once again bearing his own weight. After a few seconds the tilt of the parachute caught the still night air and dragged back against him. He skidded into a landing crouch immediately, and the black canopy rolled lightly over his head.

Once he was sure that the last folds of the parachute had sunk to the ground, Six pulled it off and started to fold it, trying to ignore the stares of the pedestrians. *It's not every night that someone falls out of the sky in front of them*, he supposed. *I wish my life were like that.*

He wondered what he would be doing right now if he wasn't superhuman. Would he be watching television or playing video games if he had been born to normal parents in a quiet neighbor-hood, instead of grown in a vat under Retuni Lerke's watchful eye? Would he have a day job at a ChaoSonic fast-food outlet? Would he be in the local under-eighteen soccer team?

It was pointless to daydream. Like it or not, he was Agent Six of Hearts. Fast, strong, smart. A tough career that was only get-ting tougher. Too few friends, too many enemies.

He would never lead a normal life. In fact, the way today was going he'd be lucky to see another sunrise. But the people staring at him could live the way they did because there were people standing up for them. Six, his colleagues, and other people like them. There was some comfort in that. He could never experi-ence normality, but he was part of it. He helped to make it possible.

It was 18:24:18, only thirty-five minutes before the drop-off, and he still didn't have a plan. He didn't even know whether Grysat had managed to deposit the bugged money into Vanish's account before the Spades had locked down the Deck. And the downside of his miraculous escape from the QS was that he'd lost almost all of his equipment: the AM-77, the Eagle, the lock-release gun, and the katana, not to mention the detonator for his Detasheet.

The silk canvas slipped out of his hands as he tried to stuff it into the backpack — it seemed to be caught on something. Looking up, he saw that a sneaker-clad foot was pressed down on the corner of it.

"You're standing on my parachute," Six said, glaring up at the teenager.

"This is my parachute," the teenager said, arms folded across his jacket.

"Sorry," Six said, standing up. "I didn't see your name

on it when I landed in front of all these people, thirty seconds ago."

"Hey, Thriek," a teenage girl said, approaching. "What's this loser doing with your parachute?"

"Says it's his," the boy said, curling one hand into a fist. "I think he's trying to steal it."

Six stared at them both for a moment. Then he looked at the group of approaching teens, the girls either staring at their hands in boredom or giggling, the boys all wearing bluntly indignant expressions. Then he burst out laughing. He couldn't say why for sure — the ridiculousness of his day suddenly hit him.

"You think this is funny?" Thriek demanded. "Are you disrespecting me?"

Six laughed even harder. *If they only knew*, he thought. *So this is how kids my age are supposed to act.*

His next burst of chuckles caught in his throat. Kids his age. Normal kids. He looked around at them. Caps, sheer jackets, loose grey jeans, button-up sneakers.

"Hey!" Thriek yelled, walking across the parachute towards Six. "What do you think you're staring at?"

"A wardrobe," Six said, a faint smile on his lips. He gave a mighty tug on the chute, pulling it out from under the approaching teenager.

Thriek yelped as he fell, landing on his backside. One of the girls standing nearby laughed, and Thriek roared as he scrambled to his feet and charged at Six, who stepped neatly to one side and grabbed Thriek's collar as he passed, pulling the teen backward. Wrapping his right arm around Thriek's elbows and holding the boy's arms behind his back, Six grabbed the wrists of Thriek's jacket with his left hand, and it slipped neatly off him. The boy thrashed out of Six's grip and swung a loose fist at his head, which

Six ducked easily as he picked up the jacket. As he put his left arm into the sleeve, he grabbed Thriek's ankle with his right hand and the boy fell to the ground. Six crouched down and pulled off Thriek's jeans, which were baggy enough to come down easily. He put them on over his own jeans, then took off the kid's sneakers and grabbed his mobile phone.

Thriek scuttled off into the darkness as Six put on the shoes, his friends following close behind.

Six needed to know whether the ransom money had been bugged and put in Vanish's account. The easiest way to find out was to call Grysat. The Spades would be listening. He'd have to try to make it innocuous. He typed the number into Thriek's phone and hit CALL.

"Yes?" Grysat's voice was strained.

"Hey, man, it's Steve," Six said, hoping Grysat would recognize his voice. "How's it going?"

There was a pause. "Oh, hi!" Grysat said finally. "Sorry, believe it or not I was actually expecting a call from a different Steve. How are you?"

"I'm good," Six said. "Are we still on for dinner at seven?" *(Are we going ahead with the trade?)*

Grysat sighed theatrically. "I've been held up at work," he said. "I would've told you, but there's something wrong with all the phones and they can't dial out." *(The Spades are monitoring all the calls, and the Deck agents can't make any.)* "But the others should still be going, so you're welcome to go without me." *(I've paid the money; you can still make the trade.)*

"That's a shame, man," Six said. "I mean, yeah, I'll go, but I wish you could come too. Are you okay? You don't sound all that good."

"I think I might've come down with something," Grysat

said, "but it's probably just a twenty-four-hour bug." *(The Spades will give up and leave soon; we'll be okay.)*

"Get well soon, buddy," Six said. "Good luck at work."

"I'll be fine. Enjoy your dinner." *(We're safe. Get to the rendezvous point.)*

"Yeah, see you around." Six hit END.

He was relieved. Grysat had managed to pay the money before the Spades had put the Deck in lockdown. Six didn't know what shape Kyntak would be in. He could have been tested, tortured, or had samples of himself sold to ChaoSonic for analysis. And Six didn't know how easily he could track down Vanish after the exchange was made. If ChaoSonic had been searching for him for as long as Shuji had suggested, he doubted that his luck would be much better.

And he didn't know how he was going to clear his name with the Spades. But Six had no doubt that if the money hadn't been paid, he would never have seen Kyntak again.

452nd Street was one of the oldest streets in this part of the City, but it was barely a street anymore. So many bridges had been put over it that it was practically a tunnel. It had been rebuilt and redirected around new buildings so many times that any resemblance to the straight line it had once been was completely lost. And eventually it had become so blocked by new infrastructure that ChaoSonic had stopped keeping it uninterrupted — there were hundreds of trenches and skyscrapers that broke it along its length, each causing a dead end and a new beginning in the street. Because of this, the spot where it hit the Seawall was essentially a T-intersection made of three cul-de-sacs — the street running alongside the wall made the top of the T, and an eighty-meter chunk of 452nd Street made the bottom. All three points were now blocked at the end by buildings. There was nowhere for cars to get in, and pedestrians entered and exited either through the subway at the center of the intersection or through one of the surrounding buildings. High above the road there was a monorail leading back to 449th Street, but while it was still connected to the massive labyrinth of monorail lines which patterned the City, business hadn't been good enough for ChaoSonic to keep sending carriages to the spot. The T-shaped intersection was known as "the Timeout." It was frequented mainly by the citizens who worked in the surrounding buildings, but there were a few cafes on the corners, luring outsiders into the area for strong, bitter coffee. And the activity didn't stop at night. Three floors of one building were taken up by Insomnia, a nightclub that slashed refracted blue lasers against its tinted windows and pumped bass-drenched beats into the Timeout from dusk until dawn.

Six had been on enough surveillance and reconnaissance missions to know that tailing someone in a nightclub was all but impossible — so if he was going to observe the Timeout and wait for Kyntak to be dropped off, behind those tinted windows might be the best place to do it. And the nightclub had two entrances, one inside the Timeout and one outside. Insomnia was probably the least conspicuous way into the intersection.

The nightclub's fluorescent sign came into view as Six rounded a corner. The blue faded smoothly to green before sliding into a violent crimson. There was a logo next to it — an eye with black-light lashes, making the painted iris glow. It was only 18:43:06 and already there was a throng of people outside the doors. Three clean-shaven heads rose above the crowd on broad shoulders: bouncers, standing by the doors with their tree-trunk arms folded across barrel chests.

Six slipped into the crowd. The bouncers weren't there to check for ID. Since ChaoSonic had replaced government in the Takeover, only about one in ten nightclubs cared what age you were. The bouncers were there firstly to scare the patrons straight — fewer rules would be broken if everyone knew there were bigger, tougher people hanging around. Secondly, the bouncers had the right to refuse entry to anyone they felt like — anyone who looked like he wasn't there to spend money.

Six bobbed up and down gently to the beat as he waited in line, trying to blend in, not making eye contact with anybody. It was 18:49:29.

The bouncer was almost half a meter taller than Six. He peered down incuriously at him for less than a second before shoving him roughly across the threshold. Six climbed the stairs quickly, dodging the people stumbling back down them. Broken glass and drinking straws flattened under his feet as he reached the top of the stairs.

Insomnia was already packed. The sea of gyrating, waving heads with bleached, dyed, gelled, and blow-dried hair on the dance floor below Six made the garishly lit ceiling seem uncomfortably low.

The noise hit him like a kick in the chest. He'd never been inside a nightclub before, and hadn't expected it to be so loud. People went to nightclubs for fun, he thought. They dressed in style, met their friends, danced wildly, and drank too much. Six didn't do any of these things himself, but he could understand the appeal of each. Dressing up impressed and attracted other people. Seeing friends signified a welcome relief from work, a life independent of employment. The physical exertions involved in wild dancing released endorphins in the brain, creating chemical happiness.

But who could enjoy music this loud? he wondered. Where was the fun in being slowly deafened?

Six had met a wide variety of people in his sixteen years. But he still didn't feel like he understood humans. *Maybe the variety is the problem*, he thought. *I should spend less time with secret agents and murderers. I need to meet more normal people.*

Six's ears were adjusting to the volume. One of the more subtle benefits of his designer DNA was a valve in each auditory canal. This was pressed up against the outside of each eardrum and would quickly dilate or contract depending on the volume of the noise surrounding him, in much the same way as pupils in the eyes of humans adjust to light. This meant that his hearing abilities were more sophisticated and robust than those of everyone else — but as with eyes, the valve could not completely close. Sudden noises still hurt, and prolonged exposure to noise of more than 110 decibels was harmful. The music of the nightclub was exceeding that. He pulled the earplugs he'd found in the armory out of his pockets and put them in his ears, dulling the repeated thuds to a tolerable volume.

Six leaned over the bar and ordered a ChaoCola. He couldn't watch the Timeout and dance at the same time, but he would look suspicious standing still without a drink in his hand.

The dance floor seemed less claustrophobic than it had from above. The waving of hands in the air and the swishing hair above heads created the illusion that people were larger than they actually were. Once Six was among them, he saw that everyone at least had space to bend their knees and sway their hips — the only movements required for nightclub dancing. Six pushed his way through, trying to look as though he was working his way towards someone.

A feathery-haired girl appeared seemingly out of nowhere in front of him, and his reflexes barely had time to stop himself from bumping into her. Her face registered surprise — apparently she hadn't seen him either — before offering an apologetic smile. Six waited for her to move out of his way.

She looked him up and down, then blushed. "Do you want to dance?" she shouted.

Six shook his head, stepped around her, and kept moving. His clothes were enough to make him blend in. He didn't need to dance as well.

Six reached the window quickly. He leaned against the sill, ignoring the bouncing people surrounding him. Kyntak would either be there or he wouldn't, but either way, Vanish would want to know who came to the rendezvous, and Six wanted to avoid being spotted.

Kidnappers were among the most information-hungry of all Code-breakers. There were many different aspects of the crime to balance: abduction, containment, negotiation, and subsequent escape. It required careful planning, swift and precise execution, and accurate prediction of the ransom recipient's actions. Four out of five kidnappings failed. The remaining twenty percent worked because the kidnappers knew everything. They had plenty of concealed surveillance before and during the event. They had tapped phones, bugged rooms, inside sources.

According to Shuji, Vanish had a large network at his disposal. Therefore, the Timeout was being watched. If Kyntak didn't appear, Six would find whoever was watching it and follow him or her back to their base. He looked at his watch. 18:54:11.

There were two monorail cars sitting on the rails above the Timeout. They were probably there for a private party, where middle-aged guests in rich tuxedos and gowns would sip expensive drinks. Six wished that this was his vantage point, instead of Insomnia.

He had absentmindedly finished his ChaoCola. He glanced around, but the only bin was the one near the exit, so he licked the last of the sticky residue off his cup and straw and placed them on the sill.

"Hey!"

Six glanced over his shoulder. A short man in a white undershirt was approaching him — wearing earplugs, Six was surprised to see.

"Were you looking at my girlfriend?" the man demanded angrily.

Six turned back to the window. "No."

"You calling my girlfriend a liar?" the man exploded.

"Go away," Six said. He wondered if the girl who'd asked him to dance was the one the man was referring to. But she had looked about Six's age — much younger than this guy.

"Want to take it outside?" The man was balling his fists.

Six gritted his teeth. *Why do I bother defending these people?* he wondered. He looked back at the man, narrowing his eyes, and held his gaze for a full second before replying, trying to squeeze every drop of his ice-cold contempt for humanity into his words. *"Go away."*

"You think you can just walk in here dressed like that," the man said, "and start ordering people around?"

The statement struck Six as odd. He was dressed the same as half the other people in Insomnia. *This man doesn't have a girlfriend,* he realized suddenly. *And he doesn't care how I'm dressed. He's just trying to start a fight.*

But why pick him? In Six's experience, men usually picked fights with people taller than them — a primitive display of bravery or ability. This man was short, but no shorter than Six. And there were plenty of other people in the club, many of whom would have committed actual slights to give the guy an excuse.

"I'm sorry," Six said, testing the waters. "I don't want any trouble. Let me buy you a drink."

A flick-knife appeared in the guy's hand, and he spun it expertly around his knuckles.

So, Six thought. *He doesn't care what I say, and he's not only armed but also trained.*

He tried another test. "Come any closer and I'll kill you," he said with as little emotion as possible.

The man didn't flinch. "Are you threatening me?" *He has combat experience*, Six thought. *He didn't pick me because he thinks I'm weak.*

Six feinted to one side, and the guy leaped towards him as though his trigger had been pulled. But his attack was a punch — the knife hand stayed back. *Nonlethal force*, Six thought. *Interesting.*

Six ducked under the punch and stepped in, throwing his shoulder against the man's legs just below the knees. The man didn't cry out as he fell forward over Six, dropping the knife and smashing through the window Six had been leaning against, vanishing into the darkness outside.

The sound of the window shattering could barely be heard over the music, but some of the nightclub patrons who'd seen what happened stopped dancing and stared. Those surrounding Six tried to back away from him, but the crowd was too thick to move through. The bouncers who had been guarding each stairway started pushing their way through the onlookers towards Six.

So much for subtlety, he thought. Getting beaten up by a half dozen bouncers would draw too much attention, and successfully defending himself would be even worse. Slipping away into the crowd wasn't an option either; the people were still backing away, leaving Six in the center of a widening semicircle.

Two options. One: He could shove his way across the dance floor, dodging around the approaching bouncers as he went, head down the stairs, and hope that the people outside weren't blocking the door.

Six chose option two.

Just as a bulky arm shot out of the mass of people to grab him, Six launched his body up into a backflip, shoes scraping stalactites of glass off the top of the window frame, and flew into the night outside. His body became vertical as he reached the peak of his trajectory, as if he were doing a handstand on the empty air, and then he plummeted down into the Timeout, ten meters below.

Broken glass crunched under his sneakers as he landed, less than a meter from the fallen body of the flick-knife man. Six glanced at him — minor lacerations and a dislocated knee — nothing serious. Unconscious, maybe concussed. One of the man's earplugs was lying on the ground, and Six nearly dismissed it as unimportant, but then he saw the tiny speaker embedded in it.

It wasn't an earplug. It was an earpiece.

Hence the nonlethal force, Six thought. Hence the weapons training. Hence the trying to get him thrown out of the nightclub so he'd be in the open, exposed. This guy was one of Vanish's men. But how did he know Six was a Deck agent? And how did he know Six was in the nightclub?

Six picked up the earpiece and glanced around. The people waiting in line to enter Insomnia were staring at him, and while the bouncers hadn't appeared yet, Six was sure that someone would be coming after him soon. He ran out of sight around the corner, into another of the Timeout's three cul-de-sacs.

The Seawall rose into the sky opposite him, a massive slab of concrete. The illumination from the streetlamps didn't reach high enough to reveal the top, giving the impression that the wall stretched right up into outer space. Six felt like he had walked in a straight line for his entire life and had now reached the end of the world. Underneath the dull thumping and yelling from Insomnia, which bounced off the smooth surface of the wall in confusingly jagged pieces, Six could feel the concrete exuding menace. If he pressed his ear against it, he knew he would hear a deep, bass rumbling, the sound of the ocean crashing against the thick barrier in an unyielding attempt to flood the City.

ChaoSonic had put up the Seawall when Six was a small child, supposedly to protect the residents of the City from terrorists in other countries. It was Methryn Crexe who had told him that this was a lie. There were no other countries anymore. Global warming had melted the polar ice caps, and the rest of the world was underwater. ChaoSonic had put up the wall to keep the City from sinking into the ocean, and to make sure the City's residents never knew they were the last people on earth.

Six removed his earplugs and replaced one with the borrowed earpiece, just as his watch ticked over: 18:59:59 to 19:00:00.

"*. . . now seven o'clock, Team Two,*" crackled a voice calmly. "*Drop off the hostage.*"

"*Copy that,*" came the immediate response.

Six peered around the corner and watched the rest of the Timeout intently. Vanish clearly had operatives working behind the scenes, but where? The only movement Six could see was the line of people slowly flowing into Insomnia, and there was nothing even remotely suspicious about them.

Six squinted into the darkness. The fog was concealing details, but something orange had appeared near the center of the Timeout, right next to the subway entrance. He looked carefully.

It was a person in an orange undershirt and shorts, sitting on the asphalt. There was an orange bag pulled over his head, concealing his face. Six took a long look, heart pounding. It could be Kyntak, he thought. The body shape was right, and the clothes were the same as those in the ransom demand video, but his posture didn't look good.

The body was sitting up, but there didn't seem to be any weight in his arms — they were hanging limply onto the road. The legs were resting flat on the ground, ankles twisted outward.

Whoever he was, he wasn't moving. And he had the posture of someone who no longer felt any pain.

Six raced into the open, not caring about being spotted by the Insomnia crowd or Vanish's operatives. As he approached he saw that the body was not moving even slightly — no breaths were being drawn into the chest. He slid to a halt and crouched beside it, pulling off the bag.

It wasn't Kyntak.

It wasn't anyone.

A white polystyrene head stared blankly up at Six, and even as he recoiled in shock he felt how light the torso was.

Vanish hadn't returned Kyntak. He had left a dummy at the rendezvous point, taken the money, and disappeared. Before Six had time to wonder what was to be gained from sending at least three operatives to leave a decoy hostage, the earpiece crackled again.

"Go, Team Two."

"Stand still," a voice boomed, "and you will not be harmed."

Six whirled around, unable to see where the voice was coming from. He looked up. The first thing he saw was a soldier with a megaphone leaning through the second-floor window of one of the buildings; the second was the sixteen snipers aiming at him from windows all around.

THE CLIMB

"Lie down on the ground, facedown." As if the instruction needed more emphasis, the cocking of rifles echoed all around the Timeout.

A bullet from an Albatross M88 sniper rifle leaves the barrel at about thirty kilometers per hour. The Albatrosses pointed at Six were each less than twenty meters away. A shot would reach him a little over one-fortieth of a second after the trigger was pulled.

Six might be able to dive aside quick enough to dodge a single bullet, if the sniper's reflexes were poor. But the remaining fifteen shots would kill him instantly. Six stared up into the goggled eyes of the soldiers, and slowly lowered himself onto his knees.

"Facedown," the soldier with the megaphone repeated. Six put his hands flat on the road and lay down. Out of the corner of his eye he saw a group of soldiers racing across the Timeout towards him, eight holding assault rifles and one holding a remote control. Six remembered seeing remotes dangling from the belts of the soldiers at the apartment block, but couldn't work out why one was being pointed at him now.

It didn't seem to matter. It was over.

A gunshot cracked through the air. The sound bounced off the Seawall and echoed through the Timeout. Six flinched, assuming one of the snipers in the windows had fired — but no bullet hit him. He looked up in time to see the head of the soldier bearing the remote snap backward at a fatal angle. The man slumped immediately to his knees. Less than a second later another shot was fired and the soldier behind the first spun around before falling lifelessly onto the road.

The other soldiers dive-rolled to the sides, moving outward, searching for the source of the shots. Six saw it first. There was a figure standing on the rooftop of the building next to Insomnia with a rifle trained on the soldiers. As Six watched, the person ejected the cartridge of the last round and fired again, this time at one of the snipers across the street. Another head shot. The dead sniper slumped out of sight below the sill.

At first Six assumed he was seeing things, but the longer he looked, the more convinced he became. The sniper was the feathery-haired girl who'd asked him to dance. And then some random neurons fired in his brain, connecting two sentences he'd heard today: *I thought you would know a trap when you saw one . . . Do you want to dance?*

One had been whispered, the other shouted. But Six was suddenly certain they'd been uttered by the same person. *She's been following me*, Six thought, watching with horror as she slowly slaughtered Vanish's team. But why?

Another soldier was reaching for the remote control, which lay next to the corpse of its previous bearer. He was shot twice in quick succession — first through his outstretched hand, then through his heart.

Six was alarmed at how quickly this simple trade-off had become a massacre, but he had no intention of letting himself be captured. He scrambled to his feet and ran in a low crouch to the cover of a corner building.

The remaining snipers and soldiers were quick. Four seconds and five shots later, they had spotted the girl on the rooftop. She fired one last shot, killing the soldier with the megaphone, before ducking out of sight below the parapet, just before the concrete was splintered by fire from the adjacent windows and the street.

Six was torn. Should he rescue the girl who had saved his life, or should he incapacitate her to stop the loss of further lives? Either way, he needed to get up to the rooftop. He started scanning the building for entrances.

One of Vanish's remaining snipers had put down his rifle. He lifted an Ostrich RIAC7 rocket-propelled grenade launcher and aimed it at the parapet that the girl had disappeared behind. The soldiers abandoned their formation and sprinted away from the subway entrance, holding their arms over their helmets. Six's eyes widened. Ostriches fired RPGs with more than enough explosive in the warhead to take the whole top floor off the girl's building. She would be blown to bits.

Six grabbed an Eagle from the hands of the nearest fallen soldier. He aimed it up at the commando with the Ostrich. His finger tightened on the trigger.

He hesitated. *Can I do this?*

He didn't have to. The soldier carrying the Ostrich twisted sideways as a bullet punched through his neck. The girl on the rooftop started to reload. As the RPG launcher tumbled forward out of the dead sniper's grip, its trigger snagged on his gloved hand.

Six let go of the Eagle and dived forward, flattening his body against the road. He heard the *shoomp* as the Ostrich discharged a grenade towards the girl's building.

The blast swept over Six's head as a chunk of the building's midsection turned to dust, showering the road with airborne debris. Concrete thumped against the road, cracking into small pieces.

The building still stood, but it looked as though a bite had been taken out of the middle. The insides of several offices were exposed; a desk and a few chairs tumbled out of the jagged hole.

Six saw the girl peer over the edge of the parapet. Her eyes flicked from the sprinting soldiers to the cavernous wound in the side of the fortress. She seemed surprised by neither. She cocked the sniper rifle once again and shot one of the fleeing soldiers. She ejected the cartridge, which fell over the edge of the parapet, and had killed another of Vanish's snipers before it hit the ground. She glanced at Six for a moment and pointed across the street. He turned to see that more soldiers were abseiling down from the roof of one of the other buildings. Two had already hit the ground and were running towards him, weapons raised, and it seemed at least a dozen more were on the way.

Six looked back up at her, but she had disappeared — presumably hiding below the parapet again.

Six couldn't see any convenient escape route. One branch of the Timeout was blocked by rubble, and soldiers were approaching from another. Panicked civilians were pouring out of Insomnia, and there was no way he was going to put them between himself and heavy enemy fire.

The half-destroyed building moaned. Its foundations strained under its shifting weight.

Six made his decision and charged towards the soldiers.

"Freeze!" One of the soldiers had his rifle trained on him. Six skipped to the right in case the soldier fired, but kept running towards the team. He was unarmed, so he had no chance of defending himself at long range, but once he was surrounded by troops, they couldn't use their guns without risking the lives of their comrades. Six was sure he could defeat them with hand-to-hand techniques. He would reach the group of soldiers in less than ten seconds.

With a final roar of protest, the building began to crumble. Six had seen enough buildings collapse to know that a safe distance was a lot farther away than this. Glancing over quickly as he ran, Six saw that the girl was throwing some kind of grappling hook over the monorail. As her platform disintegrated beneath her, she pulled the rope tight and swung out over the street, ambitious gunfire crackling around her. The building shattered downward into itself, shooting debris out from its base. Six felt tiny stones hail down on his back, and he jumped aside as a square boulder bounced out across the Timeout towards him. The soldiers all dropped into defensive crouches as rubble rained down from the sky.

The girl let go of the rope and landed deftly on the rooftop of the opposite building, hair fluttering in the breeze. Barely even pausing, she ran across the rooftop and jumped off the other side, out of Six's view.

Okay, Six thought. *She's out of the picture. That leaves a couple of snipers and at least twenty ground troops for me to deal with.*

He had almost reached the group, but the soldiers who'd made it out from under the building were already standing up again. The team leader opened fire with his Eagle. Six dodged as a line of sparks raced across the cement towards him. He needn't have adjusted his course — the shots were aimed downward, obviously intended to scare him rather than wound him, and now it was too late to aim again. Six crash-tackled the leader and rolled to his feet without stopping, driving an uppercut into the ribs of the next soldier in line and then ducking as a gloved fist whooshed over his head.

Guns clattered to the ground all around him as the troops realized that they couldn't fire while Six was in the middle of the group. Six heard the swish of knives being drawn, but not many. Most of the soldiers opted to use their fists and boots.

Six knew that when they had strength in numbers, inexperienced fighters usually attacked one at a time, trying to wear down the stamina of their opponent, and giving each attacker room to deliver a killing blow. However, trained soldiers knew that overwhelming their opponent by attacking all at once was the quickest and most efficient method — particularly if you wanted him or her alive.

If the soldiers attempted to take him one at a time, Six was sure he could defend himself adequately. But if they all attacked him at once, he knew that he could be overwhelmed by the number of limbs alone.

As Six expected, they all attacked him at once. So he jumped, just as the mass of people pushed towards him.

Six ran a few steps across the top of the soldiers, using their helmets and shoulders as stepping-stones, before jumping down to the ground.

Now he had them where he wanted them: confused, tangled up, and still too close together to use guns. At the moment, only those on the edge could see him; the others were confused as to how their target had escaped. Six scooped up an Eagle from the ground.

He readied his weapon, prepared for an attack, but it didn't come. All of the soldiers were scattering, sprinting out towards the dark, foggy corners of the Timeout.

Six was astonished that he'd managed to intimidate an entire platoon of highly trained soldiers after only a few seconds. They hadn't even bothered to pick up their weapons and back away; they were fleeing into the darkness as if simply being near him were dangerous. . . .

Six whirled around. Another Ostrich was pointed at him from one of the windows. He just had time to jump before the first shell was launched.

The flash blazed across the Timeout and cast a giant shadow of his wildly flailing body against the Seawall in front of him for a split second. Fallen dust from the collapsed building puffed back up into the air as his body slammed into the ground.

The first thing he saw when he raised his head was the remote control. He remembered the soldier reaching for it even as sniper fire dropped his comrades. It must be important. He checked the buttons as he scrambled to his feet, but it wasn't what he expected. It only had a short-range transmitter, powerful enough for about 150 centimeters of concentrated signal. There were four keys, with the words "Syncal," "Accelerant," "Morphine," and "Locator on/off." He dropped the remote into his pocket and started running just as the Ostrich launched another shell.

Six dived forward into the air. The road behind him shattered, sprinkling shards of asphalt onto the ground. Six executed a perfect rolling landing and flipped back up to his feet, instantly running again.

At the moment his best option seemed to be to keep running, jumping, and doging until the Ostrich used up its ammunition. But he was fast nearing the end of the road.

The next explosion was so close that it blasted him into the air. More dust was injected into the fog around him, making it impossible to see, and when the ground rushed up at him he barely managed to cover his head with his arms before bouncing against the pavement and landing on his behind.

The air cleared above him, revealing the opaque night sky and the Seawall disappearing into it. And suddenly he knew where to go.

Six sprinted towards one of the corners of the Timeout, where Insomnia met the Seawall. Then he turned around, preparing to run parallel to the Seawall, and waited. Every one of his instincts screamed out against standing still, completely exposed. But Six knew that his plan would take at least eleven seconds to execute, and the Ostrich was capable of shooting once every thirteen seconds. If it fired during his maneuver he could lose his balance and fall to his death. He had to wait for it to fire before he started running again.

Shoomp! There was a puff of exhaust from a window as the Ostrich fired.

Six shot forward across the asphalt, sprinting parallel to the Seawall. The shell crashed into the corner of Insomnia behind him, splattering another shower of debris across the Timeout. He figured he had at least twelve seconds before the Ostrich was ready to fire again. And he had just hit the velocity he needed.

Six pushed one foot off the pavement a little harder than was necessary, and felt the momentum suspend his body in the air. Instead of putting his other foot on the road, he put it on the Seawall and pushed down.

His body hovered for a moment, torn between gravity and momentum. He put his other foot against the Seawall, twisting his ankle to get the maximum grip, and pushed again. He rose a little higher.

Running up walls was always difficult. It had taken Six several years of practice to learn how to put his weight on a wall without pushing himself away from it, how to lean in and use his hand as a third point of contact, how to keep up momentum while running across a vertical surface, and how to judge the best angle of ascent — too steep and he would slip and fall; too shallow and he would run out of wall before reaching the top. His running across the ceiling trick was actually easier, because he was really just jumping from one wall to the other with a flip in between. He put hardly any pressure on the ceiling itself — just enough to change direction slightly if it was required.

But Six had never scaled a wall taller than 27 meters, and the Seawall was 160 meters high. Also, the section of the wall exposed between Insomnia and the building at the opposite end of the street was only 200 meters long, 180 excluding the run-up Six had already taken. He was going to have to climb at least eighty-nine centimeters for every meter of length he covered — an angle of about forty-two degrees.

One after the other, his feet slapped against the concrete surface. The wall hadn't been worn smooth above about eight meters, so gripping was much easier once he hit that altitude. Every few seconds he pressed his hand against the wall to get some extra thrust. Soon he was sprinting fifteen meters above the road and still rising.

But climbing was already getting harder. He was thirty meters up now. He had lost nearly all of the original momentum from his run-up, and he was having to press his feet harder against the wall. His thighs were rapidly becoming sore as the repetitive pushing wore them down.

Forty meters up.

Fifty.

The Timeout was becoming a little darker down below, as the distance grew the fog concealed more and more. Six was slightly relieved by this; the sight of the distant concrete, which he knew would shatter his bones and crush his flesh if he lost his balance for even a split second, was distracting. He kept running.

At sixty meters up, he estimated the horizontal distance between himself and the building at the end, where he would run out of wall: a hundred meters. He gritted his teeth — he hadn't been climbing steeply enough! He would now have to run at a forty-five-degree angle from the ground — one vertical meter for every horizontal meter — or else he would hit the building and fall to his death.

He pushed harder, trying to ignore the signals from his aching legs. *Ninety meters to go,* he told himself. *Breathe in, breathe out. Left foot, right foot, hand. Left foot, right foot, hand. Eighty meters to go.*

He could no longer see the soldier with the Ostrich. That meant the soldier couldn't see him either, unless his goggles had thermal vision. Six was probably safe.

He was a hundred meters up. *Left, right, hand.* His calf and thigh muscles burned, and he could feel his strides across the wall getting weaker. "Left, right, hand," he hissed, trying to focus all his energy reserves into the climb. He tightened his free hand into a fist and tried to halt the pain in his legs with sheer willpower. One hundred and ten meters up; fifty to go. More than two-thirds of the way there.

He looked at the building in his way again. Too close — fifty meters away. He was going to have to make his run steeper — almost fifty degrees — to reach the top.

The ground was now invisible in the black night fog, but he couldn't see the top of the wall yet. With both ends of his journey cloaked by the inky blackness, and the Seawall stretching into infinity above and below him, he felt a sudden flash of vertigo — as if the wall were actually horizontal and he were running on his side. He almost hesitated and lost his footing; he slapped his hand against the wall instead of his right foot. On the next step he nearly compensated for the mistake by pushing off too hard, before pulling back at the last microsecond as he realized that one over-industrious push would catapult him out into the void.

Breathe in, breathe out. One hundred and twenty meters up now. His leg muscles were screaming and his eyes began to water with the pain. *Keep going,* he told himself. *Pain is mental, not physical — nerves reporting injuries to the brain.*

Left, right, hand! The building was coming up too fast — it was twenty meters away, and he still had twenty-five to climb. His shoes scraped across the concrete as if it were a chalkboard, slipping more and more as his coordination suffered. His hand, its palm now pink and sweaty, scrabbled desperately against the wall. His angle of ascent became shallower even as he tried to force his body higher. The building was ten meters away now; he was about to run out of wall to climb, and the top was still twenty meters above. His run became horizontal as his calves and ankles stiffened, and soon he was actually descending.

I'm one hundred forty meters up, he thought. *If I fall, I'm dead — but I can't reach the top! If I hit that building, my momentum runs out, and I die!*

The logical part of Six's brain shut down completely, and raw instinct took over. Instead of trying to run up the wall at a seventy-five-degree angle, he ran straight at the building and jumped up as high as he could. His body rushed through the air, curling into a fetal cannonball position, and hit the side of the building shoes first, seven meters below the top of the Seawall.

The momentum of the jump pressed him against the

building's wall, but instead of grabbing on to it, he threw himself straight back into the air, spinning like a carelessly thrown battle ax, and leaped almost the whole remaining seven meters. He threw out one hand and grabbed the top of the Seawall.

His legs went completely numb as soon as the strain was taken off them, and their deadweight pulled painfully at his hips. His sweaty hand was slipping off the lip as he dangled in the air, and he tossed his other one over the edge as well.

His first attempt to drag himself onto the top of the Seawall failed, and he nearly fell. His shoulders and elbows made a muffled crack as he slipped backward, hanging on by his fingertips. He breathed deeply before trying again, his exhalations echoing off the Seawall all around him, chorusing out into the night.

He tried once more. His grazed fingers strained as they took all the weight of his torso and legs. When his shoulders were over the edge, he let go with one hand and slapped it against the concrete on the top. The Seawall was almost thirty meters thick, so there was no other side to grab hold of. Instead, he braced his elbow against the top and dragged his torso over the edge. When his weight was resting upon his chest, he dragged himself forward until he had room to lift his knee up.

With his last shred of strength, he rolled to one side, a safe two meters away from the edge, and rested.

Six lay on his back, eyes shut, thinking. The pounding of his heart in his ears had faded, and now he could hear the sea booming against the wall, each wave crashing forward, striking the concrete, then sliding back under to make room for the next.

He still had the same objective: Find Kyntak.

But where was he? With 7.5 million square kilometers of City to search, Six had no hope of finding him without a lead.

Six's eyes popped open. The monorail cars which had been resting above the Timeout when he'd arrived — he couldn't see them anymore, but they'd been there when he started running up the Seawall.

If the monorail cars were there for a party, Six thought, would they have stayed once the snipers showed up? Maybe — he could imagine a few seconds of stunned silence, when no one had gathered the sense to drive them back along the rail to safety. Would they have stayed once the girl on the rooftop started slaughtering the soldiers? Six wondered. It was possible — perhaps everyone was ducking for cover, too scared to run for the controls. Would they have stayed once the Ostrich opened fire, ripping the road to jagged shreds and turning the buildings to rubble? No way. Someone would have had the sense to hit the reverse switch.

Six's mind was racing now. The person or people inside the carriages had known that something was going to happen in the Timeout.

The only people who knew that the drop-off was taking place were the kidnappers and the Deck agents. And the monorail cars didn't belong to the Deck.

They didn't interact, Six thought. They were just there. Watching. A reconnaissance unit for Vanish. They would return to home base once their mission was complete.

Six leaped to his feet. He had to follow those monorail cars — they would lead him straight to where Kyntak was being held. He started running back along the top of the wall.

The black, inscrutable ocean swelled and deflated down below, crashing against the concrete with patient aggression. The wind blasted at Six from the water side of the wall. He ran as close to dead center as he could. Even with fifteen-meter margins on both sides, the long drops made him nervous. If he fell back into the Timeout, the impact would kill him instantly — but falling into the ocean would be just as bad. He would be stranded outside the City until he drowned, froze to death, or was slammed endlessly against the wall by the waves.

It would be hard to follow the monorail on foot without being spotted. He took out the phone he'd taken from the teenager and dialed King's office as he ran.

"King." The voice sounded tense, but not cautious. Six didn't think there was anyone listening in.

"It's me," he said. Normally he avoided statements like that, because they conveyed almost no information. But he didn't want to incriminate King, so using his own name could be a mistake.

"Are you okay? Where are you?"

"I made the rendezvous, but they didn't give him back," Six said. "I don't have a lot of time."

"What do you need me to do?"

"Put a trace on this phone. I'll call you again in half an hour, so you can tell me where it ended up. Okay?" Six looked at his watch. 19:11:08.

"Yes."

"And put the ransom money back in our account," Six added. "He's not going to take it now." He was about to pocket the phone when King broke in.

"Wait. Six?" He sounded uncertain, or nervous.

"Yes," Six said. "What is it?"

There was a pause. Six could see the end of the monorail line up ahead. "King?" he said. "There's no time for —"

"You'll be okay," King interrupted. It wasn't reassurance or a statement of fact. It was a compliment. King was telling Six that he was proud of him.

"Yes," Six said. "I will." He put the phone in his pocket, keeping the call connected.

The monorail line was directly underneath him, about ten meters down. It was an iron strip, eighty centimeters wide, stretching out across the Timeout in a straight line. Six aimed very carefully. If he missed, there was nothing to break his fall before the road a hundred sixty meters below. He took a deep breath and jumped.

Wham! Six fought to control the instinctive shuddering in his muscles as he hit the line. His hands grasped wildly as he slipped backward over the edge. He managed to hook his fingertips around the edge of the platform and dangled there for a moment.

"Agent Six is alive, unharmed, and not in Vanish's custody," the girl said. She glanced reflexively over her shoulder. She was sure that Vanish's forces were too decimated and distracted to come after her, but she didn't like the feeling of exposure that came with standing on top of a building. She felt safest with her back against a wall and a gun trained on the only door. She slept in a room with no windows, an electronically locked trapdoor under her bed, and a concealed latticework of piano wire covering the door frame.

"Excellent work." Lerke's voice was filled with satisfaction rather than relief. As usual, the girl had the feeling that he sensed her words before she uttered them, and that events had transpired exactly as he had expected them to. "How many casualties?"

"Eight," she replied. "All theirs."

There was a pause. "And witnesses?"

"Forty-one hostile, eighty-eight civilian," she said. Normally she operated invisibly. In an ideal job, no one saw her enter, leave, or do anything in between. But this mission had been different. Lerke had demanded spectacle. Unusual though this was, it had made her job easier. Subtlety was not Agent Six's strong suit. He tended to draw attention to himself, and protecting him without being noticed at all would have been difficult.

"Perfect," Lerke replied. "Shots fired?" She could hear a smile in his voice. *He's expecting a good answer*, she thought.

"Nine," she said. "All hits."

"Hostile shots fired?"

"Six hundred and twenty-six. All misses."

"Well done," he said. "Your next task is to go to Vanish's base of operations. I'll upload the coordinates to your mobile."

"What's the mission objective?"

"For now, just observe. But go prepared. If things aren't happening the way I want, I'll expect you to change them so they are."

"Yes," Nai said. "I understand."

Six could see the monorail carriages in the distance. Their shells glimmered a dull silver as the light from the streetlamps below glanced off both sides. He forced himself to run faster, his aching feet slamming down against the iron rail.

The monorail had a maximum speed of forty kilometers per hour, and Six estimated that the driver was at full throttle. But Six was gaining quickly. It wasn't long before he was illuminated in the rear lights.

The City skyline rushed past as the track joined the greater web that spanned the continent. The carriages bent at their flexible couplings as the rail curved, sending the monorail car west. Six watched another monorail clatter past in the opposite direction, on a track overhead, as he advanced on the tinted window. The rear carriage looked empty, but he could hear noises inside the others — the thumping of footsteps as people moved in between cars, the crackling and buzzing of radios, and the faint rattling clicks of guns sweeping from side to side.

Six would have liked to climb inside the train, hide somewhere, and wait for it to reach the base where Kyntak was being held. But Vanish's soldiers seemed cautious, and the two carriages were small. He would be found, and he'd have to incapacitate the troops. Then there would be no way of finding out where the base was.

He pulled the mobile phone out of his pocket and checked the screen to see that it was still connected to King's line. Then he tightened his free hand into a rock-hard fist, drew it back, and punched through the rear window of the monorail car.

The glass was shatterproof. As soon as his fist connected, it was like static on an old television. Six's view of the interior of the carriage disappeared, replaced by a matrix of white and grey cracks. He drove his hand through the glass and immediately tossed the phone inside. Then he started pulling at the edges of the hole to widen it.

Chunks of the cracked glass came away as he tugged at them, and soon the gap was wide enough for him to see soldiers running through the door between the two rear carriages. As soon as he was sure that they had seen him too, he stumbled and lost his grip on the glass. Springing up off the rails, he started sprinting after the escaping monorail car, but he didn't push his speed. He ensured that he was quickly falling back, apparently unable to keep up.

Six was about fifty meters behind the trundling rear carriage when the first soldier reached the window and fired at him. It would have been a nearly impossible shot, aiming at a moving target from a moving point at long range, but Six made the soldier think he was an excellent marksman. He hurled his body backward as if he had been hit in the chest, and fell on his rear against the track before pitching lifelessly over the side.

As soon as he was underneath the track and the monorail car had disappeared into the fog, Six broke his fall by grabbing the edge with one hand. He hung there for a moment, visualizing the scene from the soldier's perspective. He had tried to get into the carriage, had stumbled, was unable to keep up on foot, and had been shot in the chest before falling out of sight. As far as they were concerned, he was dead.

Six swung along underneath the track, from one hand to the other, heading towards the next support strut so he could slide down.

Time to take the offensive, he thought. *Nobody kidnaps my brother and gets away with it.*

MISSION FOUR
19:22:45

BEHIND ENEMY LINES

King of Hearts hit the button to unlock his office door. The QS opened the door, but didn't step inside.

"May I come in?" she asked. Her voice was casual, but not friendly.

"Of course you can," King said. "If I refused, you could have me arrested. Make this your own office, and come in whenever you like."

She sat down opposite him. "I shouldn't have to tell you that the Spades perform a necessary function here," she said.

"You're right. You don't need to tell me."

"Without a fail-safe," she continued, "the Deck would become corrupt. The Code would change, the agents would create their own agendas, and then the whole thing would either fragment into cells or become a company as bad as ChaoSonic. Neither of us wants that."

"Why are you lecturing me about this?" King demanded. "I was there when the rules were made!"

"Is that a license to break them?" the QS asked. "I just want to point out that balance needs to be maintained. The Hearts and Diamonds are useless without the Spades keeping them in line; the Spades have no function without the red suits to monitor; and we'd all disappear without the Clubs training new recruits." She leaned across his desk. "You know I have a right to be here."

"No, you don't," King said. "Agent Six of Hearts is the finest agent we've ever had. You've seen his mission records."

"You think they prove he's incorruptible?"

"He is," King said, holding her gaze.

"Less than three hours ago, we received an anonymous phone call. The caller said he had witnessed Agent Six taking money from a known Code-breaker with ties to ChaoSonic. He was able to describe Six accurately. And according to our system, Six was logged out at the time. So far, we can't find anyone to corroborate his whereabouts."

"Irrefutable evidence," King said sarcastically. "I stand corrected."

The QS smiled icily. "It's not much, but we can't let the accusation go uninvestigated. Of course, I'd like to hear Six's side of the story." She stood up and started to pace the room. "But when confronted, Agent Six of Hearts sabotaged an elevator to escape capture. He stole weapons and equipment from the armory, including a lock-release gun and plastic explosives. He ransacked the office of Agent Queen of Hearts — who, by the way, we can't seem to find either. Agent Six shot a Spade agent, admittedly with nonlethal ammunition, then attacked her with a sword. He resisted arrest once again and escaped the building with a stolen parachute. We've checked his house and discovered that he doesn't live there. He falsified his address on the Deck computers." She put her hands on King's desk. "And yet you say he's innocent? Innocent people don't behave like this."

"Did he say anything to your agents?" King asked.

The QS let a hiss of air escape through gritted teeth. "Yes. He accused me, personally, of violating the Code by trying to arrest him."

"Unless you had reasonable grounds," King said, "he was right to do so."

"Resisting arrest is, in itself, sufficient grounds for arrest!"

"Agent Six has done nothing wrong," King said. "Therefore, when an armed response team of Spades was sent after him, he could easily deduce that evidence had been fabricated to link him to a Code violation. With the knowledge that someone was trying to frame him, resisting arrest would have seemed the best course of action." He smiled ironically. "And because your teams are so efficient, the methods he used to escape are excusable. Anything less and he would not still be at large."

The QS sat down again. "Our investigative teams are beyond reproach," she said, drumming her fingernails on the desk. "If Six had given himself up, and the accusations turned out to be false, he would be back at work by now and the culprit would probably be in custody. Instead, we have a Code-breaker on the loose, whether Agent Six is guilty or not."

King raised an eyebrow. "Well, I'll help in whatever way I can. Have you investigated the caller? And who was the Code-breaker Six supposedly met?"

"You already know I won't tell you that," the QS growled, "just like you won't tell me where Agent Six is."

There was a pause.

"You believe him to be guilty," King said finally, "yet you assume that he'll call us with his location?"

"I don't believe he would conceal his whereabouts from *you*," the QS said, giving him a meaningful look. "And it wouldn't hurt you to cooperate with me."

King shrugged. "As I said, I'll help however I can. But there are other matters that require my attention." He switched on his computer monitor.

The QS understood the signal and stood up. She turned back to him when she reached the doorway. "Agent Six's exemplary mission results and test scores do not prove his innocence," she said. "No one is incorruptible, King of Hearts."

King tapped out a sequence on the keyboard, and the door swung shut as the Queen of Spades left.

The streetlamps buzzed past overhead as Six ran down the street. The shops and buildings were deserted — people had heard the gunfire and the explosions. They hadn't been drawn towards the noise by curiosity, nor had they run away in panic; they had calmly changed their routes to avoid the area, as if it were nothing more than a traffic jam.

Six had decided that the best course of action was to go home. His house was less than eleven kilometers away — a fifteen-minute run. He should arrive five minutes before King was expecting his call.

Six had figured that Vanish would only have one base of operations, for the same reason that the Deck only had one — any more would make it hard to stay under ChaoSonic's radar. Therefore the troops had probably been deployed from where Kyntak was being held.

It would have to be quite close to the rendezvous point, so Vanish could control the situation. The soldiers would need to be able to travel between the two points via ground vehicles in a matter of minutes, not hours.

Assuming that the base wasn't on the other side of the

Seawall, which seemed a fair assessment based on the number of troops they had, that left a semicircular search area with an approximate radius of twenty kilometers. And that meant 628 square kilometers of potential locations.

But Vanish wouldn't have made the rendezvous point right next door — he must have known there was a risk that Deck forces would scour the surrounding area looking for Kyntak. *We'd be doing it now if the Spades hadn't messed it up*, Six thought. So he would have left a safety buffer — enough distance between the base and the rendezvous point so that the Deck wouldn't have the manpower to search far enough. At least ten kilometers — that took a semicircular chunk out of the original area: radius ten kilometers, area 157 square kilometers.

This left a curved strip of possible locations ten kilometers wide and more than a hundred kilometers long. Approximately 471 kilometers in area, Six calculated. Not a big part of a 7.5 million-square-kilometer City, but still way too much to search on his own.

Six hoped the troops in the monorail hadn't found the phone. Beyond stumbling on the base with blind luck, it was his only chance.

As he was without a mobile or any money (and no way of getting any unless he stole it or used his card, which would attract the attention of the Spades), Six had decided to use the landline at home to call King. And if he was going to break into an enemy base with no information and no backup, he was going to need weaponry and equipment, which he could no longer get from the Deck.

His house was just around the corner. He slowed to an inconspicuous walk. It seemed unlikely that the Spades would have found it, but it was best to be cautious.

The house and the lawn surrounding it looked exactly as he had left them that morning. Six disarmed the four locks, opened the door, and punched in the alarm code. A barely audible beep of consent emerged from the panel, and Six shut the door behind him.

He did his usual sweep of the house. No intruders. Harry was standing perfectly still in the training room, showing no sign that he had moved since Six left the house fourteen hours ago.

Was that only this morning? Six wondered. *It feels like it's been days.*

"Harry," he said.

The robot didn't respond, but that was normal. Six hadn't asked a direct question.

"Has anything unusual happened in the house today?"

"You left approximately ninety-five minutes before you usually do on Mondays," Harry growled.

"Anything since I left?" Six asked.

"No."

That was good enough for Six. He glanced at his watch: 19:37:51. The monorail might not have reached its destination yet, and he didn't want to call King prematurely. He started his computer and opened up his in-box.

Six raised an eyebrow in surprise. There was a new message from King, sent just eight minutes previously. It had an attachment entitled *OIvanish.doc*. Six read the e-mail first.

Six

I hacked into the ChaoSonic security mainframe and pulled their file on Vanish. It raises more questions than answers, but might be useful to you.

I had a visit from the QS a few minutes ago and I think

she's still suspicious of me, so my phone may be tapped by now — but I've uploaded the program tracking your phone to the following web page: http://cww.prog91167/sim2305 3306.ds.

The Spades don't seem to know about Project Falcon. Someone's trying to set you up to look like a double agent. I'll let you know if I can work out who.

Watch your back.

King

Six opened the attached document and text flooded the screen. It was a dossier on Vanish, apparently written by a ChaoSonic security analyst named Serfie Thaldurken, whose contact details were at the top of the page. Six was already discouraged. ChaoSonic had its analysts writing dossiers on Vanish, and therefore large security forces looking for him. They'd clearly been trying to find him for a long time. How was Six going to fare on his own, racing against the clock?

The first section of the dossier was a list of events believed to have been orchestrated by Vanish or linked to him, categorized in reverse chronological order. These included numerous assassinations, abductions, and even bank robberies. There were also several break-ins at ChaoSonic scientific facilities, and a ransacking of the ruins of the Lab, Six was surprised to see, less than a month after Kyntak had rescued him from there.

Six scrolled down, sifting back through time. The most common activities seemed to be robberies and abductions. Vanish had stolen a vast amount of equipment, data, and weaponry from various ChaoSonic facilities, along with many rare valuables, each of which would fetch a small fortune if offered to the right buyer. He had kidnapped dozens of people, usually asking for a ransom but only sometimes receiving it, and even then rarely setting the prisoners free.

Just like Kyntak, Six thought. Vanish's victims were all taken for some kind of strategic value less obvious than monetary — they had information, or a high public profile, or an important position within an organization. Several ChaoSonic executives, security chiefs, and shareholders had been kidnapped by Vanish; in fact, this seemed to be what had brought him to the organization's attention.

He believes Kyntak is me, Six thought. *So what does he want with me, if not the ransom?*

The next section of the document was a list of people suspected of being involved with Vanish's operations. There were more than a hundred names, but most had no more than a brief physical description and the reason they had come under suspicion. Many were soldiers, either suspected of working in Vanish's army or killed and identified later. None had been captured alive. Six saw that most of the soldiers were ex-ChaoSonic — presumably having changed sides because the pay was better. He knew that ChaoSonic rarely paid its employees generously.

Some of the suspects — in fact, all of the people who'd been abducted and later released — were higher-ranking ChaoSonic employees. At first, Six assumed that the fact Vanish hadn't killed them was the grounds for the suspicion against them, but he then saw that all had been guilty of stealing information or technology which quickly found its way into Vanish's hands.

So he only lets them go if they agree to work for him? he thought. *How does he keep them to their word?*

Six saw Earle Shuji on the list. The picture of her was an old one — Six could still see the greed in her beautiful dark eyes. The caption stated that Vanish had been a potential buyer for her soldier bots, but that the deal had been aborted when Shuji disappeared; apparently she had been telling the truth. The paragraph concluded with "Missing, presumed dead."

Six felt a touch of satisfaction. The Deck had hidden her well, and it seemed she had made no move to contact old friends.

He kept reading.

Retuni Lerke was on the list too. Apparently he had leaked Lab data to Vanish's organization. This didn't surprise Six. Eight months ago Lerke had stolen a sample of Six's DNA and tried to sell it to a ChaoSonic security official. Methryn Crexe had been planning to have Lerke killed, but Six and Kyntak had arrested Crexe before he could do this.

Six assumed that Lerke, like most high-ranking ChaoSonic employees, was extremely greedy if not actively cruel. But he also suspected that Lerke was actually insane. Project Falcon could not have been conceived by a normal brain, and double-crossing Crexe was madness. Six hoped that Lerke was not involved in today's events. Vanish was scary enough on his own.

He didn't make eye contact with Lerke's picture. He knew what Lerke looked like, and glimpsing that face staring out of the screen unnerved him. He scrolled down immediately, seeing the bald head and pale eyes only in his peripheral vision.

There was a picture of the red-eyed woman who had recited the ransom demand, Niskev Pacye. There wasn't much information — she had lived an unremarkable life before being hired as a neurologist in a ChaoSonic hospital. She'd risen to the rank of senior neurosurgeon before disappearing completely, and then showing up two years later as Vanish's representative in a data trade. There was no indication she'd ever joined his soldiers in battle. Her role seemed limited to adviser and spokesperson.

Six was alarmed to see Chelsea Tridya on the list. She knew

too much about him, Kyntak, and the Deck. But his panic subsided when he saw that the grounds for her inclusion were slender. ChaoSonic suspected that Vanish was the one who had stolen the Lab's supply of Tridya's aging drug. To do this, he would have to have known it existed, and it was more palatable for ChaoSonic to assume that Tridya had told him about it than that there had been a leak within their organization.

Six didn't recognize any of the other names. The next section was the shortest — known information about Vanish himself. Six looked at the picture first and recoiled in horror.

It was a black-and-white mug shot, taken in a ChaoSonic cell. The man in the photo was about thirty, bald, slightly chubby, and 174 centimeters tall, according to a text box in the corner. But it took Six a moment to notice any of this because his eyes were drawn to the scars on the man's face.

Three broad gashes split the flesh, one from his right nostril to his chin, one from above his right eye to his cheekbone, and one from the left side of his forehead up to the top of his skull. A series of minor scratches latticed his left cheek, and there was a small triangular gouge under his left eye — it looked like mascara that had run.

The man's eyes were closed. The background was an uneven grey-and-white gradient — a pillow, Six realized. He was asleep.

The wounds had been cleaned before the picture was taken, so there was no blood, but this only made it more horrific. Six thought he could see exposed bone in the gouge in the left cheek, and he looked away, heart pounding.

Six had once gone undercover in a ChaoSonic jail to break out an agent, and he'd seen plenty of brutality there. And vivid images of the prisoners at Earle Shuji's factory still haunted him.

But he'd never seen wanton disfiguration like this. He started reading the caption.

This was the only known photo of Vanish. One of his soldiers had defected, informing ChaoSonic that Vanish was planning a raid on one of their satellite uplink stations. He said that Vanish wanted to use equipment which was integrated into the building, and would therefore have to be there in person. ChaoSonic left the facility minimally guarded, and ambushed Vanish's fifteen-person team once they were inside. Thirteen of Vanish's soldiers were killed. Only he and the defector were left alive.

The ChaoSonic troops put Vanish in an armored personnel carrier so he could be transported to a secret prison facility for processing. But when the APC arrived, he was rushed straight into the emergency room. Apparently Vanish had mutilated his own face with his fingernails.

According to the document, he didn't speak a single word the entire time he was in their custody; but that wasn't long. His troops broke into the emergency room less than three hours after his condition had been stabilized. It was unclear how they'd found it. The picture was taken ten minutes before their arrival.

During the rescue, Vanish's team killed three doctors and nine guards, leaving one doctor and one guard alive. A week later, the defector's body was found under the ChaoSonic security chief's desk, with a high concentration of Syncal in his bloodstream — almost double the amount that had been injected into Six that morning.

Thaldurken drew special attention to the fact that twenty-six people had been killed: thirteen of Vanish's and thirteen of ChaoSonic's, including the defector. Thaldurken suggested that Vanish may have been trying to send a message to ChaoSonic —

that he had only reacted defensively, with force that was precisely equal to that used against him.

He also said that he didn't believe Vanish had wounded himself just to get into the emergency room for an easier escape. With so much damage to his face, he couldn't be identified by any witnesses to his crimes or by previously taken photographs — not that there were many of either. As long as Vanish maintained his silence in ChaoSonic custody, his real name would never be exposed.

But this seemed illogical to Six. By gouging out his own face, hadn't Vanish made his appearance so distinctive that he would never be able to conceal his identity again?

Six recalled an old story about a criminal whose head had been shaved and who had shaved the heads of a dozen other men as they slept so he could not be identified the next morning. He imagined Vanish inflicting injuries identical to his own on the faces of thousands of innocent people so ChaoSonic would never find him.

He shook off the image with a shiver. Not only was that completely insane, it wouldn't work. Presumably the doctors in the emergency room had taken a sample of Vanish's blood and compared it to their DNA database.

He scrolled down. Yes, they had, but it hadn't helped identify him. Vanish's DNA wasn't on file, and his blood was of the most common type, O positive. Six knew that trying to identify someone by blood type was nearly impossible. He could think of twenty people at the Deck who were O positive, including himself. He scrolled back up and kept reading.

Vanish hadn't mutilated thousands of strangers to stay hidden. He had just disappeared. While his forces occasionally turned up and wreaked havoc on ChaoSonic facilities, the man himself had not been seen again. And his capture had taken place . . . almost thirty years ago?

Six went over this again, just to make sure he hadn't misread it. He hadn't. Vanish had scarred himself and disappeared twenty-eight years, eight months, and three days ago.

He scrolled farther up, looking at the list of crimes Vanish was believed to be responsible for. The first one was eleven years earlier, and they got older as Six read. Abduction of a ChaoSonic official, twenty-two years ago. Bombing of the Gear munitions factory, thirty-eight years ago. Assassination of a security chief, forty-seven years ago. There were more events listed. ChaoSonic was the result of a small merger almost fifty years ago, so that was as far back as the records went.

In fact, the people who'd been kidnapped, set free, and then discovered working for Vanish were rarer than Six had thought. Each kidnapping only happened once the previous victim was dead. Because he usually picked people in such extreme positions of power within ChaoSonic, Vanish only seemed to need one at a time.

No wonder they suspect Chelsea Tridya, Six thought. This implied that Vanish was at least seventy, in a city where most people were dead at sixty. The Lab's supply of Tridya's drug was stolen only a few months ago, and it couldn't actually make someone younger. It couldn't even keep their age at a complete standstill. The Lab was using an inverted formula anyway — they were making children age quickly. So ChaoSonic assumed that Vanish collaborated with Tridya, and had access to the drug in some form for at least a decade. Tridya hadn't designed her formula back then, but maybe they didn't know that.

Six held the theory in his mind, testing it, feeling its weight like a ball being tossed lightly from one hand to the other. Did he believe that there was a seventy-year-old, hideously scarred puppet-master behind today's events?

No way. ChaoSonic had had the wool pulled over their eyes.

Vanish wasn't a man at all.

Vanish was an organization.

It only took Six a few seconds to connect his spare mobile phone to the web page King had sent him. Soon the location of the teenage boy's mobile was a blinking red dot on the screen, superimposed over a map of the City. There was a white line which showed where the phone had been since King set up the tracking program. It seemed that the monorail train had gone more or less straight from the Timeout to a warehouse thirteen kilometers west of it, and stopped.

It's in my search area, Six thought. *And it's a warehouse, so it'd be a suitable base of operations for Vanish, particularly if there's an underground area — that way ChaoSonic wouldn't know how big it is. And there's an airfield right next to it, so the troops can get all over the City quickly.*

He stared at the screen of his phone intently, searching for anything that would contradict the signs. There was nothing.

I think I've just found Kyntak, he thought.

It was 19:39:45. He needed to get going as soon as possible, but had to get some equipment first. Six walked into the training room and pressed his palm lightly against the wall. It slid aside, revealing four rows of weapons.

For Kyntak's safety, he was going to have to enter the facility silently and invisibly. This meant lightweight equipment that could be used quietly — no shotguns, no automatic rifles. But he was going to have to get out as well — and once he had rescued Kyntak, he expected the alarm would be sounded quickly.

He picked out a quarterstaff, which could be separated into two halves for carrying, and an Owl semiautomatic pistol. He screwed a silencer to the gun, then took a nylon rope from the rack and started spooling it over his shoulder.

"I'm going on a suicidal rescue mission," he said to Harry as he worked. "Want to come?"

"*No*," Harry said. He didn't turn his head to look at Six.

Of course not, thought Six. *It's not that he's scared; it's that he doesn't want anything. He's a robot.* "Do you want to stay here?"

"*No.*"

Six thought about it. He couldn't use Harry to create a diversion for easier entry — any disturbance would be either too subtle to help or so obvious the alarm would be raised. And taking him inside wasn't an option. One intruder would have a far better chance of staying hidden than two.

But when he and Kyntak were on their way out, possibly with the entire Vanish army behind them, they would be able to use his firepower.

"Harry, get out the motorbike," he said. "I'm going to find an outfit for you."

Harry walked out the door, and Six started sifting through his wardrobe.

Two minutes later, the house was locked up and he was outside, helping Harry get dressed. Six didn't have a garage or a backyard. His bike was kept on the thin strip of concrete between the back of his house and the wall separating his property from his neighbors'. He had built the motorcycle himself from parts of other bikes. He'd had to scan each piece for bugs as he went, because ChaoSonic made them all, and ChaoSonic often bugged their products. But it was worth it. Six's bike was better quality than even the most expensive models; it had a six-cylinder engine, a carbon-fiber chassis, and a softail-style monoshock suspension. The fiberglass fairing was polished to an obsidian-like shine.

Six had chosen to dress Harry in one of his long black coats, a pair of grey jogging pants, and a thick woolen beanie. Harry was taller than Six, so the pants didn't quite reach his ankles, but not enough plastic skin was exposed to look suspicious. His synthetic feet and hands could pass as shoes and gloves. Other than his fingertips and the soles of his feet, Harry's plastic exoskeleton was coated in PTFE, an almost frictionless fluoropolymer, so Six had to attach the belt very tightly around Harry's waist to keep his pants from falling down.

There was really nothing Six could put on Harry's face — a ski mask or even sunglasses would be too suspicious. He resolved that Harry would sit behind him on the bike and they would go fast. Anyone who happened to look would be much more likely to think *mask* than *robot*.

Six himself had changed into a black spandex catsuit — the clothes he'd borrowed from the teenage hoodlums were useless from a stealth point of view. He had the two halves of the quarterstaff strapped to his back, with the climbing rope looped over the straps and the silenced Owl in his belt.

"Do you know how to ride a motorbike?" Six asked Harry as he climbed on.

"*No.*"

"Fair enough," Six said. Why would a robot that could run at sixty kilometers an hour need to know how to ride a motorbike? "Hang on tight."

Plastic forearms crushed his abdomen. "Not that tight," wheezed Six. "Just don't fall off." Harry's grip loosened, Six revved the engine, and the motorbike thundered into the night.

Driving didn't take much concentration, so Six was free to consider the facts as they traveled. *If Vanish is an organization rather than a man, this changes everything,* Six thought as the wind blasted past his face. It would explain the hundreds of highly trained troops, the half century of crimes attributed to one man, the deals with so many Code-breakers and the co-opting of so many officials. A single person couldn't do all that, even assuming that he was able to live to the age of seventy. Sooner or later he'd be found out, or betrayed, or murdered by a rival.

It was like struggling to assemble a jigsaw puzzle and discovering halfway through that the wrong picture was on the box. An organization could achieve many things that a lone person could not — ChaoSonic had shown everyone that. Corporations were not subject to human ailments; they didn't die naturally and were hard to kill. They didn't have emotions, and their actions could affect many people, requiring just as many people to affect them back. And the value of extra manpower could never be underestimated.

But there was something that gave lone operatives an advantage — concealment.

ChaoSonic had never allowed another corporation to rise. It was clinging to its monopoly over the City with every white knuckle it had. There were thousands of ChaoSonic operatives whose sole purpose was to find fledgling corporations and crush them, eliminating competitors in advance. Finding the Deck was not their top priority yet, partly because it was so well hidden, partly because it was a nonprofit organization, and partly because its interests so often overlapped with ChaoSonic's own. ChaoSonic lost money to thieves, and employees to murderers, and the Deck was constantly shuffling them away. But anyone else who was a member of a non-ChaoSonic group had better be looking over his or her shoulder.

But now Six was picturing something new: a secret organization that had been established more than fifty years ago, before ChaoSonic had tightened its grip; that had stayed secret until now by attributing all its actions to a lone enigmatic man, recruiting more and more people, remaining invisible even as it grew, welling up towards ChaoSonic from beneath, like a volcano under the City that was slowly getting ready to explode.

Pedestrians crossing the street hurried as Six and Harry rocketed past through the fog, pulsing in and out of visibility as streetlamps rushed by overhead. Six saw a small child tugging on the trouser leg of a man and pointing at Harry. He twisted some more power into the engine with the throttle, giving them an extra boost into the next wall of gloom.

The situation seemed both simpler and more complex than Six had guessed a few hours ago. On the one hand, the bizarre variety of Vanish's actions so far — breaking into the Deck, killing Methryn Crexe, kidnapping Kyntak, attempting to abduct Six, then trying to kill him when they failed — could be explained by the fact that a conglomerate had more motives than a single operative. No group was ever perfectly unified, because different people would always have different agendas. The strongest teams used their diversity to support their efforts, King had once said, while the weaker ones let their differences tear them apart. He had been trying to explain the value of cooperation to Six, and failing. Six had seen why other people might need to work together, but there was nothing he was incapable of doing on his own.

So Vanish was a group of people, each of whom had something to gain from today's events. But this realization didn't help Six much — one man would have been easier to investigate than fifty.

But for now, Six had a single goal — rescue Kyntak. Kyntak would get the Spades off his back and help him keep Vanish from exposing them.

Six clenched his hands around the grips on the handlebars as other thoughts swirled in his brain. *Unless I can't rescue him. Unless I'm not strong enough and I die trying. Unless he's already dead and I'm on my own again.*

They were getting close now. He slowed the bike down to a manageable seventy kilometers per hour. *Other people are addictive*, he thought. *You don't need them at first, but once you've been exposed, you can't get by without them. A year ago I was completely satisfied being on my own. Not happy, but satisfied. And now I'm on a suicide mission, looking for my twin brother. Not just because it's right and because I owe it to him. And not because I like him all that much. Because I need him. I can't go back to the way I used to live.*

He switched off the headlight and clicked on the ChaoSilent muffler. He'd taken the chip from a pair of stealth boots and attached it to the exhaust pipe when he built the bike; the small subwoofer and tweeter amplifiers, which he'd pilfered from a guitar amp and placed under the suspension, now emitted the phase opposite of his motor and tire noise. His bike glided along with a barely audible clicking sound as the volume settings adjusted themselves.

The giant domed shell of the warehouse materialized on the horizon. Six slowed the bike even more, scanning the area for soldiers. None yet, but he was still outside the perimeter.

As he'd guessed, the barrier was no more than a chain-link fence, about four meters high. He had no doubt that Vanish could afford something better: automated sentry guns, electrified razor wire, or even a small-scale replica of the Seawall around the warehouse. But spending so much money in such a public way would shatter the illusion that the warehouse was privately owned and unimportant. It would draw ChaoSonic operatives to it, like rats to rotten meat.

Six thought it was safe to assume that there'd be some form of security between the fence and the warehouse, again probably something not too flashy. He eased the bike to a halt, hooked his fingers through the fence, and pressed his face against the wire, peering into the darkness. The warehouse was still just a silhouette to him. The fog shielded the details from his gaze.

"Harry," he whispered. "Can you see any guards?"

"*Yes*," Harry said. His voice was muted to the volume of Six's own, but there was no difference in tone — a robotic equivalent of whispering that still unsettled Six. "*There are three sentries in towers on the three visible corners of the warehouse, each armed with Wedge-tail FBN2 sniper rifles. There are two guards standing near the main door, and another near the side door, each carrying Raptor pistols.*"

"Any sensors?" Six asked.

"*Yes. There is a ChaoSonic Mark 3 security light on each wall of the warehouse.*"

"What range do they have?"

That model of security light was older than Harry, so he had the specifications in his CPU. It took him less than half a second to recall the data. *"They can be tuned to detect movement at a maximum range of fifty meters,"* he said.

Six nodded. That meant that if they crossed the fence, they could only get about ten meters before a spotlight would click on, exposing them.

He tensed as something moved at his feet, but relaxed as soon as he looked down. It was just a rat, sniffing his shoe as it scurried past. Harry's head turned to follow it; he'd never seen an animal before, Six guessed.

Six picked the rat up by its tail, holding it at arm's length. It hissed in panic and waved its claws in the air as it swung from side to side. Wrinkling his nose with disgust, aware of how many germs were likely to be rubbing off onto his skin, Six pushed it flat against the fence, and it wriggled through one of the holes and landed on the ground on the other side.

As he had expected, the rat scampered in a direct line away from him. It vanished into the darkness between the fence and the warehouse.

"Harry, can you hit the sensor closest to us with your paintball gun?"

"Yes," the bot replied.

There was a pause. Six sighed. He'd asked instead of instructed. "Do it," he said.

Harry raised his arm and fired a round into the darkness. The security light snapped on as the ball of goo slapped against the sensor, illuminating the concrete surrounding the warehouse. Six could see the sentries in the towers now, and the guards. None of them were wearing night-vision goggles, so they were relying on the security lights to alert them. The warehouse was painted red, stained black in parts by the darkness. There were five sedans and two construction vehicles parked outside the giant door, all too close to the building to offer any cover. There was a narrow ladder attached to the warehouse wall, but a sentry was standing right next to it. The rat had changed direction; it was running parallel to the fence about twenty meters away.

There was a long pause. Six waited for the timer to switch the light off again.

The distant crack of a sniper rifle echoed out from one of the towers, and the rat skidded sideways across the concrete. Six winced. *Sorry, buddy,* he thought. *I didn't expect that.*

The light clicked off. With the sensor blocked by paint, Six figured it was now safe to cross. He curled his fingers around the links in the fence.

"Harry," he said, "follow me." He climbed the fence easily, crossed the tip before the wire had time to buckle under his weight, and dropped nimbly down to the other side. Harry didn't climb — he jumped, lifting his legs up so they didn't scrape the fence on the way over, and landed with a silence that belied his weight. He rose slowly out of his crouch to stand beside Six.

Six took cautious steps forward. Enough to bring him within range of the sensor.

The darkness was impenetrable. He couldn't see the guards or the sentry towers. The security light stayed off.

They were inside the fence, but they still had to make it past the sentries and the door guards, and Six had to assume there would be more troops inside. They would see him as soon as he walked through the door.

Six peered into the gloom, picturing everything he had seen when the light was on. Two towers on the corners nearest him, with a sniper in each one. Neither was as high as the warehouse, or he'd be able to see them above the silhouette of the domed roof. Five sedans and two construction vehicles.

He could go a little closer and open fire. Disable all the sentries before they raised the alarm, and get inside before their command realized anything was wrong. Then use the same strategy when he got inside — keep his gun out and shoot anyone who got in his way.

Would he turn into a killing machine, exactly what the Lab had designed him to be, in the hope that Kyntak might be saved? Was that any worse than condemning Kyntak to death so he could keep his vow to never take a human life again?

It was 20:01:45. Every second decreased the likelihood that Kyntak was still alive. Six drew out his Owl and aimed it into the darkness by instinct alone, lining up the sights with where the sniper's head had been.

The gun felt heavier when it was aimed at a person — as if the bullet itself was already weighed down with the life it might be about to take. Six slipped into his firing crouch. He felt Harry's gaze on his back: not judging, but watching nonetheless. He pictured the sniper, staring coolly down the barrel of his rifle, unaware that his skull could be shattered at any moment by a bullet.

Six holstered the Owl. "We're going back," he said.

"*No, we are not,*" Harry said. "*We're standing still.*"

Six rubbed his eyes with his empty gun hand. "We're going to go back to the fence," he said. "We're going to get my bike."

THE SLEEPERS

"Agent Six has reached the warehouse," Nai said.

The phone hissed quietly. She pictured her father thinking.

"Is he inside yet?" Lerke replied eventually.

"No. Should I stop him?"

Nai knew that Lerke had hoped Six wouldn't come this far. He'd sent her to warn him at the apartment block. He'd called the Spades to try to trap him at the Deck. He'd posted her at the rendezvous point to protect him from Vanish's soldiers.

She watched Six through night-vision lenses as he and the robot lifted the motorcycle over the fence. Lerke had wanted him to give up, to leave Kyntak for dead, before Vanish got him too. But now here he was at Vanish's base of operations. Apparently planning to break in.

"Can you do it safely?"

Nai thought about it. She could overpower Six if she caught him by surprise. But there were guards, so she would have to do it silently and invisibly, or they could both die. And he had a robot with him, who would presumably try to intervene.

"Seventy percent chance of success," she told him.

She waited for him to think about the numbers. If he told her to proceed, there was a seventy percent chance that she and

Six would survive, but Kyntak would die. There was a thirty percent chance that none of them would survive. But if he told her to stay back, Six's and Kyntak's chances dropped to less than twenty percent, and hers went up to a hundred percent.

She didn't weigh up the pros and cons in her head. That was his job. The decision was his to make. She waited patiently.

"Don't follow him," Lerke said finally. "But stay on the perimeter. If he and Kyntak make it out alive, you know what to do."

"Understood." Nai hit END. She lay down on the asphalt and trained her sniper rifle on the warehouse. She wriggled until she was comfortable. It could be a long wait.

The giant construction vehicle had been well maintained. The joint of the tailgate was lightly oiled and turned in its socket as easily as if it had never been used. Six lowered the tailgate gently until its edge was resting on the concrete, and climbed into the bed. The sides were almost a meter high, which would provide good cover from the door guards if the security light was switched on again. But the snipers would see him instantly. He tried to be as quiet as possible.

Six wriggled cautiously towards the front of the bed until he was touching the rear window of the cabin, then peered down through the Plexiglas. *The battery must be dead*, he thought. *There should be a warning light blinking on the driver's display, stating that the tailgate is open.* It didn't matter.

Looking down, he saw that the hand brake was on. He climbed out of the tray, leaving the tailgate on the ground. He bent down to look at the angle it made — about fifty degrees. Good enough. He put his palm in the center of it and pressed. It didn't bend — probably cadmium, he guessed.

He stared into the inky blackness where he knew the nearest guard tower to be. No sign that anyone could see him. But if he was spotted, he knew there would be no warning — just a gunshot that would kill him before he knew it had been fired. With a deep breath, he slipped back into the darkness to where he had left the bot and his bike.

"You understand what you have to do once I'm inside?" Six asked as he approached.

"*Yes*," Harry replied.

"You'll have to go back to the fence the same way we came," Six said, "or else you'll trigger the security lights."

"*Yes*," Harry repeated.

Six climbed onto the motorbike and started the engine, arming the ChaoSilent fittings as he did so. He clicked a switch so only the engine noise was canceled out. If the sensors near the tires were activated, they would pick up the sound from Harry's jet pack and interfere with the bot's own noise cancellation equipment. This left a risk that the guards would hear the rolling of the wheels, but with their helmets on and the security light out of commission, Six was confident that his plan would work.

"This time, do hang on tight," he said. Harry's arms squeezed his torso and Six gunned the motor. The clicking of the guitar amp grew louder for a moment. *Here goes nothing*, he thought.

He twisted the throttle and the motorcycle shot out across the concrete. The silhouette of the warehouse grew larger before them. Six's hair was blasted back by the acceleration and his triceps strained to keep him close to the handlebars. He kept accelerating. He couldn't see the speedometer, but he knew that if he hit the construction vehicle too slowly the guards would be the least of his worries.

The motor screamed softly. Harry switched on his jet pack, and Six's cheeks rippled with the extra burst of speed. The vehicle appeared out of the darkness just ahead — Six tightened his grip on the handlebars, squeezed the bike between his calves, and lifted his rear slightly off the seat.

Thump! The front wheel slammed into the lowered tailgate, which acted as a ramp, and the bike shot up into the air, the wheels spinning wildly as they lost their traction. Harry held Six's torso tightly as the jet pack added to their upward momentum. Six gripped the bike with his hands and legs to stop it from falling out from underneath them.

They reached the peak of their trajectory above the sentry tower and rapidly began to fall. Harry braced one mechanical palm against the bike to stay upright, directing the thrust from his boosters downward to slow their descent. Six swung his legs off the seat as the roof of the warehouse reared up out of the gloom below, hanging his feet as low as he could underneath the bike.

His shoes clunked against the aluminum roof, and he bent his knees to soften the impact as he reached up and wrapped his arms around the chassis of the motorcycle. He held it in the air, letting the wheels spin themselves down to a halt as Harry hovered next to him, then slowly lowered himself down to the roof.

Six put the bike down, keeping one foot against it to stop it from sliding backward down the sloped metal. He listened carefully; there was no audible movement from below.

He turned to look at Harry. Flames were licking up his clothes. "You're on fire!" Six whispered urgently.

Harry turned invisible, using his cloak to suffocate the flames on Six's trench coat, and reappeared a second later. Six looked down ruefully at the ragged ends of the coat. "Last time I lend you my clothes," he muttered. "Has your skin melted?"

"*I am undamaged*," Harry said.

"Good," Six said. "Go back to the fence and wait for me to come out."

Harry picked up the motorbike, walked to the edge of the roof, and jumped off, switching his jet pack on again once he was in the air. He and the bike glided down quickly into the gloom.

Six paced slowly from one end of the roof to the other, checking for weak points. A roof this large and thick wouldn't be a solid piece of metal — it would be giant slats, held together with rivets. All he had to do was find a seam.

He discovered what he was looking for exactly in the center of the dome — it was made from four aluminum plates, overlapping one another by a meter where they met in the middle. Six braced his feet against the metal and pulled as hard as he could on the lip of one of the plates.

The giant shard of metal bent slowly, the edges grinding softly against girders underneath it. Soon Six had folded the corner up, exposing a triangle of light large enough to squeeze through. He put his head into the hole, checking that the coast was clear, and then slithered inside.

Six tried to hang as still as possible from the girder. All the giant halogen lights dangling from the roof by chains were underneath him and pointed downward, keeping him in shadow, but he wasn't kidding himself — a loud noise or a sudden movement would be enough to make the soldiers in the warehouse below look up, and he'd be spotted.

190

And there were plenty of troops around. In stark contrast to the deathly stillness of the night outside, the floor of the warehouse was a matrix of slow activity. Soldiers stalked along the perimeter wall, their boots making hardly a sound. Four guards paced in pairs from side to side by the main door, and another three were stationed next to the side entrance.

Most warehouses looked much the same. This one closely resembled the one he and Kyntak had raided fourteen hours earlier, except for the contents. There were no crates here. No cranes. Only a few ground vehicles — three vehicles like the two outside and a large sedan.

But there wouldn't have been room for much else. Not with a forty-meter, four-engine jet plane resting in the middle.

Six stared down in disbelief. He could believe that Vanish could get away with employing a few hundred troops without ChaoSonic cottoning on. But a plane?

When he had discovered that the warehouse was right next to an airfield, he had assumed this meant the troops could travel by air easily — but by buying tickets from ChaoSonic, like everyone else. Even a small airplane flying over the City without a ChaoSonic permit would be picked up on dozens of radar screens only seconds after it reached useful altitude. How did they manage to fly this plane without being detected?

It didn't matter. Six couldn't think of a way to make it relevant to his current situation. It might be a plausible escape vehicle for him and Kyntak, except that to use it they'd have to open the warehouse door, and if they were going to do that, they might as well leave on foot.

On the wall of the warehouse opposite from the doors there was a metal panel about three meters square. It had a seam down the center — *A door*, Six thought. *Looks like iron. Strong, tough.* It would lead to the rest of Vanish's facility — the only other doors in the warehouse led outside. There was a guard standing by it, weapon holstered.

Six reached up and slowly folded the aluminum roof back into place. It was more flexible the second time. He had the feeling that stealth would not be an issue by the time he was back here, so the hole wouldn't be a useful exit. But if it started raining between now and when he found Kyntak, the soldiers would notice it and sound the alarm.

He swung out across the roof, slinging his body carefully from one girder to the next as if he were on a giant maze of monkey bars. The temptation was to move his legs to increase his momentum and keep his center of gravity steady, but he was afraid that waving them might attract attention.

One of the bars rattled in its slot as he gripped it. He lifted his body up on top of the girder immediately and lay still. There was no cry of alarm from down below. He waited five seconds before peering over the edge.

The soldiers were patrolling as normal. It suddenly struck Six how quiet they were. Not only were their footsteps almost silent, but not a single word had been uttered since he'd entered. There was something almost mechanical about all the troops he had fought today. They had superfast reflexes and incredible accuracy, and were also uncannily professional. He knew that they were human — he had almost strangled one to death eight hours ago and had felt his pulse. And he doubted that they could be genetically enhanced, like he was. Project Falcon was the first major development in that field, and it was only twenty years old. Vanish had been employing highly trained crack troops for at least fifty years, according to the ChaoSonic file.

But there was definitely something strange about them. Despite their differing physical attributes and voices, they all seemed somehow the same. Identical training regimes never produced identical soldiers, Six knew. Some would be better than others; all would have particular strengths and weaknesses. But there was no human error here. No mistakes, no disloyalty, and no unprofessional conduct.

Six had reached the wall, so he tied his climbing rope around the girder in a highwayman's hitch, and threaded the free end through the protruding loop. He looked down. The iron doors were right beneath him, the guard standing impassively in front of them.

He thought about his options. He could drop straight down from the ceiling onto the guard's head, hoping that the blow would knock him out before he made a sound. But that was risky — he'd have to catch the guard before he hit the ground as well, or else the noise would attract attention.

He could lower himself down on the rope and grab the guard by the throat to stifle the scream. But he'd need one hand for that and the other to hold on to the rope, so he'd have no way of stopping the guard from drawing his weapon.

He was a little relieved that he didn't have to consider shooting the guard with his Owl. The silenced pistols weren't actually silent. Indoors, they made a dull thud which was easily audible at a range of many meters. In a quiet environment like this, with no soft surfaces dampening the acoustics, the noise would reverberate around loud and long enough to get the attention of every soldier in the warehouse.

Before he had time to think about it any longer, the guard put his hand to his ear, apparently receiving an order. He pushed a button beside the doors and they slid aside immediately. He walked through them, out of sight, and they slid closed once again. The door was now unguarded.

Six swept his gaze around the warehouse. There were three guards patrolling the perimeter at a speed of approximately one meter per second. The warehouse was sixty meters long and forty wide, and the soldiers were patrolling one meter away from the wall. Therefore each guard walked 192 meters in each lap. They were evenly spaced, which made it sixty-four meters in between each one, and one had passed the door five seconds ago. *Fifty-nine seconds before the next patroller passes the door*, Six thought. *Make it thirty before he's in visual range.*

Plenty of time.

Six slid down the climbing rope and landed gently on the cement floor of the warehouse. He tugged the other side of his giant loop to undo the knot up above and gathered the coils of the rope quickly as they fell. He pushed the button with his thumb.

The doors didn't open.

Six pushed it again. An orange light blinked; there was no other response.

A countdown started automatically in his head, recording the number of seconds remaining before the patrolling soldier would spot him.

Twenty-six, twenty-five, twenty-four . . . Six didn't panic. He squeezed his eyes shut and pictured the guard opening the doors. The guard had reached down, pushed the button, and the doors had opened immediately.

Six looked at the button panel. There were no other buttons on it. He pushed it again, and the orange light blinked again. The doors still didn't open.

Nineteen, eighteen, seventeen . . .

He rewound his memory. Before the soldier pushed the button, what did he do?

Nothing. He was standing there, then he put his hand to his ear, then he pushed the button, then the doors opened. Was the order he'd received significant? Was it a message from someone in control — someone who'd disarmed the doors so they could be opened?

The patrolling soldier was walking alongside the adjacent wall, getting closer and closer to the corner. When he reached it in perhaps ten seconds, he would see Six. Give him another three, maybe, to determine that Six wasn't the door guard. Another two to raise the alarm, then one to fire.

Eight, seven, six . . .

Six looked around for a hiding place. The plane was too exposed; the soldiers would see him moving towards it. There was no way back up to the roof — he had no grappling hook to go with his climbing rope, and it would take too long to improvise one.

Six slid the two halves of his quarterstaff out from under the straps on his back and clicked them together smoothly. If he ran towards the patroller, he might be able to knock him out before he could raise the alarm. He dropped into a sprinter's crouch.

The doors slid open behind him, and Six dived backward through them without even checking what was on the other side.

The doors slid shut a moment later. Six disassembled the quarterstaff as he took a look around. Now he saw why the doors had not opened for him immediately. He was in an elevator.

There were no buttons inside. Apparently the elevator only traveled between this floor and the one below. This made Six nervous — the fewer floors there were, the more likely it was that there would be someone on the other side of the doors when they opened. He scanned the elevator for a hiding place, but except for the doors it was a featureless cadmium box. The ceiling was a single plate of stainless steel with a coin-size puncture in it, containing a low-watt bulb. The corners were —

Six flattened himself to the floor and dragged himself back to the wall. There was a tiny surveillance camera in the corner, pointed at the doors. He had been standing right in front of it. He hoped that he hadn't noticed it too late. A monitor somewhere would have displayed an image of him as he jumped backward into the elevator. He could only hope that no one had been watching.

The elevator hadn't stopped, which was a good sign. *If I'd been spotted,* Six thought, *surely they would stop the elevator. Or they could just mobilize the troops outside the doors on whichever floor the elevator is headed to.*

Six reattached the halves of his quarterstaff and passed it to his left hand, drawing his pistol with his right. He rose into a crouch, carefully staying below the camera's field of vision. This was his worst nightmare — outnumbered and outgunned in an enclosed space with no escape routes. He could feel the elevator slowing as it approached its destination.

It stopped. The doors slid open.

No one was standing on the other side.

Six darted out as quickly as he could, away from the camera.

He was at the end of a narrow corridor, the walls almost invisible behind racks upon racks of equipment. Helmets were closest to him, hundreds of polished black domes on wall hooks, their expressionless dark visors staring into the corridor. Beyond them were rifles; neat rows of identical Eagle OI779s nestled side by side, ready to be pulled out and used. Six touched the pad on the butt of one of them, switching on the tiny display screen on the stock. The gun was fully loaded. Eighty rounds.

Six switched off the gun and kept walking. There was a grid of spare magazines, at least a thousand resting on the shelves. Beyond that there was a pipe with belts hanging from it, each fully equipped with the weaponry Six had seen on the soldier in the apartment building: one Feather knife, one fully loaded Raptor sidearm, a string of six PGC387 grenades. But the remotes weren't attached, he saw.

Six now knew more or less what he was looking at. When they were being sent into the field, the soldiers would be funneled through this corridor. They'd grab their weapon belts, their spare magazines, their Eagle automatics, and then throw on their helmets before piling into the elevator and heading for the surface.

Not all the equipment was here, Six noted. The soldiers would need clothes, boots, earpieces. They probably kept those near where they slept.

He was nearing the end of the corridor, and he peeked around the corner. As if reality were mimicking his thoughts, he saw three men asleep in a column of bunks, all lying flat upon their backs, their feet pointed towards him. Six watched them for a moment, checking for movement. There was none. They appeared to be fast asleep.

He edged around the corner, keeping his breaths shallow and quiet. He looked past the column of bunks and saw another. Two women and a man, fast asleep, identical posture. Another column: three men. None moving.

As Six walked forward, he saw that he was no longer in the

armory. There was at least a hundred bunks, each holding a sleeping man or woman, stretching into the distance.

He had found the barracks.

Six eyed the aisle between the bunks apprehensively. He could be quiet when he wanted to be. He could sneak up on someone better than anyone else he knew. But it was one thing to slip by a guard when he or she was looking the other way, and quite another to tiptoe eighty meters past a hundred soldiers as they slept.

Nevertheless, that was what he was going to have to do. The layout to this facility seemed to be very linear — so far there had been only two doors per room. He had been forced to come this way, and even if doubling back were an option, it wouldn't help him find Kyntak.

Six took a deep breath and started to move through the room.

None of the soldiers stirred as he passed. He assumed that most of them must be fairly deep sleepers — the room was air-conditioned to a cool fifteen degrees Celsius, and none of them had blankets — they were covered only by thin cotton undergarments. The lights were on too. The whole hall was bathed in a fluorescent bluish glow, casting sharp indigo shadows of the bunks onto the bald cement floor. But all the soldiers were faceup, and none wore blindfolds.

Six noted that almost a third of the sleeping soldiers were female. This seemed unusual to him. More than ninety-five percent of the soldiers in the City were male. There were still plenty of jobs for women in ChaoSonic security and various private armies, but they were usually strategic, administrative, or medical. Six wondered why Vanish had so many women in the infantry.

He couldn't imagine the organization caring about equal-opportunity employment.

Six was halfway across the barracks when he saw an empty bunk ahead. One of the soldiers wasn't in bed.

Six caught the eye of the soldier as he stood up beside the bunk. He had removed his armor and was wearing the same cotton undergarments as the sleeping soldiers. His shirt was in one hand, his pants were dangling from the other.

He stared at Six in astonishment for a fraction of a second that seemed to last an eternity. Then they both moved at the same time, Six starting forward, raising his quarterstaff, and the soldier grabbing the strut of one of the bunks and swinging his legs out.

Six ducked under the flying kick and whirled back to face the soldier, quarterstaff first. The soldier blocked the blow by raising his forearm above his head and he drew his other arm in close to his body, ready to parry any punches Six threw at him.

Six swung around and kicked him behind the knee. The soldier's leg collapsed and he slipped backward to the floor. On his way down he tugged Six's Owl from its holster. Six saw it fall too late to catch it. It dropped into the soldier's waiting hand.

Six slid aside swiftly as the soldier hit the floor and pulled the trigger, sending a bullet crashing into the ceiling. He fired a second shot immediately, and a puff of foam exploded into the air as it hit the side of a top-bunk mattress; Six guessed that both bullets had been intended for his abdomen. Soldiers often aimed first, then fired three shots before aiming again. This one hadn't had much time to line up his shot, but he'd still fired two before realizing that Six had moved.

His reflexes didn't seem as quick as those of the other troops

Six had fought today — but he had been caught by surprise, and he was in his pajamas.

Six slammed his foot down on the soldier's gun hand, pinning it to the floor. The soldier howled as one of his metacarpal bones cracked and the gun fell from his wriggling fingers.

Six quickly slapped his palm over the soldier's mouth and drove the index finger of his other hand into the flesh behind the soldier's ear. The soldier went limp instantly. Six lifted the man's eyelid with his fingers. The pupil didn't contract. He was unconscious.

Six stood up immediately and lifted his quarterstaff. There were no soldiers in the aisle between him and the armory. He turned to face the other way. No one there, either.

He frowned, heart still thumping in his chest. Was it possible that not a single person in the entire barracks had been woken up by all that scuffling and two gunshots?

He stood on tiptoes so he could see all the bunks. The soldiers were lying exactly as they had been before. No one was rubbing their eyes or sitting up. No one had even rolled over.

Six knelt beside the nearest bunk and poked the soldier there gently. No movement. He prodded him again, harder. He didn't react at all. Six's eyes widened as a drop of blood appeared on the soldier's undershirt; Six rolled it back to expose his stomach. It was unmarked, but as he looked at it, a drop of blood appeared in the same spot. He looked up; a red stain was spreading across the underside of the mattress above, and blood was dripping from it onto the bunk underneath.

He stood up, and saw that the second shot the soldier had fired had not only punctured the mattress; it had clipped the thigh of the mattress's occupant.

An occupant who was still *asleep*?

Six had the sudden overwhelming sense that everyone in the room was dead, that he'd been sneaking past rows of corpses rather than sleeping troops. He touched his fingers to the throat of the soldier with the wounded thigh.

Yes, there was a pulse. *So what's going on?* Six thought. *Who sleeps through a gunshot wound?* He tore the man's shirt into strips and started tying them around the injury. The bullet had gone straight through and had missed the femoral artery, so it was easy enough to stem the blood flow. He looked around the room. Some of the unconscious soldiers were lying with their eyes open, staring blankly at the ceiling.

Only now did Six notice that every bunk had a synthetic rubber holster clipped to its side. In each holster was a remote. He lifted out the one closest to him and examined it. It was identical to the one he'd found at the Timeout, with the same four buttons. SYNCAL, ACCELERANT, MORPHINE, and LOCATOR ON/OFF.

Six had seen the equipment the soldiers had: guns, clothes, knives, ammunition, earpieces. Nothing that needed a remote control, certainly not one with those buttons. So why would every single soldier need one?

A piece of the puzzle resurfaced suddenly in Six's brain. Vanish, or one of the people who had used that title, had been a nanotechnology expert. *He used to be a scientist*, Shuji had said. And Ace had told him that Syncal, the fluid in the tranq gun he'd been shot with, was a sedative. Enough to put most people in a coma, she'd said, but creating a refreshingly deep sleep in small doses.

Six was no nanotech expert himself, but he knew the basic principle of nanotechnology — microscopic robots, sometimes injected into the bloodstream for medical reasons. Could these robots each be given a tiny sensor and a capsule filled with chemicals? Syncal or morphine, ready to be pumped into the bloodstream when a button on a remote was pushed?

Six had never heard of it being done, but he was sure that it was possible. And it made more sense than any other explanation he could come up with. Vanish's soldiers all had nanomachines in their bodies, controlled by the remotes they always carried. He knew that Syncal could put people in a deep enough sleep to ignore a gunshot wound, and morphine was one of the strongest known painkillers. A soldier-locator that couldn't be removed would be invaluable to field troops, and while Six didn't know exactly what an "accelerant" was, he was betting that it could explain the abnormally fast reflexes he'd observed. Possibly the high percentages of women, too — gender wouldn't matter much if drugs were being used to enhance ability. The soldier Six had just fought hadn't been expecting a fight and hadn't had his remote within reach. He'd seemed like a normal, if well-trained, soldier.

Six thought back to the soldiers who'd been captured and taken to the Deck. They'd been unconscious much too long, and Ace found Syncal in their bloodstreams. What if the soldiers had dosed themselves up with their remotes? Or, more likely, a signal had been broadcast from here, or from a satellite, knocking them out so they couldn't be interrogated by their captors? If Vanish had access to an orbiting transmitter or a broadcasting tower, troops could be reclaimed by switching on the locator function in their nanomachines, hitting the SYNCAL button, and sending out a rescue team to recover the sleeping bodies.

He recalled the document he'd read about ChaoSonic capturing the man they believed to be Vanish, who'd wounded himself to get to the emergency room. The writer hadn't known how the Vanish troops had found the facility holding their leader, but now Six thought he did.

And then he thought of all the people who had been captured, released, and then co-opted into stealing ChaoSonic secrets. Now he knew how they had been kept to their word. There were nanobots in their blood. "Do as we say or you'll fall asleep" was quite a fearsome threat, and Six figured that worse chemicals could be carried by the tiny robots. Arsenic, cyanide, peroxide — any of a dozen poisons.

Six put the remote back in the holster. This presented a problem. What if Kyntak had been injected with the nanobots? It seemed likely. A hostage with nanobots in his blood would be much easier to interrogate.

Even if Six found Kyntak and got him out without the alarm being raised, there would be nowhere to run. Kyntak would have microscopic beacons coursing through his veins, beaming his location to every monitor in the facility.

THE VICTIM

Apparently there were no surveillance cameras in the room. Kyntak couldn't see any, and the neck clamp was loose enough to allow his head to turn and scan the whole area. He figured that Vanish had weighed the risks of putting additional equipment in this otherwise sterile room against the benefits of watching him lie on the table and decided that it was better to make the cell featureless.

All the better. Kyntak wasn't sure what he'd do once he got off the table, but being watched would severely limit his options.

The wrist clamps were tight, but they'd been left loose enough to keep his circulation flowing. Kyntak gritted his teeth as he pulled. His theory was that if he tugged with enough force, he could dislocate the bones in his hand and make it slip through the clamp. Then he could reset the joints with his teeth and use the hand to hit the buttons that unlocked the clamps around his other joints. Then he would wait for Vanish to come in, kick the stuffing out of him, and run.

One, two, three. Pull! He drew his breath in sharply as the flesh of his hand was squeezed between the metal and his bones. He stopped before there was a risk of the cuff cutting him — this was hard enough already without having to worry that his skin would be scraped off his hand. Not to mention that if Vanish came back too early, he might notice that Kyntak was bleeding.

One, two, three. Pull! He crushed the base of his palm against the rim of the clamp, and a whimper of pain escaped his lips. His freakishly strong bones and joints withstood the pressure. He stopped once again. *I'll have some impressive bruises if I live long enough*, he thought.

"Yeeaargh!" He tried to throw his body into the air, hips first — there were no restraints around his torso. He held himself up like a crooked bridge, straining against the clamps at his knees and elbows, the restraint around his neck choking him.

Thud. He landed back on the table, the impact sending a shock of pain into his coccyx. He breathed quickly and deeply, saturating his brain with oxygen to numb the pain, and flexed his aching wrist.

One, two —

The wall started rolling aside. Kyntak immediately slumped limply against the table, heart pounding. He lifted his head as the door opened, as if he had just woken up.

"We must stop meeting like this," he said as Vanish and the red-eyed woman entered. She stood silently in the corner, gun in one hand.

Vanish approached the table. "How do you feel?" he asked. "Headache gone? Any nausea?"

"My back is a little itchy in a spot I can't quite reach," Kyntak said.

"Cold?" Vanish asked, ignoring him. "Thirsty?"

Kyntak was thirsty, but he doubted that saying so would get him anything to drink. "Your torture methods suck," he said. "It's like the water torture, but with dumb questions instead of drips."

"I don't want you damaged," Vanish said. He began to pace slowly from one side of the room to the other. "Not yet."

"You want me to win a beauty competition first?" Kyntak asked. "The kidnapping makes sense now — you'd never win one on your own."

Vanish smiled. "No, I'm just waiting for Agent Six to get here."

Kyntak's heart thumped faster, and he was suddenly certain Vanish could hear it. He kept his voice level. "I don't get it," he said.

"Yes, you do," Vanish said. "Your twin brother? Or should I say triplet brother — Sevadonn may be dead now, but he was part of Project Falcon too."

"Now I am thoroughly confused," Kyntak said. "The Deck didn't pay up, so you assume I'm not the real deal?"

"You know what the secret to a good plan is, Kyntak?" Vanish pierced him with a cheery grey gaze. "Fluidity. Let's say I want to capture the remaining two Project Falcon kids. I stage a prison break as bait, and leave a trail to an empty apartment building by planting the blood of one of the residents I've disposed of. So far, so good. But then what happens?"

He laughed. The noise bounced off the walls, hitting Kyntak from all sides. "They both show up! Not just the one from the Deck, but the freelancer too! And, of course, I've given my troops orders to take the agent with the superhuman abilities, but I've never imagined two would show up and confuse them. After all, when every scientist wants you dissected and every vigilante wants you dead, you don't expose more than you have to, right? Sending two Falcons to a job that only requires one is stupid, correct?"

Kyntak tried one last time. "You got me," he said, slipping a little sarcasm into his tone. "I'm not Agent Six of Hearts, I'm just an impersonator. Guess you're going to have to let me go now, huh?"

Vanish shook his head. "I've known who you are since you first spoke to me," he said. "I've studied both of you. The real Agent Six would have pretended to be another Deck agent, a generic. A regular human being. But not you. 'My reputation precedes me?' you said. Because secretly, and I find this fascinating, you were *glad* when I mistook you for him. He's becoming a big name in the criminal underworld, and you're jealous. And the fact that Six sees it as a liability, that he wishes he could remain anonymous, that's conducive to celebrity, and that just makes it worse."

"Yeah," Kyntak said. "I've been knocked out, abducted, clamped to a table, drained of my blood, bored to death by this empty room and by your ranting. But it's really hard to concentrate on all that when I'm so busy wishing I was my brother."

"But when the two of you showed up," Vanish said, ignoring him once more, "did my plan collapse? Of course not, because it was fluid. I was originally expecting to take one and get the other when he came to the rescue, and Six's surprise appearance didn't stop me. I sent the ransom demand as planned and told my troops to take Six alive if they could. The fact that Six showed up to collect you instead of you showing up to collect him didn't change a thing."

"Yeah, it did," Kyntak said. "You obviously didn't catch him."

Vanish's grin broadened. "You're right. He's evaded my capture twice. He must be the competent one. He brought a friend with him who killed a few of my troops. But did this mess up my plan? No. Because it's fluid."

He leaned down close to Kyntak. "Six has been headed our way for the better part of an hour. He's in this facility right now, looking for you. I didn't need to bring the trap to him — he came to it. And as soon as he's on the floor . . ." Vanish's white teeth showed as he smiled. "See? Both the Project Falcon kids are mine."

Kyntak's breaths were becoming tighter. It was as if his lungs were slowly crystallizing, or caking over with ice. "You think the Deck will give you more money if you hand over both of us? After you let down your end of the bargain last time?"

Vanish sighed, as if disappointed in Kyntak. "You thought this was about money? The ransom was a secondary objective — there are easier ways to get a hundred million credits." He beckoned to the woman and walked towards the wall. She muttered something into her radio and the wall rolled aside.

"I don't want the Deck's money," Vanish said on his way out. "I want *you*."

Six found the remote of the soldier he'd knocked out, held it against the man's skin, and hit the button marked SYNCAL. There was no outward sign of change, but Six hoped this meant he wouldn't wake up anytime soon. He dumped the soldier on his bunk, straightening his limbs so his posture was identical to that of all the other sleeping troops. Six saw the shirt and pants on the floor where the soldier had dropped them and, after a moment of hesitation, he put them on. The soldier had placed his boots neatly under his bunk. Six slipped them on too.

The whole outfit was too big for him. The bulletproof plastic in the shirt hung below his collarbone instead of reaching his throat, the pants bunched up slightly around his ankles, and the soles of his feet lifted off the insoles in the boots every time he took a step. But it was a better disguise than nothing, and he didn't have time to check all the bunks for a shorter soldier.

He jogged clumsily back to the armory and took a sample of the standard gear: knife, pistol, Eagle, grenades, spare magazine. Lastly he jammed a helmet onto his head.

He hesitated before leaving. His job might be made easier later by a little sabotage. He swept his arm across the row of Eagles, hitting the EJECT button on each one. All the magazines fell to the floor. He gathered them up and dumped them in the darkness behind the pipe with the belts hanging from it. The automatic rifles now each had only one bullet in them, the one that was loaded into the chamber. They would click empty almost as soon as the triggers were pulled.

He grabbed a hundred or so of the spare magazines, quickly emptied the bullets into an upturned helmet, and put it underneath the spares. He put the empty magazines back on the shelves, at the front.

There wasn't much else he could do without being too obvious, and he didn't want to waste any more time. He moved quickly back through the barracks and headed to the other end of the aisle.

There was no elevator at this end, just a giant stairwell with concrete walls and thick, strong stairs. It looked like it was designed so all the soldiers could run down at once. But there were only four flights — Six reached the bottom in a matter of seconds.

The stairwell led directly into a short corridor. He peeked around the corner, checking for soldiers — and froze.

There was another entire warehouse beyond the opening, identical in construction to the one two floors above. But this one held more than a few cars and an airplane; it was a massive labyrinth of equipment.

Six could see four huge motors and two electrical generators propped up on metal stilts, with tables covered in repair equipment underneath them. The hollowed-out shell of a bus was resting upside down, and an enormous spiderlike machine was poised over it, steel claws locked around the one remaining axle. There were dozens of airtight Plexiglas chambers, with rubber gloves built into the framework. Judging by the shrink-wrapped lumps of grey plastic next to them, these were for making bombs. In the center of the warehouse there was a giant cube of thick tinted glass, through which Six could see a web of tubes and valves, occasionally lighting up as sparks blasted back and forth along exposed wires.

Six didn't have enough general mechanical experience to recognize the functions of everything in this room, but he had a gut feeling that the device in the enormous glass box was manufacturing nanomachines. *If there's time,* he thought, *I should smash the glass to break the vacuum seal on my way back. The more I can do to sabotage Vanish's operations, the better.*

A huge creature of iron and steel rested in the corner of the warehouse. Six stared, unsure of what he was seeing. There was a short, hollow tube attached to the front, like a pitiless black eye on a stalk, and instead of wheels or legs, the thing had great rollers covered by strips of armor plating the color of engine grease.

An illustration from a history website flashed through his mind, and Six's eyes widened as he realized what he was looking at — it was a tank. It didn't look quite finished — the hatch on the top had no seal, and the gun was only half as long as it should be. But there was no mistaking the shape. Vanish had acquired a tank, and was restoring it for some reason.

There were five soldiers in the warehouse, pacing slowly back and forth like the ones upstairs. Six adjusted his overly large costume self-consciously as he scanned the warehouse for the exit. On the opposite wall there was an elevator, just like the one in the previous warehouse. Six checked the positions of all the guards. If he timed this right, he wouldn't have to walk too close to any of them.

He took a deep breath. *Now!*

He strode into the warehouse, at a pace that felt neither urgent nor aimless. He passed one of the bomb-making chambers on his right and resisted the urge to glance at it, focusing his gaze on the elevator doors up ahead.

There was one soldier walking past the elevator, and another one patrolling in Six's peripheral vision. Neither of them had stopped to look at him — either they were unconcerned by his presence or they hadn't seen him yet. He kept walking, passing the giant glass cube on his left.

Four of five soldiers were now behind him. He kept his eyes on the elevator doors, but listened carefully, waiting for the sound of approaching footsteps. His breathing seemed painfully loud inside the helmet.

Almost there. He passed another of the bomb-making chambers on his left. He was almost level with the hollow bus. He forced his gaze away from the mechanical spider, as if looking at it would draw the focus of one of its many plasma lenses. He was ahead of all five soldiers, but one would reach the elevator in less than a minute. He planned to get there first.

He kept his carefully measured pace. *Left foot, right foot. Not too fast, not too slow. You're fine,* he told himself. *You're invisible to them. They're not expecting any trouble, and you're nothing out of the ordinary. Unless you do something stupid, like running. So just keep walking and you're okay.*

He reached the elevator doors and pushed the button, just once. Then he waited patiently. The next guard wouldn't pass him for at least twenty seconds. *Relax.*

His breaths boomed against his visor. He imagined that he could feel the eyes of the five soldiers watching him. That he could sense them slowly creeping towards him, rifles raised, communicating with hand signals and slowly surrounding him.

The doors slid apart. Six started to walk in, and then paused — there was a soldier in it already. Six stepped aside, leaving him room to walk out. The soldier's helmet turned to Six in acknowledgment, but there was no nod of approval or grunt of thanks. He kept walking, disappearing behind one of the machines.

Six stopped watching and turned to the elevator again. *Behave normally,* he told himself. *Like you do this every day.* He stepped into the elevator and waited for the doors to close, ignoring the security camera. Through the opening he watched the soldiers slowly pace the perimeter of the warehouse until the doors slid shut.

The elevator hummed smoothly downward. Now there were three floors of enemy soldiers between him and freedom. *How did I expect to get away with this?* he wondered. *Once the alarm is raised, I'm as good as dead — even if they don't shut down the elevators, there will still be a hundred or more troops after me. And this facility is too small and linear to hide in.*

He clenched one hand into a fist and thumped it lightly against the back wall. He didn't want to die like this. His body would never be found, so King would never know what had become of him. Kyntak would suffer the same fate. The Spades would continue hunting for him, but he would be unable to prove his innocence and be branded a traitor forever. Harry would wait loyally outside the warehouse fence for hours, days, maybe even weeks — however long it took for him to get spotted by bystanders or soldiers. And who knows what would happen then? Nai would never be rescued, wherever she was, and she would grow up believing that he and Kyntak had abandoned her.

It's not too late to turn back, he thought. He was well disguised, and certain that the alarm hadn't been sounded yet. But he was immediately ashamed. To abort the rescue now would almost certainly mean condemning Kyntak, his brother, his closest friend, to death. Logically, he knew it was the best course of action, because there was almost no hope of both him and Kyntak making it out of here alive. But it would also be the most selfish thing he had ever done.

The elevator stopped and the doors slid open. Six hesitated. Could he walk right back out the way he came, and still live with himself?

No, he decided. *I'm doing this. There's nothing left for me out there. Nai is missing, Two is dead, King is under investigation, and the Deck has disowned me. If I leave now, Kyntak dies and I'm completely on my own.*

He was ashamed of that thought too. *I consider backing out for selfish reasons, then I decide to stay for even more selfish reasons.* "Everyone was right about me," he whispered to himself. "I am a monster."

He stepped out of the elevator and turned left instinctively. He was in a long corridor with only one wall. Instead of the other, there was a row of huge roller-doors with dark alcoves in between so they had room to slide. They didn't end at the floor or the ceiling — they disappeared into narrow trenches at each end, giving Six the impression that they were probably several meters taller than the corridor.

Cell doors, he guessed. More surface area than the walls, almost impossible to open from the inside. He felt a thrill of adrenaline run through his veins. He was close.

He could see one soldier patrolling the corridor, walking slowly away from him. Six figured he had perhaps three minutes before the soldier reached the end and turned around. He risked a quick glance over his shoulder. There was a guard behind him as well, standing impassively in front of one of the roller-doors. He wasn't looking in Six's direction.

One soldier patrolling, one stationary, he thought. *What are the chances that the one standing still is outside Kyntak's cell?*

But there was no sense in approaching the guard until he knew for sure. Doing so would almost certainly lead to the base being put on alert status, and if Kyntak was in a different cell, then soldiers would be coming down ten at a time in the elevator while he searched all the others.

Each giant door had a circular blue button on the edge. Six pressed the first one and heard a solid click as the mechanical dead bolt disengaged. He put the palm of his hand against the edge of the door and pushed.

The door was heavy, but it rolled aside in silence. Six didn't open it all the way — just enough to peer through. This room looked less like a cell than an infirmary or a surgical operating room — there were two people-size tables with padded headrests on the ends, two long white desks with several drawers, a stainless-steel sink in the far corner, and a polished glass cabinet filled with sharp instruments.

No Kyntak. No anyone. Six retreated into the corridor and pushed the door slowly closed.

He glanced up and down the corridor again. One soldier still patrolling, one standing guard. Each a fair distance away, and neither facing him. So far, so good. He walked to the next door, pushed the button, and rolled it open.

This wasn't a cell either, just a dark, empty room with a window and a small button panel on one wall. The window looked into the next room, which did appear to be a cell — it had reflective walls and a block in the center, topped with restraining clamps and a headrest.

One-way glass, Six realized. This was where Vanish officials could watch the prisoners. But why? If they were clamped to a table, what would they be doing that was worth watching? Perhaps one of the buttons on the panel released the clamps.

Again, no Kyntak. He stepped back and closed the door.

He skipped the next door, knowing that it led to the empty cell. He pushed the button on the door after that, opened it, and poked his head inside. Another cell, identical to the one he'd seen through the one-way glass of the observation room. Empty again. There was probably another observation room on the other side.

He stepped back, about to roll the door closed, when he heard a noise — a thin wheeze. He turned his head sharply. The patrolling soldier hadn't turned around yet, and the stationary one hadn't even glanced his way. He looked back into the cell and frowned. There was someone — or something — inside.

He stepped across the threshold and bent down. A figure was crouched beside the table, a skinny teenage boy who scampered backward across the floor as Six moved. There was something ungainly and graceless about the way he was crawling, something not entirely human, and as soon as he hit the corner and could retreat no farther, Six saw what it was. The boy had only one arm — his left one had been amputated at the shoulder.

Six approached him slowly and carefully. The boy in the corner didn't look up at him. He had some kind of mask over his mouth, a clear plastic bulb with a valve on the side — the wheezing gasps Six had heard were coming from it harder and faster now. A respirator, Six realized. Something had to be wrong with his lungs.

As the boy's long, greasy hair slid aside, Six saw that the missing arm wasn't his only physical oddity. Half of his face and neck was scarred a dull brown, as if he'd had first-degree burns on one side of his body. Both of his ears were missing. The eye on the burned side of his face was cheap glass and didn't even match — it was chocolate-brown instead of blue. There was no eyelid to cover it — it stared crazily over Six's shoulder.

"What happened to you?" Six asked, aghast.

The boy let out a rasping squeal, shoved off the wall, and scurried across the cell to another corner, farther away from Six. Six kept walking towards him. "I'm not going to hurt you," he said quietly. "I'm here to help." Inside, his horror was slowly being eaten away by fury. Who would do this to a child? And why?

With a thin groan, the boy threw himself at Six, arm outstretched, fingers clawing at Six's face. He didn't quite make the distance, and Six had to step forward and catch him as he fell. The boy's respirator hissed again and he looked up at Six, his real eye widening with fear.

Six gasped, icy spiders crawling up his spine. The eye was the same as his own. The undamaged half of the boy's face was a precise copy. And now Six saw that the boy was exactly his height. He considered again the respirator mask, the missing ears, the missing arm — the skin which had not been burned, as he first thought, but stolen for grafts. And he was willing to bet that if he removed the boy's shirt, he would see surgical scars over the heart and lungs.

He didn't know how the boy had come to be here, and he didn't know why, but there was no doubt about it — he was a clone of Six. He'd been created just eight months ago, solely for the use of his organs and limbs. Six stared in horror at his own left hand, flexing the fingers unconsciously, as its previous owner howled and tore himself out of Six's grip.

Six had wondered how Vanish had got a sample of his DNA to compare to Kyntak's, given that the Lab computers had been wiped. Now he knew. After making the clone and taking parts of it to heal Six, Crexe had kept it alive with a respirator, a pace-maker, and probably some kind of artificial kidney. When Crexe was arrested and his soldiers had either fled or been incarcerated, the clone must have been left lying forgotten on a hospital bed at the Lab. Vanish troops broke in less than a month later and probably brought him straight here. He had doubtless been carefully studied and relentlessly tested since then.

The clone whimpered and bashed his fist into the floor; the blow was pathetically weak. Six's pity was almost unbearable — *It's so unfair*, he thought. *His eyes are barely open before surgeons cripple and disfigure him for life, then he lives off an IV drip until he's abducted and locked up. He can't speak English. He can't hear, or see, or breathe properly. All he's ever felt is pain, fear, and confusion.*

Six looked at the sinews in the boy's arm and legs — he was skin and bone. Six knew that his own genes weren't the sole cause of his incredible strength and speed; they had only provided potential. It had taken years of strenuous exercise, training, and dieting to make the most of them. This boy had been fed minimally and had probably never even been outside.

Then Six heard footsteps, approaching slowly. They were distant — presumably coming from the soldier patrolling the corridor outside. Six's three minutes were up. The soldier had reached the end of the corridor and turned around.

Six pressed his palm against the roller-door, thinking. *If the door is still slightly open when the soldier passes, he'll raise his gun and open the door the rest of the way. I'll be completely exposed.*

I could slide the door closed now, he thought, *but then I'd be trapped in here until they bring the clone his next meal, and that could be hours — someone could easily see me through the one-way mirror before it happens. Not an option.*

Six approached the opening and pressed his back against the edge of the door. The footsteps drew closer.

Six knew that perceptions were affected by expectations. A person could search for something right in front of him and fail to see it, simply because it wasn't where he thought it would be. An obscurely shaped scribble or an inkblot could reveal things about the viewer, who would perceive it differently depending on his thoughts. And a soldier who saw an open door which he expected to be closed would experience a split second of confusion as his brain tried to reconcile his vision with his imagination.

The footsteps faltered — the soldier had hesitated. Six threw the roller-door aside and exploded into the corridor. He lashed out with his foot, the heel slamming into the soldier's visor and cracking the shatterproof glass.

The soldier reeled back with the impact, his shoulder slapping against the wall, but he recovered quickly. Six dived after him, not wanting to give him time to aim his Eagle. He shoved the soldier against the wall and held him there, forcing the wrist of his gun arm against his torso. The barrel of the gun was trapped sideways, pointing at the empty end of the corridor.

The soldier had reached for his knife with his free hand. Six yelped as it slashed up across his forearm, slicing through the sleeve of his disguise. Droplets of blood splattered onto his visor, and he whirled around, twisting the guard's arm out in front of him and holding the blade at a safe distance.

Now he was facing away from the soldier, crushing him between his back and the wall. The soldier's gun was pressed flat between them, and Six was squeezing the wrist of the hand that held the knife, trying to cut off the circulation.

Apparently realizing that he was going to lose this scuffle, the guard pulled the trigger of his Eagle, firing into the empty corridor. The noise of twenty rounds being discharged right behind Six's back was deafening, and he could feel the burning of the muzzle against his arm. He twisted around, reached down, and grabbed the soldier's remote, tearing it off his belt. He leaped backward, pointing the remote at the soldier, who was swinging his Eagle to face Six, and jammed his thumb down on the SYNCAL button.

The soldier went limp instantly, falling against the wall. Six was already turning back towards the elevator as he slid heavily to the floor.

The other guard was running towards Six, presumably sounding the alarm with his helmet mike. Six couldn't hear it — his radio was either off or on the wrong frequency. The guard had raised his Eagle, but Six lifted his Raptor and fired three shots.

The first round missed, but the second hit the armor on the soldier's left shin, and the third clipped his right ankle, punching straight through. He tumbled over as his leg gave way underneath him, sprawling on the floor of the corridor. He stretched out a hand towards his fallen gun, but couldn't reach it. As Six ran towards him he retracted the hand and flopped awkwardly onto his side like an asphyxiating fish, reaching for his Raptor.

"Don't," Six yelled as he ran. "Put your hands on your head."

The guard ignored him and pulled his gun out of its holster. He fell back onto his front, bracing his elbows against the ground and aiming at Six. Six fired immediately, the first two rounds splintering the guard's fingers and the third shooting over his head and grazing his ankle.

The guard howled as the gun fell from his ruined hand. "Why doesn't anyone ever do what they're told?" Six muttered as he approached him.

Does one remote work for any soldier's nanomachines? he wondered. He pointed the stolen remote at the guard and hit MORPHINE. The whimpering quieted, and then stopped. The guard writhed slowly on the ground, apparently disoriented by the drug. Six hit SYNCAL and the guard's head fell to the floor, face-first, and all his limbs went slack.

Six made only a cursory examination of the guard's wounds. He might limp for the rest of his life and never be able to shoot again, but the bleeding wasn't life threatening. *Good,* Six thought. *If he raised the alarm, I don't have time to be dressing wounds.*

He started running back up the corridor, heading for the room that the soldier had been guarding. That was the most probable location for Kyntak, and they needed to get moving.

The elevator doors slid open as he was approaching them. Soldiers started pouring out, enough to block the corridor. Six immediately dropped into a gunman's crouch, dropping the Raptor and the remote and raising his Eagle instead. He opened fire, sending forty rounds into the legs of the soldiers.

They wobbled, but none fell. Their armor hadn't been penetrated. "Freeze," the team leader ordered as the soldiers advanced on Six, raising their weapons.

Six ran towards them, drawing the two halves of his quarterstaff out from behind his back. No time to put them together. He could have used the remote, but its range was very short, and he didn't know the technology well enough to trust it with his life.

Six swung half of the staff down in a vicious arc, slamming the end onto the helmet of the team leader. The fiberglass snapped, denting the helmet and popping out the visor; Six drove his elbow into the back of the soldier's head, cracking his face down onto his knee. Satisfied that the leader was out for the count, Six spun around and smacked the other half of the quarterstaff into a soldier's chest, winding him, then slammed a gloved fist up into his jaw.

He hadn't even hit the ground when Six thrust a leg over him in a mighty kick, knocking the soldier behind him into the wall. He lashed out backward with half of the quarterstaff without even looking, and heard a yell of pain as it connected. He whipped a fist out to the side, and it thumped into armored flesh. *Four or five down*, he thought.

There was a sharp buzzing in his ears, and the flesh all over his body tingled for a moment. He stumbled forward. *What was that?* he wondered. *Do they have tasers?*

He spun around, his muscles suddenly slack and unresponsive, searching for the threat. As he turned, every single soldier in the corridor fell to the floor and lay still.

Six's eyes widened. He walked slowly and awkwardly backward into the wall, his legs feeling numb. He barely registered the impact.

"Think," he mumbled, tongue loose against his teeth. "Think! What's going on?"

Syncal, he thought. Someone hit a remote, and the nanobots flushed Syncal into all the soldiers' bloodstreams. So where'd this person go?

He suddenly realized that he was on the floor. He tried to push it away and stagger to his feet. *Someone hit a big remote*, he thought. *A mass transmitter, or a satellite — it knocked out all the troops on this floor. I'm safe — or I would be, if I could walk. What's happening to me?*

A memory echoed through his head. *I dug out the dart they hit you with*, Ace was saying. *Less like a dart than an automatic syringe.* Her voice faded and he remembered wondering how Vanish's man in Insomnia knew where to find him. He saw again the other soldier running across the Timeout, pointing a remote at him.

Now he couldn't even lift his head off the floor. The linoleum smelled faintly of grease. *There were robots in the tranq gun*, he thought wildly, *and now they're in my blood! Broadcasting my location — they knew I was here; knocked me out at the push of a button . . .*

His entire body was numb. His eyelids were dragging themselves closed. He tried to scream, but only heard the noise in his head. *No*, he thought. *Fight it! Don't sleep. Find Kyntak — open*

the door and he'll help you out. He'll carry you. It's just a few meters.
You can do it.

He saw his arm slap against the floor, and saw it slide back towards him. He couldn't tell if he was dragging himself along or just wriggling his arm. The whole image was fading. No corridor, no soldiers, no arm.

Don't give up!

Six's eyes slid closed.

Fight it!

So tired . . .

And then there was nothing.

IMMORTALITY

This can't be happening. You were so careful.

The soldiers are storming the house, rifle barrels swinging from side to side, orange goggles glowing like bonfires. You usually call them cockroaches, because of the clawlike gloves and the tubes leading from their black masks to the air purifiers on their chests.

They've smashed in the front door, sending walnut-brown fragments of wood skittering into the hallway. The windows have been shredded to razor-sharp glitters of dust that seem to hang in the air much longer than they should. Dozens of holes have been punched in the roof so more troops can abseil in. The helicopter is still overhead, dropping more — you can hear the thundering of its blades, and see the spotlight slicing across the windows.

You were prepared for this. You bought the City's best security devices and reconstructed them to make them even better. You turned your whole house into an elaborate booby trap, preparing for the day they would come for you.

But this isn't your house. This is Kyntak's house, and it was a mess even before ChaoSonic troops showed up. How can you defend it on your own?

Forget the house. Nai needs you. She should still be in her bedroom. Her cot could be knocked over, she could be crushed under their boots. You have to find her, get her out of here before she's hurt. You try to run down the hall, but there are cockroaches blocking the way. One of them knocks you to the ground with the butt of his rifle. He's bigger and stronger than you are. Stronger than any man has a right to be.

You scramble back onto your feet, shove him aside. The corridor stretches to an impossible length — no matter how hard you run, the bedroom seems just out of reach. And somehow you know what's happening in there — a soldier scooping Nai out of her cot, ignoring her thin squeal of protest, and walking slowly back towards the shattered windows.

You round the corner, swinging through the bedroom door with one hand on the door frame. Someone grabs you and shoves you away, but you push right back. The soldier carrying Nai has just disappeared through the window. You run and jump, but as soon as you're outside you see that it's a long way to the ground. A freezing wind scrapes your skin as you plummet through the night air, briefly catching the beam of the helicopter's spotlight.

Thud. *Your bones crack, but you feel no pain. There's a ringing in your ears, and Kyntak's house vanishes into the darkness. The soldier with Nai has gone, but there's another — a Vanish trooper. He's aiming his pistol at your head.*

You try to throw yourself at him, but you've fallen too hard — it's like you're glued to the concrete. The soldier fires once, and a trapdoor opens beneath you. You tumble into the darkness.

Solid ground appears beneath your feet. It's black and silent here. There's a ladder leading back up to the light, but it's twisted; the rungs are straight but the sides spiral around one another as they rise. It looks as if it's made of bone — you're not sure you want to climb it. You're alone right now, but maybe Kyntak is on his way. Nai might be too.

Hiss. *The noise is painfully loud. It echoes out of darkness which is steadily becoming brighter. You try to cover your ears with your hands, but there's a sudden pain in your wrists and you can't move your arms . . .*

Six woke suddenly, thrashing against his bonds. The copper clamps around his wrists and ankles scraped his already tender skin, and the restraint around his neck choked him. He slumped back against the table, coughing, and squinted into the bright light.

He didn't need to look around to know where he was. He could see his reflection in the mirrored ceiling. He was wearing orange shorts and an undershirt, and he was clamped to a table. He was in a cell, probably only a few meters away from where he had fallen.

He hadn't rescued Kyntak, and now they were both doomed.

He scrunched his eyes shut for a moment. *No,* he told himself. *Don't think like that. You're alive. You don't know what they want from you, but they obviously can't get it once you're dead. There's still hope.*

The hissing stopped, prompting him to look up. There was a clear plastic hose with a valve on the end attached to the ceiling — providing oxygen, he guessed. They didn't want to give him an air vent to escape through. But the room couldn't be completely airtight, or the pressure would be increasing each time there was an oxygen burst, and sooner or later the valve would stop opening.

If there was a way out of here, he'd find it.

The roller-door slid open and two men walked in. One was a Vanish trooper, dressed in the same fatigues that Six had been wearing; he slid the roller-door shut behind them. The other was a large man wearing a T-shirt and jeans. He was smiling broadly.

"Six of Hearts," he said. "It's a pleasure."

Six twisted his head from side to side, stretching his aching neck. "Who are you?"

The man rested his hands in his pockets. "They call me Vanish."

"So you're on the board of directors?"

Vanish blinked. "I'm sorry?"

Six snorted. "I worked it out. Vanish isn't one person; it's an organization, operating as an individual so ChaoSonic doesn't exterminate it. How else could Vanish have been operating for more than fifty years?"

There was a long silence. Six held Vanish's gaze. His heart thudded softly in his chest, like a ticking clock.

"Do you know what telomeres are?" Vanish asked finally.

Six frowned. "Scraps of DNA?"

"Close enough. They are strings of DNA at the ends of chromosomes, making sure your cells don't lose genetic information as the chromosomes are replicated. Every time that happens, the telomeres get a little shorter, and eventually they run out, causing every age-related ailment from wrinkles to cancer." He paused. "Your telomeres, however, are self-copying."

Six drummed his fingers against the table, confused by this change of topic. "How?"

"I don't know!" Vanish shrugged. "Theoretically it should be impossible. But when I acquired the one-armed clone of you and started testing him, it only took a few months to notice that his telomeres weren't getting any shorter. So I put a microcamera into him and watched it happen. His telomeres were copying themselves right in front of my eyes!" He smiled hungrily. "And I needn't remind you that you have the same DNA."

Six stared at him. "So what are you saying?" he asked. "That I'll always be young?"

"Yes!" Vanish exploded. "You can't die of old age!" His hands fidgeted excitedly in the air. "Your DNA will never corrupt!" He lowered his voice. "That was Retuni Lerke's secret gift to you. He never told Methryn Crexe about it — Crexe would have tightened his leash, because he didn't need soldiers who never got old. But Lerke rigged up your genes so if you stayed away from external danger, you would live forever."

Six was starting to feel claustrophobic. He was clamped to a table in a sealed room with a raving lunatic. "So you have the same thing?" he asked. "You can't grow old, so you've been a thorn in ChaoSonic's side for more than fifty years?"

Vanish laughed. "No, not quite the same," he said. "My genes are very average — but not for long." He walked over to the side of the table and rolled up Six's left sleeve, tracing his finger across the line where the clone's arm had been attached.

Six shivered at his touch. "You're going to steal my DNA?" he demanded. "But how? Genes are inseparable from the body."

Vanish rolled the sleeve back down and withdrew his narrow fingers. "Oh, I know that. So I'm going to take your body, too."

Six's eyes widened in alarm. "What are you talking about?"

"Well, perhaps Kyntak's rather than yours. That's why I was hoping to get both of you, so I could make sure I got the best one.

Sure, your genes are the same, but genes aren't everything. You're probably fitter than he is — you've had a stricter diet and training regime, I'll bet — but I need to see if the surgery the Lab did on you last year has adversely affected your health."

"You can't take my body! That's impossible!"

Vanish raised an eyebrow. "No, it's not. My surgeon will remove your cerebral cortex and most of your limbic systems, then replace them with mine. You'll get a stem cell injection to make sure the neurons remap and the cells bond properly. The parts of your brain that keep your heart beating will be untouched, and we'll put you on a respirator to keep the lungs going during the surgery. Your sensory systems and motor system will be unchanged, so that I can use your body more easily when I have it. But my hippocampus, my orbitofrontal cortex, my nucleus accumbens, and my amygdala will all be stitched into your skull, so I'll be able to keep my memories, emotions, thought processes, and feelings, as well as my likes and dislikes. Things will taste different to me, look different, and feel different — but I'll still be me."

Six's heart was racing. It felt like there was a block of ice inside his stomach. "A successful brain transplant has never been done before. You'll die."

Vanish smiled. "Do you honestly think I'd risk this if it had never been done before? The whole point is living, after all." He leaned down close to Six's face, and Six shrank away from his luminous grey-green eyes. "Forget the fifty years of crime that ChaoSonic knows about. I'm more than a hundred years old; this is my fourteenth body. But I'm sick of all the surgery, the searching for new bodies, and the fear that someday I won't find one and old age will finally catch up with me. So now I'm going to live forever. In your body."

One, two, three. Pull! Kyntak howled as the bones in his hand were crushed against the copper clamp. He had concluded that the room was soundproof — he never heard Vanish and his guard coming, and his ears were hypersensitive. This meant that he was free to yell and scream as much as he liked as he mutilated his hand.

His bruised skin stung with the pressure. He could feel the thick copper bending slightly, but that wasn't what he needed — he knew that the copper would never stretch far enough to let his hand slip through. He needed his bones to become disjointed.

One, two, three. Pull! Pain throbbed through his wrist, and suddenly he couldn't find the energy to pull anymore. He slumped helplessly against the table, fatigued and miserable. He stared up at his reflection in the ceiling through watering eyes. He hadn't expected to die like this: pale, bruised, bald, and dressed in mandarin underwear. Statistically it had been more likely for him to be killed by a bullet — a lucky head shot by a ChaoSonic grunt. So many people had fired guns at him in his pitifully short sixteen years that one of them was bound to hit him eventually.

How long had he been in this cell? He hadn't been fed or given water to drink, and he was still alive despite having had several liters of his blood removed, so that meant less than a week. It felt like longer — like months or years. And how much longer would it be? How long would this psychopath keep him before killing him?

The door rolled aside, and Kyntak laughed weakly. He wondered idly if he was going mad.

Vanish walked in, holding a syringe. The woman stood on

Kyntak's left, pointing a gun at him. "Oh, come on," Kyntak rasped. "Surely I don't have any blood left."

"You wouldn't think so, given that you haven't had anything to eat or drink since I brought you in." Vanish smiled as he jabbed the needle into Kyntak's vein. "But somehow you keep generating it at a steady rate. My working hypothesis is that you're able to convert your fat reserves into blood, almost like a backup metabolism."

"Remind me to send a thank-you note to Retuni Lerke when I get out of here."

Vanish withdrew the needle from Kyntak's arm. "Neither you nor Six is getting out of here," he said. "But I'll pass on the message to Lerke when I next speak to him."

Kyntak closed his eyes. "You have Six?"

"Oh, yes. He's just a few cells down. Speaking to him is fascinating from a nature versus nurture point of view — same DNA, same situation, but he responded quite differently from you when he woke up."

"He's going to kill you," Kyntak whispered faintly.

"He's not in a position to kill anyone," Vanish said. "But it's strange that you should say that. Six has a reputation for restraint when it comes to murder. In fact, he stopped to bandage up one of my soldiers on his way down to this floor."

Kyntak smiled. "Yep, that's him. Six the merciful — but not weak. He's escaped from every cell he was ever put in, shuffled every Code-breaker who so much as looked at him sideways, and broken into half the maximum-security facilities in the City without working up a sweat. It's true he's pretty levelheaded. It'd be hard to make him angry enough to kill you. But if you really wanted to, you could."

He started to laugh, a thin, wheezing chuckle. Vanish's smile faded slowly as he watched.

Kyntak cleared his throat before continuing. "In fact, you know what I'd do? If I really wanted him out for my blood — not that I would, of course, because he could be the world's greatest assassin if he tried — but if I was suicidal and wanted to send Six of Hearts completely over the brink, I know exactly what my first move would be."

There was a long silence. Vanish stared at him.

"I'd kidnap his twin brother!" Kyntak howled, and then he burst out laughing again, a rattling, hysterical cackle. His chest heaved and his throat scraped against the strap around it.

Vanish moved away from the table, the syringe still in his hand. He beckoned to the red-eyed woman. She muttered into her radio and the door slid open. Vanish walked out backward, watching Kyntak with a frown of disbelief, and the door closed.

Kyntak stopped laughing and smiled grimly. *There*, he thought. *Maybe Six and I will die here, and maybe no one will ever know what happened to us. But I've had my revenge on our captor — I've scared him. He will see our face in his nightmares for the rest of his life.*

The loss of blood was making him dizzy. He closed his eyes and rested.

Six was thinking hard. There had to be a way out of this. There was already a way.

He'd reassembled all the new data in his head to get what he finally believed was the complete picture. Vanish had been a criminal many years ago, rich enough to afford a new body to transplant his brain into. Presumably it was a desperate measure. His crime syndicate must have been falling down around him, perhaps because some not-yet-extinct form of law enforcement was closing in on him, but more likely because he'd trodden on the turf of a criminal empire with more manpower. He'd dumped his old body somewhere with most of his brain missing in order to fake his own death. He had probably mutilated it so the surgery wasn't obvious. He wouldn't have wanted the people looking for him to know what he had done.

So he starts recruiting again, Six thought. *Goes somewhere new. Hires a load of soldiers and at some point begins injecting them with nanomachines. Now he has an elite force: better fighting through chemistry. He changes bodies a few more times, using the technique as a disguise rather than a last resort.*

Something clicked in Six's mind. He remembered the list of senior ChaoSonic officials who had been captured by Vanish, and who had the stolen ChaoSonic information for him after being released. He remembered that there had only been one at any given time. He had assumed that they were coerced into working for Vanish because he had tagged them with his nanomachines, and that he had only needed one at a time because they were so well placed within the company — but now Six had a much more frightening thought. Each and every one might have been Vanish himself. He had started stealing not only bodies, but also identities. He used his assistant/brain surgeon to represent him anywhere he was supposed to be in person. Niskev Pacye was currently filling that position, but there must have been others before her.

Hiss. The valve in the corner opened, releasing some more oxygen into the room. Six ignored it.

So ChaoSonic chokes the vestigial government and rises to power, he thought, continuing his mental timeline. *The Takeover. Vanish stays in hiding and keeps sending his soldiers out on missions, but starts stealing exclusively from ChaoSonic because they now have a virtual monopoly on everything. And sooner or later, they notice him and try to hunt him down. Presumably they managed to get one of their own operatives into this force — and that would be why he showed up as a potential buyer for Earle Shuji's robot army. Robots are more loyal than people.*

Anyway. ChaoSonic lures him into a trap and captures him. He scratches on his own face so he can't be connected to any of his previous crimes, and to make his appearance so memorable that later no one will suspect a normal-looking man of being him. Someone in his team, probably one of Niskev Pacye's predecessors, takes the initiative and uses the locator in Vanish's own nanomachines to find him, then storms in with a bunch of troops. They decimate the ChaoSonic forces to send a message, then Vanish changes bodies again, while ChaoSonic searches for a hideously scarred man they're never going to find.

Fast-forward thirty years, and Vanish is well established. He's got his new assistant, his own private army, a fistful of credits, and a century of experience. So what made him go to the Lab eight months ago?

Project Falcon? Six thought. *Was he interested in replacing his army with a team of super-soldiers, each carrying my designer DNA?* It was possible, Six supposed, but this was after they had gone to see Shuji, not before. Wouldn't Vanish rather be investigating the bot angle? Particularly when one of his troops had betrayed him before: Project Falcon made them strong and fast, but not incorruptible.

Six took a quick breath. *Of course! At this point, Vanish no longer treats the body-swapping as a defense against ChaoSonic. He sees it as his defense against age — his road to immortality.* Breaking into the Lab was only indirectly linked to Project Falcon. What

Vanish really wanted was Chelsea Tridya's formula! He'd heard about its ability to slow the rate of cell division and mutation, and figured he could enormously extend his own life span without having to switch bodies.

It would have been a ruin when he broke in, Six thought. Sevadonn dead, Crexe and the soldiers gone, Nai taken away by Kyntak and Six. The inside of the tower was smashed and burned. But they didn't know that the clone was in there, too — Vanish found him and took him. He would have been furious to find the drug missing . . . but only until he discovered the self-replicating telomeres in the clone.

So he spent the next few months planning a way to get Kyntak and/or Six to his facility. Kidnapped Methryn Crexe as bait. . . .

The thought of never going back to the Deck and leaving his fate a mystery to his friends was bad enough. The idea of letting a madman steal his identity and wear his face for the rest of eternity was far worse.

He tried to flush the image out of his head. This wasn't helping. He wasn't going to die. Not here. Not now.

He considered trying to pull his hand through the copper clamp — it might be possible if the bones dislocated or broke. But he could safely assume that Kyntak had tried that, and he had a head start of at least nine hours, depending on how long Six had been unconscious.

Hiss. Six wondered if there was some way he could use the oxygen valve — but he couldn't think of anything that didn't involve getting off the table first. Dead end.

The roller-door slid open again. Six looked towards one of the wall mirrors and saw Vanish's face through the widening gap. He rested his head back down against the pad.

"I haven't decided which of you to use yet," Vanish said. A soldier entered with him and stood impassively in the corner. "You're both very similar from a medical and health standpoint. So I've decided to use the opportunity to run a few tests first."

"Whose body are you wearing now?" Six asked. "Just out of curiosity. Who died so you could wear their face? Another ChaoSonic official?"

"You can't make me feel guilty." Vanish laughed. "It's every man for himself in this City. I was given the intelligence and the tenacity to survive, and I don't believe it was wrong of me to use them. If I hadn't started taking bodies, I'd be long dead by now. That makes it justifiable homicide. Call it self-defense, if you like."

"If you didn't feel guilty," Six said, "you wouldn't feel the need to twist logic into a moral defense of your actions. Inside, you know you're preparing to kill two innocent people to save your own worthless skin."

Vanish laughed again. "Worthless? I am the only living link to pre-Takeover times — the City's oldest person! I'm a national treasure! What have you seen or learned in your sixteen years that gives you more right to live than me?" A syringe appeared in his hand, this one full of a shimmering golden liquid. "If it makes you feel better, think about all the people I won't have to kill once I've taken your body. In a way, you're saving their lives."

He jammed the needle into Six's arm, and Six winced. "Since you asked," he continued, "I can't remember the name of this body's previous owner — I rarely remember their names unless I need their identities. I have it written down somewhere, I think. He was a music teacher. I chose him because he played rugby on the weekends, and I wanted the strength." He smiled. "I suspect it hasn't prepared me for a Project Falcon body, though."

"More nanomachines?" Six asked as Vanish withdrew the needle.

"No. This is accelerant — my own formula. Mostly a mixture of epinephrine, NENB, and mateine. It decreases reaction time and increases strength. You've seen it work on my soldiers. It should take about a minute to kick in fully."

Six's jaw dropped. Mateine was just caffeine, and epinephrine was basically synthetic adrenaline; neither of them would do him any serious harm. But NENB was a dangerously strong stimulant. "Won't that also cause brain damage?"

"The possible side effects include dehydration, addiction, paranoia, and exhaustion once it wears off," Vanish said calmly. "It can also suppress the immune system, but we have ways of combating that. The nanomachines don't secrete very much into the bloodstream, though, so there's rarely any permanent damage."

"But you're not giving me nanomachines," Six said. He was already feeling queasy. "You're giving me a pure dose!"

"Yes," Vanish said. "I'm hoping that your extraordinary metabolism will give you greater resistance than my soldiers have to the negative effects. But I obviously want to test it before taking your body rather than after, just in case I'm wrong." He shrugged. "If it kills you, I'll just take Kyntak's body instead of yours."

His voice seemed to be getting slower and deeper. The room was getting brighter. Six's mouth felt dry.

"I'm going to send in an opponent for you to fight to test your accelerated reflexes," Vanish said. "It'll be recorded so that I can watch it later. Then I'll come back in and examine you for damage."

He gestured to the guard and the door slid open. Six felt the accelerant course through his veins. Every muscle in his body tingled with energy. He tried to lunge at Vanish, and he felt the copper clamps bend a little. Vanish and his guard walked out the door, but it didn't slide shut.

Six tried again, bracing his arms against the table and pulling his wrists against the clamps. The table groaned encouragingly, but nothing moved. Six felt his heart palpitate in his chest. The accelerant was making him feel sick. But he knew that was his best chance to escape. The door was open and the soldier he was supposed to fight hadn't arrived yet.

He tried to pull his legs against the clamps. The sinews in his ankles were crushed against the copper, but the accelerant numbed the pain.

He froze as he heard heavy footsteps outside. *Thud, thud, thud.* That didn't sound like a soldier.

Six's eyes widened as it appeared in the doorway, familiar features shining in the light, silvery eyes gleaming.

"Harry?" he asked.

MISSION
FIVE
04:39:02

INTO
THIN AIR

The door slid shut and the clamps popped open. The strap around Six's neck slithered away into a hole in the table. He rolled off and fell slowly, as if he were on the moon. He landed on his feet and stood up.

"Harry?" he repeated. "Is that you?"

The bot didn't reply. It stood stock-still, staring impassively at the wall.

Six remembered Earle Shuji telling him that Niskev Pacye had approached her to buy bots. She had known the address Vanish used for deliveries. And Six remembered that she had seemed nervous, as if she were hiding something from him.

Now he knew what. *Vanish has a prototype bot too*, he thought. *If he'd sent a human soldier for me to fight, I'd have won, accelerant or no accelerant, and then I might have been able to coerce him or her into opening the door. There's no chance with a robot. It can't be threatened, bribed, or reasoned with.*

The oxygen valve hissed above him, but it seemed to take longer than before. His heightened consciousness stretched the sound out — from a burning fuse to a hissing snake.

He bounced restlessly on the balls of his feet, feeling the accelerant sweep into full effect. With every thrust he seemed to hang in the air, as though he were moving in real time but the universe had slowed to a crawl. Gravity barely seemed to touch him. His hands curled into fists that felt tougher than ever before. But his tongue was burning and his already sensitive retinas stung with the light blazing through his dilated pupils.

The robot still hadn't moved. Six assumed that it was waiting for a radio signal from Vanish. Probably less time had passed than it seemed, considering his accelerated thought processes.

He braced a foot and a hand against the table and gripped one half of a clamp with the other hand. He pulled with all his might and felt his turbocharged muscles strain. With a shriek that seemed to last forever, the copper tore at the base, and Six fell slowly backward. He drifted towards the wall and smacked into it, clutching his prize: a thick, square blade. It glinted reddish-bronze in the bright light.

Six waited.

The bot waited.

Then it lifted its arm and fired at him with its built-in Swan.

Six launched himself sideways into the air as bullets streaked around him. The accelerant had pumped so much power into his reflexes that he could actually see the bullets coming — fast and blurry, but visible.

The first few rounds hit the glass wall behind him, drilling holes into it and sending fine cracks spiraling outward. The glass was too thick to shatter, and there was a layer of metal behind it — probably steel, Six thought, like the door. No way out there.

As he fell behind the table and smacked onto the ground, he couldn't see the bot, which stopped firing immediately and walked towards the table. *Thud, thud, thud.*

The first time Six had met Harry, he'd challenged him to

combat. But Harry had been in a nonlethal mode. He couldn't use his gun. This was a far more dangerous situation.

Six didn't know how many bullets remained in the clip of the Swan, but he suspected it would be more than he could dodge — and the bot might be capable of reloading.

He had two plausible strategies. One: Keep circling the table in a crouch, never giving it a clear shot. Two: Charge. Shuji's bots were programmed to use hand-to-hand rather than gunfire if their opponent was closer than two meters.

The thumping footsteps had stopped. Six listened carefully.

The table groaned noisily, then lurched to one side with a sickening crack. The bot ripped it out of the floor with both synthetic arms and held it above its head, cords with loose wires trailing to the floor. It threw the table towards the wall. To Six's eyes it seemed to drift as slowly as a cloud before slamming into the glass with a shower of sparks.

With an earsplitting *thunk*, the table landed on its side, propped up against the cracked wall. Now nothing separated Six from the bot except a flat square of plastic on the floor with a few tufts of shredded steel poking up from it, where the table had been attached.

The bot raised its gun and Six lunged forward, stopping just inside the two-meter mark. The bot swung a fist at him; Six ducked underneath it. The bot's arm whipped over Six's head like a helicopter blade.

I know things about this bot that Vanish may not know, Six realized. *Like the code that shuts down all its systems. What was it — something that sounded like Latin?*

"Cerfitipus talotus!" he shouted triumphantly.

The bot punched him in the stomach.

Six doubled over and slid backward across the floor.

*   *   *

Kyntak looked up as Vanish entered his cell. This time, the red-eyed woman didn't stand in the corner; instead, she stood beside the table and held her gun close to the left side of Kyntak's head. Vanish walked to the other side of the table, holding a syringe and two large vials filled with dark-red liquid.

"I'm going to return some of your blood," he said, pocketing one of the vials and removing the cap from the syringe.

Kyntak said nothing.

"I've more or less condemned Six to death," he explained, jamming the needle into the lid of the vial he was still holding, "or serious injury, at least — which means it's probably you I'll be using for the surgery. So it's safest if I start bringing your stats up slowly."

Kyntak didn't ask what surgery Vanish was talking about. He threw his head to the left, stretching his neck strap. The gun was just out of reach of his teeth.

Vanish stayed back. "Kyntak, you'll live longest if you cooperate with me." He signaled to the woman, who stepped back. Her gun was still pointed at Kyntak's head but was now above his hand. He stretched his fingers up but wasn't even close to reaching it.

The phrase hadn't worked. Shuji's bots must have had individual shutdown codes.

The bot lowered its arm to shoot again, and Six scrambled to his feet and dived forward. He reached the two-meter perimeter just as he heard the bot's internal safety catch click off. The bot immediately lowered its arm and lifted its leg, aiming a kick at

Six's chest. Six stepped aside at the last moment, letting the metal and plastic foot swish into the air beside him. He wrapped his arm around it and twisted. The bot lost its balance and slammed face-first into the floor.

Six aimed a stomp at the bot's head. *Maybe I can damage some of its eyes*, he thought. But the bot swiped an arm out at Six's other ankle, and he had to jump over the blow. The stomp missed. Six stepped back, and the bot rose to its feet. Six kept the two-meter distance — close enough so it wouldn't use the gun, but far enough away that punches would fall short and he would see kicks coming.

The bot lunged forward, and Six ducked back. It swung a kick in his direction, and he sidestepped. It feinted a right hook, and Six dodged again.

It's figured out my strategy, Six realized. *And now it's trying to drive me into the corner farthest away from the door.*

He threw a punch at the bot's head, which connected. The accelerant didn't completely mask the pain in his knuckles, and the bot seemed unharmed. It drove an elbow towards his ribs, and he had no choice but to retreat farther.

Six drove his copper blade forward, and it scraped through the plastic shell covering the bot's metal chassis, but did no more damage — the bot just shoved him backward. His eyes widened as he hit the wall and the bot aimed a skull-crushing punch.

And then, in his moment of necessity, Six came up with a plan. He ducked to one side, and the bot buried its fist in the glass where Six's head had been. While it was extricating itself, Six leaped up and tore the oxygen hose from the seam between the wall and the ceiling. The long-dried glue made a sucking sound as it was ripped away. Six immediately jammed his thumb over the valve, just as it opened.

He could feel the pressure building up against his thumb as the steady flow of pure oxygen looked for a place to escape. He held the hose tightly as he approached the bot again. It started towards him, but as soon as its rear foot left the ground, Six kicked it in the chest and it stumbled backward. Without giving it time to recover, Six drove a fist into its abdomen, ignoring his aching knuckles. The bot tried to kick his head, but Six ducked under its leg and charged forward, pushing it back farther until it was pressed against the door.

Six kept his forearm against the bot's chest, pinning it against the glass-covered metal. His face was so close to the bot's that he could see synthetic irises spinning in its silvery eyes. The bot tried to claw him off, but he grabbed its arm and pressed it against its chest.

He couldn't hold it much longer, and the pressure against his thumb was becoming unbearable. He held the hose up to the door and released the valve. In the same instant, he slashed the copper blade down against the bot, creating a shower of sparks.

He jammed the hose into the groove he'd made in the robot's chest, and some internal mechanism squealed with protest as the oxygen combusted and the sudden heat expanded and softened the metal. The bot drove a plastic fist towards Six's head as its internal cooling mechanism kicked in.

Six ducked the blow and, before the metal could harden again, drove his copper spike into the bot's exoskeleton.

It didn't go right in — the blade stopped just a few centimeters after punching the chassis. Six released the blade and it fell to the floor as the bot twisted its torso, trying to land a blow on Six.

The stabbing didn't appear to have done any serious damage to the bot. Six put his foot on its chest, slammed it back against the door, and hoped his plan would work.

There was a sudden beeping sound.

The robot looked down foolishly at its torso.

Six was hurled backward across the cell as the thirteen hundred grams of C-4 detonated, the primary force of the blast exploding out of the exhaust valve beside the robot's spine. Half of the roller-door was smashed out into the corridor, leaving the other half shaking on crooked tracks. The glass on the walls and ceiling splintered under the pressure, sending pricks of light out all over the cell. The noise exploded through the enclosed space. Six slammed into the rear wall shoulder first and watched with accelerant-enhanced vision as the robot tumbled lifelessly through the air, surrounded by spinning shreds of glass, like a planet among the stars. Its back was twisted and melted, and its luminous eyes had faded to a dull grey.

Then everything hit the floor — the roller-door, the robot, and the million chips of glass. It all came crashing down in a deafening symphony of shrieks and crunching thuds. Then there was silence. Six was alone with the ringing in his ears.

"Don't get in the way of the exhaust valve," Six muttered to himself. "Thanks, Shuji."

Vanish paused, the needle above Kyntak's flesh. "Did you hear something?" he asked the red-eyed woman. Kyntak turned his head towards her. She was still pointing the gun at him. He aimed very carefully.

The woman yelped as Kyntak's tooth hit her in the ear at a speed of ten meters per second. She dropped the gun and it fell towards Kyntak's shoulder. He threw his torso up into the air and the gun bounced off his collarbone, landing in his left hand.

Vanish dropped the syringe as he jumped back to get out of Kyntak's range. But Kyntak wasn't aiming at him. He fired four shots into the mirrored ceiling in quick succession. They ricocheted back down; the first one missed the table altogether, and the second narrowly avoided his bicep. But the third and fourth punctured the clamp around his other arm, and Kyntak ripped his wrist through the fractured copper like it was paper.

The red-eyed woman was reaching for her Eagle but Kyntak shot the magazine, making it unusable. He swung his free arm over to his gun hand and slapped the release button. The clamp popped open with a *clank*, and now both his arms were free. Vanish and his assistant lunged forward to hold Kyntak down. Kyntak lifted Vanish up with his right arm and threw him over the table, onto the woman. Kyntak sat up and slammed his right hand on the button operating the right knee clamp, and the gun butt on the button for the left.

Clank. Clank. Clank. Clank. His legs were free. He rolled off the table and dropped into a firing crouch.

Vanish had recovered quickly. His jeans had apparently concealed a gun, which was now trained on Kyntak's heart with a perfectly steady hand.

"Drop it," Kyntak said.

Vanish laughed. "I think I'm the one with the advantage in this situation," he said.

"I have Project Falcon reflexes, agility, and strength," said Kyntak. "There's nothing to stop me from killing you."

"But you're weakened," said Vanish. "Hungry, thirsty, exhausted. Not enough oxygen is reaching your brain. I'm healthy and alert, and I've had eighty years of marksmanship practice. And if you kill me, there's no way out of this room."

"Eighty years?" Kyntak snorted. "Yeah, right. You must really cleanse, tone, and moisturize. You can tell your incompetent assistant to radio out and get this door open, or else I'll take a few shots at you." He kept his gaze level. "I don't want to hurt anyone, but I will. And I'd rather hurt you than her."

"You're bleeding," Vanish said, and suddenly Kyntak knew it was true. His wrist hurt, and there was a warm wetness on his forearm. "You shot yourself," Vanish continued. "The bullet went right through the clamp and hit your wrist. Or maybe the pieces of the clamp were sharp, and you cut yourself on them. Either way, you're already weak and getting weaker." He smiled. "Kill me and you'll bleed to death in this room. Get back on the table and I'll stitch you up."

He was right. Kyntak could feel his arm becoming numb. The gun was starting to tremble in his grip.

"What's more important, Kyntak?" Vanish asked. "Your dignity or your life?"

Kyntak smiled. "I'm going to die anyway. But I'm keeping the sights on you as long as I can lift this gun — because I know that inside you're scared to death."

Vanish's smile faded. "I can save your life, Kyntak. And I want to. I wanted both the Project Falcon kids, but Six is probably dead by now, so you're all I've got."

"Tough," Kyntak whispered. Then he shouted at the red-eyed woman, "Hey, butterfingers. Open the door or you'll need someone else to sign your paychecks."

The door slid open behind him. She hadn't spoken a word, so Kyntak backed away towards the wall so he could see the doorway while keeping his gun trained on Vanish.

Six was standing there, clothes shredded, face blackened, scratches all over.

"Six," Kyntak rasped. "You look terrible."

"At least I still have my hair," Six pointed out.

"Okay, now you're fired," Kyntak replied. Then, to Vanish, "Stop right there!"

Vanish had moved behind the table. His gun was still pointed at Kyntak; Six was unarmed. "That wasn't a good strategic move," Kyntak said. "You can't beat both of us, and we're between you and the door. How long do you think that table's going to protect you?"

"Longer than you think," Vanish said. A mad smile flitted across his face.

"Toss me your radio," Six said to the woman. She didn't move.

"Do it," Kyntak said. "Or I shoot your boss and then take it from you. You don't have a whole lot of leverage here."

The woman threw the radio. And as it was in the air, Vanish opened fire. Two bullets had hit the ceiling before Kyntak squeezed off his first shot, which missed Vanish, who had ducked behind the table. Kyntak and Six stooped into identical crouches, minimizing surface areas as the ricochets sparked off the ceiling and the walls.

The bullets ground to a halt after their second or third deflection, and clinked harmlessly on the floor.

Kyntak was feeling weak, and his aim was shaky. He threw his gun to Six, who caught it and aimed it at the table.

"Put down your weapon," Six said. "Hold up your hands. You have until I count to five, then I come around the corner firing."

There was no response from behind the table. "One," Six began. "Two."

"He's gone," the woman interrupted. Her face was white and sweaty — there was fear in her expression. "He's disappeared."

Something in Niskev Pacye's voice struck Six as raw truth. All her icy confidence from the ransom video was gone. She was scared. Six leveled his gun and walked around the table in a slow circle. There was no sign of Vanish anywhere.

"Cool trick," Kyntak whispered from his position on the floor. "How'd he do it?"

Six remembered the plastic plate he'd seen on the floor when the bot picked up the table in his cell. He kicked the side panel of the table. It didn't budge. "The doors to the cells can't be opened from the inside," he said, pressing his palms against various spots on the panel. "And he wanted them closed while the prisoners were inside, even while he was in there with them, to minimize the risk of escape. Therefore there was some small chance that he'd get trapped in one." A part of the table depressed under the pressure from his hands, and the side folded in, exposing the hollow inside of the table. Six rapped his knuckles on the plastic square embedded in the floor underneath. It sounded hollow.

"So he built tunnels," he finished, standing up. "Escape routes, well hidden and hard to open without the know-how."

"Do we follow him?" Kyntak asked. He had clamped his hand over his wounded wrist, trying to slow the bleeding.

"No," Six said. "We don't know where it leads, and he'll be waiting for us. We have to get out of here."

He ripped the tattered shirt off his chest and knelt down beside Kyntak. "Let go."

Kyntak released his wrist, and Six wound the shirt around it. He looked at Kyntak's face. He was pale, and his eyes were unfocused. *He's lost too much blood*, Six thought.

"Kyntak," Six asked. "Can you hear me?"

"It's not that bad," Kyntak whispered. "Barely hurts."

Six glanced around for something he could use. He'd stopped

the bleeding, but he might have done it too late. He saw a syringe lying on the ground, filled with blood, and he reached over and grabbed it.

"Kyntak," Six said. "Stay with me. Is this your blood?"

"Stole it," Kyntak breathed. "Wanted me weak . . ."

Vanish was draining him, Six realized. That's why the blood loss seemed so bad — he was already depleted. He rolled up Kyntak's shorts, tapped the syringe, pushed the valve to get the oxygen out, and put the needle in Kyntak's femoral artery. "Can you feel that?" he asked as he pushed the valve.

"I knew you'd show up," Kyntak said. "You always . . . you . . ." His eyes drooped. He was still as white as a sheet.

"Stay awake," Six said. "Stay awake!"

The syringe was empty, and Six took it out, pressing his thumb against the needle mark. He'd never done a blood transfusion before — he hoped he had done it right. But it didn't look like enough; Kyntak's lips were still blue, and he was now unconscious. Six felt for a pulse. It was faint and slow.

Of course, he thought. *Kyntak and I have the same blood type!* He pushed the needle into his arm, ignoring the sharp sting, and filled it with his own blood, then tapped it again and pushed it into Kyntak's leg. "Come on," he whispered. "I didn't come this far to watch you die."

Kyntak's chest was no longer visibly rising and falling. Six filled the syringe again from his arm, and gave Kyntak another transfusion. He was starting to get dizzy now, and his head ached from dehydration. *I can't give any more blood*, he thought, *or I'll lose consciousness myself.*

He felt for a pulse again.

There wasn't one.

DESPERATE

Don't panic, Six told himself. He put his hands on Kyntak's ribs and pushed down repeatedly. *One, two, three, four, five.* Kyntak had stopped breathing. Six pinched Kyntak's nose, held his mouth open, and exhaled into it twice. He put his hands back on Kyntak's chest. *One, two, three, four, five.* He was pushing hard enough to crack ribs on a normal human, but Kyntak's bones were stronger than most. Six put his ear to Kyntak's lips; the only sound was the frenzied pounding of his own heart. He put his mouth over Kyntak's again and breathed: *one, two.* Kyntak's chest rose and fell with the breaths, but there was no movement once Six stopped forcing air into him.

He touched his fingers to Kyntak's neck. Still no pulse.

"Give me your remote," he shouted to Pacye.

She looked up in alarm. "Why?"

Six picked up the gun and aimed it at her. "Just do it!"

She tore the remote from her belt and threw it to Six, who pointed it at Kyntak and jammed his finger down on the ACCEL-ERANT button a few times. He hoped that the benefits of the epinephrine would be greater than the danger of the NENB.

He dropped the remote and bashed the heels of his palms

against Kyntak's chest. *One, two, three, four, five!* He put his mouth to Kyntak's. *One, two!*

There was no response. There just wasn't enough blood in Kyntak's veins, and no amount of CPR was going to change that. Six's brother was becoming little more than a still-warm corpse.

Six stuck the needle into his arm again, but hesitated. If he pulled the plunger, he would lose consciousness in seconds — long enough to give Kyntak the transfusion, maybe, but not long enough to do any more CPR. Kyntak would die. He was nearly dead already.

"What blood type are you?" he demanded, turning to Pacye. But she had disappeared — either run out into the corridor or followed Vanish down the tunnel.

Six thumped his fist into the floor next to Kyntak's drained flesh. They were both O positive. They needed someone who matched, or someone with O negative blood, the universal type.

Think, Six commanded himself. *There has to be a way. There's always a way!* Vanish had O positive blood. He couldn't transplant his brain into a body that didn't match. But they had already ruled out catching him as a possibility, let alone taking some of his blood and running back to the cell. There were soldiers out in the corridor, but they were unconscious and there was no way to tell what blood type they were. If he gave Kyntak the wrong kind of blood, he would poison him.

Six's eyes widened. There was another candidate, someone close by who had O positive blood. Six's mind recoiled from the idea, but he knew it was Kyntak's only shot for survival. He lifted Kyntak in his arms and carried him out the door.

He couldn't run; he was too dizzy and exhausted. He staggered slowly down the corridor, Kyntak's lifeless body flopping sickeningly in his arms. "Stay with me, Kyntak," he whispered.

He stumbled in as straight a line as he could: *left foot, right foot, left foot* . . .

As he passed the elevator, he kicked the gun of one of the fallen soldiers between the doors. They wouldn't close with it in the way, so the elevator couldn't move. No reinforcements would get to this floor for a while.

He reached the cell door and opened it. The clone looked up at him with the same terror in his gaze that Six had seen before. Six laid Kyntak down on the table and pulled the syringe from his pocket.

He fell to his knees and shuffled across the floor of the cell toward the clone, who backed into a corner. Eight months ago, Six had unwittingly stolen this boy's body parts to save his own life; now he intended to steal more to save Kyntak. A part of him felt like he was no better than Vanish. But he knew that he had run out of options.

Six held the syringe in his right hand, bracing himself against the floor with the left arm that he would never again think of as his own. The clone stared at the tip of the needle, his breath coming in rattly hisses from the mask that half concealed his deformed face.

"I'm sorry," Six whispered. "So sorry."

And he lowered the needle to the clone's skin.

Kyntak's chest arched, his arms thrashed, and his whole body shuddered as a cough exploded out of his lungs. Six fell backward onto the floor of the cell as Kyntak gasped for air, hacking and wheezing on the table. Six stared at him, wide-eyed. A part of him had accepted that Kyntak was dead. *The logical part*, he thought. *It's a miracle!*

Kyntak rolled off the table and fell to the floor beside Six. "That," he choked, "was the least pleasant experience . . . I've ever had in the line of duty."

"All you had to do was lie there." Six coughed. "I was doing all the work." He forced himself to think about the potential harm that the heart failure could have done to Kyntak. Brain damage was the most likely. "Do you remember who I am?"

"I don't feel brain-damaged, Six of Hearts," Kyntak said. He stared gloomily at the floor of the cell.

"It's not something you feel," Six replied. "What's twenty-eight multiplied by seventeen?"

Kyntak frowned. "Four hundred and seventy-six?" he said after a pause.

Six nodded. "What color is the bandage around your wrist?"

Kyntak grimaced. "Orange with red splotches."

Six shut his eyes and slumped back against the floor. Kyntak's memory, sensory, and calculation apparatus all seemed to be okay.

"Are we safe?" Kyntak asked. He thumped his chest with his fist and coughed again. "Are there guards coming?"

"The elevator is disabled and all the guards on this floor are unconscious. We're okay for the moment."

The clone in the corner whimpered — a muffled, hissing squeak. Kyntak saw him for the first time. "Who, or what, is that?" he demanded.

"Our little brother," Six said. "The clone that Crexe made last year to harvest body parts for me. Vanish stole him and kept him as a test subject." He kept his eyes closed. "And I took his blood to replace the amount you lost."

"Wow," Kyntak said, staring in horror at the boy's glass eye, the respirator mask, and the stump where his arm should be. "That sucks."

"I didn't have a choice," Six began. "If —"

"I know," Kyntak said, cutting him off. "I'd be dead if it weren't for you. And him. It just sucks, that's all."

Six longed to remain lying on the floor and go to sleep. Every muscle screamed for rest. But there was still more to do.

"Come on," he said, grabbing the edge of the tabletop and dragging himself to his feet. "Vanish knows what floor we're on. Soldiers are probably blocking off the exits as we speak, and since the elevator isn't working, they'll be looking for another way down. We have to get out of here."

Kyntak stood up slowly. "How? Even if we weren't weakened and exhausted, we're still hopelessly outnumbered. There's no way we're walking out the front door."

Six looked Kyntak in the eye and was frightened by the despair he saw there. He had given up, Six realized. Vanish had wrung the hope out of him like water from a sponge, and now all that was left was sorrow.

"There's always a way," Six said. He wanted to put a reassuring hand on Kyntak's shoulder, but couldn't — it would seem too weird. "Always."

When they went back to the surgery room Six had passed on his original search, they discovered that some rations were kept in one of the drawers — small, heavy bars of protein, sugar, and vitamins. Six felt better after he had eaten four or five of them; the pain in his muscles died down, his headache disappeared, and he could already feel his body metabolizing the food and replenishing his blood. There were also clean clothes, both hospital scrubs and orange prison garb. Six told Kyntak everything that had happened since waking up in the morgue while Kyntak munched on the bars in silence. Six applied some styptic to Kyntak's wrist to stop the bleeding properly as he talked, and replaced the torn-up shirt with proper gauze. He treated his own wounds too — the knife cut on his arm and the bruises from the fight with the bot. Then he grabbed a pair of scissors, a razor, and some shaving foam from one of the drawers — a plan was forming in his mind.

They offered some food to the clone as well, but he wouldn't touch it. The fear was gone from his gaze, replaced by a heavy-hearted resignation, an acceptance that no one was ever going to help him. They unwrapped the bars and left them on the table in his cell, hoping that he would eat them after they were gone.

Six considered closing the cell door, so the clone would be safe until they came back for him. But he decided against it. There was a chance they weren't coming back. If they died trying to escape, he didn't want the clone left at Vanish's mercy.

"We'll come back for you," Six said. "We can't take you with us now, but we'll be back with help." The clone stared helplessly down at the floor as Six rolled the door towards the wall, leaving a narrow crack. Hopefully any soldier who happened to look wouldn't be paying enough attention to notice.

Someone had called the elevator. The doors were sliding back and forth, starting to close and then backing off when the lasers sensed the gun lying in the way. Six suspected they didn't have a lot of time. They went back to the sleeping troops.

He started pulling their helmets off, looking at their faces. This one's skin was too tan. The next one's hair was blond — useless. The third was female. He kept looking.

Kyntak was doing the same thing; he pulled the helmet off a

sleeping soldier and held up the body so Six could see — it was a man in his early twenties. "What do you think?" he asked Six.

Six nodded. "It'll do."

"Give me the scissors," Kyntak said.

Six threw them to Kyntak, who started work immediately. Six kept pulling helmets off. Another woman, a guy who was too stocky . . . There! Perfect.

"Six," Kyntak said, pocketing the scissors and prodding his soldier. "This one's waking up."

"Grab their remotes," Six said. "Hit the SYNCAL button on them; keep them asleep."

We'll have to hurry, he thought. He took a watch off the nearest soldier's wrist and put it on. 05:27:27.

There were sixteen soldiers in the room. Two on each side of the elevator door, three on each side of the stairwell entrance, and the remaining six distributed randomly throughout the room, crouching behind the bomb-making chambers, pressed up against the half-constructed vehicles, and standing guard by the glass cube.

They had been thoroughly briefed on the situation. There were two escaped prisoners on the loose in the lower level. The elevator was the only way up, and the fugitives were expected to try to take it. The orders that the soldiers had been given were very clear. The mission priority was to keep them from getting past; the secondary objective was to leave them undamaged; and the escapees were to be considered dangerous even when unarmed. They had nanomachines in them, but they had jammed the elevator. This meant that there was no point in sending the "sleep" signal to the bottom floor. It would overdose the soldiers who were still down there, and the fugitives would wake up before anyone could get down there to recapture them. So instead, they guarded the elevator. The soldiers down there should wake up soon and take control. But if the escapees tried to come up, they could be taken down with the remotes. And the soldiers had been issued with AM-92s as backup.

All heads turned and guns were raised as the elevator doors slid open. There were two soldiers in it. The prisoners were slung over their soldiers, apparently unconscious.

"Stand down," the soldier carrying the bald prisoner said, walking forward out of the lift. "Holster your weapons. The situation has been neutralized."

"Don't come any closer," commanded a soldier standing next to the glass cube, not lowering his weapon. "Our orders state that the fugitives are not to pass this checkpoint. Why did you bring them up here?"

"The cells have been compromised," the soldier carrying the dark-haired prisoner said. "The lower level is no longer suitable for holding the prisoners."

"That information doesn't match ours," said one of the soldiers standing beside the elevator doors.

The soldier carrying the dark-haired prisoner kept walking. "Then recheck with command. I'm prepping the hostages for transport."

"I said no closer!" repeated the one near the cube.

"Well," Six muttered under his breath, "it was worth a try." He threw the orange-clad soldier at the one who'd just spoken and stepped backward, cracking his fist down onto the helmet of one of the door guards. He lunged forward, driving a solid uppercut into the ribs of the other guard beside the elevator, then he ducked. A Syncal dart cracked against the steel doors where his head had been and clinked uselessly against the ground. Six curled into a ball, exposing as little surface area as possible — Kyntak would take care of the threat.

Kyntak did. He'd just finished wrestling two stunned troops to the ground when his head turned to face the sound of a tranq gun firing. Six watched him fly forward, energized by the transfusions, the rations, and the accelerant, slamming his left foot against the soldier's right shoulder. The AM-92 went flying, and Kyntak pushed the soldier over backward with his palm.

Six stood up again. That was six soldiers down, ten to go. He scooped up the AM-92 as he ran to the opposite side of the warehouse. One of the commandos was yelling into his helmet mike, "We need reinforcements at the Basement Two checkpoint," when Six shot him. The Syncal dart zipped through the air, visible to Six's accelerant-charged eyes, and slipped into the flesh under the soldier's chin. He dropped like a stone.

A dart was fired somewhere to his right — he spun to face the sound, ducking at the same time. The shot had been fired at Kyntak, not him, and Kyntak had dodged it, but there was a second guard taking aim. Six was about to charge forward to help when a gun butt hit him in the back of the head. He collapsed forward in surprise, dropping the tranq gun. The shock of the impact reverberated around the inside of his helmet. His vision swam and his ears hissed as he tumbled towards the floor.

As soon as his palms hit the concrete he kicked his legs backward, but it was a blind strike and his feet didn't connect. Trying to predict the actions of the soldier who'd hit him, he rolled aside — his instincts were good, and a Syncal dart snapped down into the ground where he had just been. Six lay faceup as the soldier readjusted his aim. At Six's heart.

Tough break, Six thought as he pointed his remote at the

soldier and clicked. The soldier fell like a puppet whose strings had snapped, smacking lifelessly down onto the floor.

Six scrambled to his feet, picking up his AM-92 and that of the fallen soldier. Then he aimed them both across the room. He lined up the sights of the first at the soldier Kyntak was currently battling, and of the second at the soldier approaching Kyntak from behind.

Bang! Bang! Both the soldiers fell, and Kyntak looked around, confused. Six waved before turning to face the remaining soldiers.

Three had retreated back into the stairwell, presumably to wake up reinforcements from the barracks, but five stood their ground beside the doorway. Six stepped aside as a dart zipped past, and then fired the AM-92s again. *Bang, bang* — two down. Kyntak was coming out of a dive-roll towards the two troops closest to him, and he landed in a firing crouch, holding out his remote. The soldiers fell limply.

The remaining soldier had dived to one side to avoid Six's shots and was out of Kyntak's range. She aimed at Six as she rose to her feet, her gun arm as steady as a rock, and pulled the trigger.

Six saw the dart coming, but didn't have time to throw himself out of the way. Instead, he reached up and caught it, stopping its flight only centimeters away from his shoulder. Then he threw it back as hard as he could, striking the soldier on the inner shin. She doubled over, half reaching for it, the accelerant in her blood fighting the Syncal for control — then she slumped to the ground.

"I could get used to this 'accelerant' stuff," Kyntak said, flexing his muscles. "Do you think we could take some with us?"

"No," Six said, walking back to the nanomachine factory cube. He picked up two more AM-92s as he went, and hooked them into his belt. "It's bad for you." He looked at his watch — it was 05:51:22. It seemed years ago that he had been raiding a warehouse looking for Nai, but it had been less than twenty-four hours.

"Not as bad for you as getting killed in battle because you were too slow," Kyntak said. "And if we — wait, what are you doing?"

Six was leaning up against the giant cube, trying to push it. He had felt it move a centimeter — which meant it wasn't bolted to the ground. "Moving this to cover the doorway. Shut up and help."

"Earth to Six," Kyntak said. "That doorway is our escape route. It leads to the surface."

"No it doesn't," Six said, grunting as he pushed the cube. It crackled as it slid slowly across the gritty concrete. "It leads to a hundred freshly woken soldiers, who are being pumped up with accelerant as we speak, and who will soon be coming down this stairwell to get us."

"If we block the doorway now, how are we supposed to get out?" Kyntak demanded. "You think they'll just forget we're down here and leave?"

"I have a plan," Six said. "Now, are you going to stand there whining, or are you going to help me push?"

Kyntak braced his arms against the cube. It started to grind steadily across the floor. "This plan," he said. "It had better not involve running, falling, fighting, explosions, or gunfire, because I've had enough of those for one day."

They had barely moved the cube to cover the doorway when Six heard a thumping from the other side. He could dimly make out the silhouettes of Vanish's soldiers pounding their fists against the glass. He had hoped that they would show concern for the safety of the equipment, and would be hesitant to try breaking through it. No such luck. But his second instinct had been correct. Because the glass cube had to be airtight and vacuum-sealed, it was structurally solid and the glass was very thick.

The pounding ceased for a moment. Six saw a muzzle flash and heard the dim report of an Owl being fired at the glass, which didn't break. Good.

Six knew that if he and Kyntak had been able to push the cube all this way, a group of the soldiers would be able to push it back without too much difficulty, and it wouldn't take them long to think of it. He ran over to the giant mechanical spider which had been working on the hollowed-out bus — it was now lying prone across the two remaining wheels, apparently having been shut down when the alert was sounded.

Six hit the power button. A few eyelike lenses clicked sleepily open. He looked at the keypad — the controls seemed reasonably straightforward. He pressed a few keys, and the spider lifted the bus, rotated it so it was the right way up, and put it back down. Six touched four more buttons and the spider extended a long steel claw, pushing the bus across the room towards the cube. It stopped a few meters short, and Six didn't think he'd be able to get the spider to relocate and keep pushing, so he hit the power switch again and ran over to the bus, beckoning to Kyntak.

They pushed it up against the glass cube, adding its weight to the barrier. The thumps on the other side had stopped — Six hoped that the soldiers' next strategy would be pushing rather than something he hadn't foreseen.

"Now what?" Kyntak asked.

Six walked over to an electrical generator and started to unscrew the bolts on one side of it with his Feather knife. A metal plate came free as he pulled, exposing the inner workings. Wires and cords were tangled everywhere — Six ignored them. In moments he had found what he was looking for — a vacuum tube. He pulled it free and rested it on the ground. There was a heavy coil of iron built into the inside wall, which he unscrewed and pulled free.

Six left the vacuum tube and the iron coil on the floor and went over to a bomb-making chamber. First he removed the ChaoPull — a device for sucking air out of a sealed chamber. Then he punched the shatterproof glass, cracking it, and ripped the pane from its rubber seal. He grabbed the lump of grey plastic: C-4, he now realized.

Kyntak gaped. "What are you making? An explosive-powered radio?"

Six was stuffing the C-4 into the vacuum tube. "The soldiers outnumber us — and as long as their nanomachines function, they'll have the edge."

Comprehension dawned in Kyntak's eyes. "You think you can make an electromagnetic pulse bomb out of these scavenged parts. You think that if you set it off, the nanomachines will short out. Not only that, but you think that instead of pumping all of the Syncal, morphine, and accelerant into their systems and therefore either supercharging all the soldiers or killing them — and us, come to think of it — the nanos will become inert, and the accelerant will wear off. Then we'll be able to move the bus and the cube, fight our way through the hundred or so soldiers, and walk out of here alive." He paused. "Is that the plan, more or less?"

Six looked up as he was screwing the iron coil onto the vacuum tube. "You have a problem with that?"

"Heck no," Kyntak said. "With you all the way."

A fuse, Six thought. *I'll need a fuse, and some cover.* He went back to the electrical generator. "For the record, there's more to this plan than just the EMP," he said, pulling out wires. "We're going to create a distraction to draw troops away from this floor. I need to radio out before the EMP fries all the transmitters in the building. Does the radio in your helmet work?"

Kyntak pulled it off and tossed it to him. "It's short-range radio — you can't contact the Deck with it."

"Watch me," Six said, fiddling with the frequency and putting the helmet on. He muttered a few words, then took it off and threw it back. "This is what I want you to say."

The mobile phone groaned, vibrating its way slowly across the QS's desk. She hit SAVE on her computer menu and picked the phone up, staring at the screen.

Caller: unknown.

That was unusual — unprecedented, even. This was her personal cell phone. She kept her work and personal life completely separate. That way she didn't need to surround herself with security at home. Only her husband and his daughter had this number, and neither of them had blocked their caller ID. More to the point, the phone was rigged with a descrambler that should theoretically reveal the identity of the caller even if he or she had blocked it. Whoever was calling her had more sophisticated encryption than her decryption, which she had thought would be impossible.

That rules out a wrong number, she thought. *And it probably means that the cell phone won't be able to record the call.*

She wanted to see who it was; in fact, she needed to. This marked a security breach, and one that couldn't be investigated unless she answered. But she wanted the conversation recorded.

She had a minidisk recorder in her desk. She slipped the mike into a groove she'd cut into the phone. It should record the actual sound rather than the signal. It would be good enough.

"Who am I speaking to?"

"The Joker," came the whisper. "Authorization code one seven one two one nine seven five. You can confirm that with any of the Queens and Kings of Hearts and Diamonds, but I'll change it very soon. I needn't tell you that I wouldn't be calling you except under dire circumstances."

That can't really be one of the Jokers, she thought. *What "dire circumstances" could there be? But no good will come of contradicting him — keep him talking. Collect info.*

"How did you get this number?" she demanded.

"I've tracked down harder things than that. You don't believe me — I would expect no less until you've confirmed the code. But do it later. I have information for you."

"What kind of information?"

"An agent and an employee will soon be in need of immediate evacuation from a hot zone. Agent Six of Hearts and Kyntak."

The QS gripped the side of her desk. "Where?"

"A warehouse near an airfield — you'll see the coordinates at http://cww.prog91167/sim23053306.ds."

"What do you mean, *hot zone?*" the QS asked. "What kind of hostiles, and how many?"

"Private army, at least two hundred strong, probably heavily armed, but they'll be disoriented, due to a situation that Six will brief you on later. More soldiers will arrive soon, perhaps as many again, but they're not reinforcements — they'll create confusion and panic."

"Are you going to tell me exactly what is going on?" the QS demanded.

"The decisions are not yours to make — you are to follow my instructions." The voice was even, cold. "Validate the code I gave you. Get as many agents as you can and go to the warehouse, but stay outside the perimeter. When Six and Kyntak come out, evacuate them. Be invisible. Don't get caught in the cross fire. Understand?"

"Will they want to be evacuated?" the QS asked. "My troops have orders to arrest Agent Six of Hearts, and he knows it."

"The evidence against him was fabricated in order to sabotage his investigation. He resisted arrest under my orders. Argue protocol later — you will be needed soon."

The line clicked dead. The QS placed her phone gently on the desk, rubbed her temples for five seconds, and then picked up the landline to dial King of Hearts.

"So if the Deck agents are being invisible," Kyntak said, as he threw the helmet back to Six, "then who's the distraction? Who's going to break in and save us?"

Six had removed a battery from the first fallen gun he had found, and was now pressing the metal nodules against his tongue. A tangy, hot tingling raced across his taste buds, and he withdrew the battery hastily. It was fully charged. Excellent.

He jammed the helmet back onto his head and recited another phone number to Harry as he stuck the ends of the wires into the lump of C-4 inside the vacuum tube and used the ChaoPull to remove the air from it. He beckoned to Kyntak and they left the improvised EMP device on the floor and ran to stand behind the tank.

"I am connecting you to that number now, Agent Six of Hearts," Harry said in Six's radio.

"When the Deck agents arrive, get out of their way," Six told him, "and cloak so no one sees you."

"Seriously," Kyntak said, still waiting for the answer. "Who you gonna call?"

The line clicked, and a voice answered.

"Serfie Thaldurken."

"I know the location of Vanish's base of operations," Six said. "And I know that he's trapped there right now. I got your number from a dossier you wrote about him, and thought that you might be interested."

"Who is this?"

"Your enemy's enemy," said Six. "Listen carefully . . ."

PANIC

Six told Thaldurken most of the things he had learned about Vanish since reading the dossier. Not just the nanomachines and the body switching, but also further details about his past crimes: that Vanish had purchased a bot from Earle Shuji, now destroyed, and that he had broken into the Lab to steal Chelsea Tridya's drug.

He didn't reveal that he himself worked for the Deck, or that he was one of the Project Falcon kids. He also left out the parts about the self-replicating telomeres and the clone in the cell. The last thing he wanted was ChaoSonic abducting the clone and starting its super-soldier project all over again.

He listed the information he knew about the facility and its inhabitants. Thaldurken seemed keen to let him talk — probably so the call could be traced. That didn't bother Six. Even if the trace was better than Harry's shielding mechanism, it would just lead ChaoSonic forces to the facility, which was exactly where he wanted them to be.

"If I were you, I'd get to the facility ASAP," Six finished. "Something tells me Vanish isn't going to be there for much longer." He terminated the call before Thaldurken could say anything else.

Six knew that he and Kyntak could never fight their way out

through so many Vanish commandos. And there was nowhere to hide, which ruled out his usual strategy. So the plan was to give those troops bigger problems to worry about. If the base was being attacked by ChaoSonic forces, hopefully the two of them could get out during the confusion.

The battery was in his left hand and the wires leading to the vacuum tube filled with C-4 were clenched in his right. He peered out around the edge of the tank, looking at the tube on the floor, and trying to calculate which direction it would fly off in when the plastic explosive inside detonated. *Impossible to tell*, he thought — *it's completely sealed. I hope it doesn't crack. That will fragment the pulse and make it useless.*

A large enough EMP would short out any electronic device switched on within its blast radius. Six hoped it would kill the nanomachines. But even if it didn't, it would shut down all the remote controls. That would be almost as good. Vanish's soldiers would no longer have the advantage.

"Are you ready?" he asked Kyntak.

Kyntak put his fingers in his ears. "Why do I get the feeling that this is going to hurt?"

"Here goes nothing," Six said. He jammed the wires against the nodule on the battery.

Nothing happened.

Six frowned. What had he done wrong? The battery was charged, the wires were embedded in the C-4, no air was in the tube, the coil was firmly attached. Why hadn't the EMP gone off? He tapped the wires against the battery a few more times.

"Six," Kyntak said, pointing at the battery, "that side's positive; the other side's negative."

Six grudgingly turned the battery over and held the wires near the correct nodule.

"Where would you be without me?" Kyntak asked smugly.

Six touched the wires to the metal.

With a noise like a giant champagne cork being popped, the vacuum tube exploded upward, slamming into the roof of the warehouse. The wires burst out the end, cracking backward towards Six and Kyntak like a burning bullwhip. They both spasmed as the EMP fried the microscopic circuits in their nanomachines, blasting throbs of electricity through their arteries.

The vacuum tube clanked to the ground and the burning wires twisted slowly down through the air like streamers at a party.

Kyntak raised an eyebrow. "Okay, that was pretty cool."

Six picked up the remote and reattached the battery. He pointed it at himself and clicked ACCELERANT.

Nothing happened. He waved a hand in front of his face and it appeared to move at normal speed. He pointed the remote at Kyntak and pushed SYNCAL.

"Hey!" Kyntak yelled, snatching it away from Six. He didn't fall asleep, and it looked like his limbs were responding normally.

"Well, it worked on us," Six said, dropping the remote. "Now let's just hope it worked on the guys outside."

Six walked over to the glass cube, sandwiched between the doorway and the bus. He could no longer see the silhouettes on the other side; either the soldiers had given up and gone away or, more likely, they were momentarily stunned by the EMP. From now on they would be functioning without accelerant, morphine, or locators. He and Kyntak might make it out alive after all.

Kyntak was approaching behind him. "Well done for making it this far, but there's one part of your insane plan I still don't quite get. Why'd you call the psychoanalyst? Isn't the presence of

ChaoSonic soldiers going to make it harder for us to walk out of here, rather than easier?"

Six turned to survey the room again. His eyes settled on the almost-finished tank. "Who said anything about walking?" he asked.

The controls were nothing like those of a car. Six didn't know what the cabin of a tank was supposed to look like, but the interior seemed new. Vanish had probably designed his own control mechanism. There were two levers with a wheel in between, and Six had spent almost a full minute trying to move the tank using the wheel before realizing that it was probably designed to aim the gun, which hadn't been completely built yet. After that it only took him a moment to establish that the two levers controlled the treads on either side. He could make the tank roll forward by pushing them both and backward by pulling them, and he could rotate the tank on the spot by pulling one and pushing the other.

This seemed to be the first time the tank had been switched on, which made sense given that it was incomplete. The EMP hadn't busted any of its circuits, but the downside was that Six had no idea which functions would work and which wouldn't. The missing gun wasn't the only handicap. The interior had no seats, so Six had to operate the controls standing up. There was no lock on the inside of the roof hatch. If someone outside wanted to open it, all they would have to do was pull. The screen for observing the outside world wasn't connected to any digi-cams, so Six had to make do with the narrow view through the dark strip of bulletproof glass that circled the cabin. Kyntak was providing additional surveillance — he was currently testing a pull-down periscope he'd found.

But it was still a tank — and Six was confident that it could take them out.

They had pushed the bus out of the way. Now only the nanomachine-manufacturing cube stood between them and the stairwell. They had decided not to move it — pushing it aside would leave a gap wide enough for soldiers to pour through long before it was wide enough to drive the tank past. Besides, the cube was made of glass — thick enough to repel bullets, but not to stop a tank. And ChaoSonic soldiers would be arriving any second — Six knew that the nanotechnology was not much safer in ChaoSonic hands than in Vanish's.

"Ready?" he called to Kyntak. He could feel the engine growling beneath his feet.

"Ready," Kyntak said. He gripped the sides of the periscope with both hands — the closest thing possible to bracing himself in the seatless cabin.

Six threw both levers ahead, and the front of the tank lifted slightly off the concrete as the treads spun into motion. Six braced his feet against the floor as he leaned forward, making sure that the momentum didn't throw him over backward or weaken his grip on the levers. Dust and grit exploded out from under the tank as it thundered towards the glass cube. Six watched it rush up to the nose of the tank through the darkened glass.

The wall of the cube didn't shatter; it cracked into jagged splinters, and the tank bounced slightly backward. Six was hurled against the controls, and he used the extra momentum to push the levers as hard as he could. The treads kept whirring underneath the tank, and it shoved against the glass, bending the fragments inward with an earsplitting creak. Soon they were crumbling to the floor and the tank crushed them under the treads.

"Are you okay?" Six yelled back as he plowed the tank through the matrix of machinery inside the cube and slammed it against the opposite panel of glass.

"I'm fine," Kyntak shouted. "Keep going!"

Through the web of cracks in the remaining pane, Six saw the soldiers raising their guns as they retreated. Sparks exploded out from the nose of the tank as it scraped against the shuddering glass.

The drive through the first panel had taken away too much momentum. Six pulled both levers back, and the treads shrieked as they changed direction. The tank rolled backward until it was half-outside the cube, spitting shreds of machinery from underneath as it went.

The soldiers were apparently smart enough to realize that Six and Kyntak weren't giving in — the tank was taking a run-up. They started to flee up the concrete stairs. Six threw the levers forward, the giant motor roared beneath him, and the tank thundered across the debris-strewn floor.

This time the glass did shatter. Huge blades of it exploded out into the stairwell, and the tank smashed through, knocking out chunks from the sides of the doorway as it went. Bullets crashed against the steel roof, fired by the soldiers on the flight above. Kyntak left the periscope and stumbled across the cabin to the hatch, where he employed all his weight to keep it firmly closed. *Good instinct*, Six thought as the gunfire stopped and he heard boots land on the roof of the tank. *They know they can't penetrate it with weapons, so now they'll try to board us.*

"What are you waiting for?" Kyntak demanded, dragging the hatch down as hostile fingers pried at it from above. "Let's go!"

Six slammed the levers against the panel, and the tank

lurched on towards the staircase. He heard stumbling from above as the soldiers on the roof lost their balance. "Hang on," he yelled back to Kyntak as the treads reached the steps.

The whole cabin lurched as the tank mounted the concrete stairs, treads clanking as they fought for grip. Six heard panicked screams as the soldiers who'd been trying to pull open the hatch flew backward off the roof. The first step crunched when the weight of the tank cracked it, but there was more concrete underneath; the stairs were climbable. Six crouched with his knees bent, the balls of his feet pressed against the lopsided floor of the cabin as if he were waiting for the starter pistol. His knuckles were white around the control levers.

The staircase was huge, but only just wide enough for the tank. Sparks flew off the stairwell wall as the armored shell scraped past. The tank ground its way to the top of the flight of stairs, and Six heard bullets ricocheting off the hull once again. He ignored them — he was headed for the wall. *Turn left!*

He pulled the left lever back, but kept the right as far forward as it could go — the tank spun left with surprising agility, turning towards the next flight of stairs. The right treads mounted the wall and tilted the cabin sideways — Six pulled the left lever back even farther, making the left treads roll backward. The ground shivered as the tank smacked down onto the landing with a thud.

The motor growled in anticipation as Six rotated the tank to face the next flight. The bullets rained down from above and starbursts of sparks fizzed near the window. Wasting no time, Six pushed the levers against their hinges again, and the tank thundered up the second flight of stairs, cement dust shooting out from under it as it went.

Six thought back to his original journey down these stairs. There had been four flights. The tank lurched as it reached the second landing — two to go.

Kyntak was looking into the periscope. Suddenly he staggered backward and grabbed the hatch again. "Six," he roared. "Incoming!"

A pair of boots landed on the roof, and footsteps clanked above Six's head. He pulled the right lever back and thrust the left one forward, spinning the tank to the right, and then pulled them both back, reversing into the wall. The cabin shook and the concrete gave way with a crack; Six heard the thumps as the soldier stumbled backward and hit the wall. He shoved both levers forward again, and the tank climbed the third flight of stairs.

A trench was splintering its way up the wall. The stairwell was crumbling. Sturdy though the steps were, they had been designed to carry people, not tanks. Six kept the treads spinning as fast as they would go, and the tank bounced upward as the concrete cracked beneath it. It mounted the third landing, and Six turned it around again. He couldn't see the last landing and the doorway through the narrow window, but he knew the soldiers must be on it. The hail of bullets chipping the nose of the tank had intensified.

Why haven't they retreated through the door to the barracks? he wondered. That could be much more easily defended than this last landing, and they'd be closer to the armory. Without heavier artillery they had no hope of stopping the tank.

But if they didn't want to retreat to a more easily defended location, that wasn't his problem. He jammed the levers forward, and the tank clambered up the first few steps of the last flight.

An ominous creaking noise reached Six's ears, muffled by

the tank's thick shell. He saw the stairs shudder, and a chunk of concrete snapped off the side of the stairs and tumbled down into the dusty darkness. Six's instinct was to reverse — this flight of stairs wasn't solid — but he knew their best chance was to drive up it quickly, before it had a chance to collapse completely. If he drove the tank back to the third landing, the stairs might crumble anyway, leaving them trapped there.

The bullets stopped hitting the nose, and now that the tank was facing upward Six saw that the soldiers were ducking for cover as they raced through the doorway. They didn't want to be in the stairwell when it fell to pieces under the strain.

Six gritted his teeth as he held the levers as far forward as they would go, pressing them against their hinges — he actually felt the steel bend slightly under the pressure. Chunks of the concrete wall rained down upon the roof of the tank, some small enough that they merely bounced down into the stairwell, and some so large that Six felt the cabin shake as they hit. The treads squealed as they scraped against the stairs, the motor howled as gravity dragged the tank backward, and the concrete boomed like thunder as it splintered under the tank's weight.

Six kept pushing. They had almost reached the landing. The treads were about to touch it. Almost . . . there . . .

The flight of stairs snapped off the landing completely and plummeted down into the gloom. The tank remained, half on the landing, half hanging out into open space, the treads skidding uselessly against the ground. Six eased the levers back slightly and the treads caught. The tank rolled forward, away from the precipice, coming to rest a few meters away from the stairwell doorway.

Six exhaled a deep breath that he hadn't realized he'd been holding. "You all right?" he called.

Kyntak appeared by his side. "Sure. That was the coolest thing ever!"

Six grimaced. No matter how many near-death experiences they went through, Kyntak never seemed to take things seriously. But then he remembered the look of despair in Kyntak's eyes when he had first been resuscitated, when he'd thought that they were both doomed. He hadn't been talking about how cool it all was then. It was impressive that he'd bounced back so quickly . . .

And suddenly Six realized something about Kyntak that he should have already known. His smiles were convincing, but they weren't real. Like Six, Kyntak had been in constant pain since his awakening sixteen years ago and, like Six, he had hidden it from everyone else. But while Six had done it by limiting his social interactions, Kyntak had done it by forcing them — creating a happy image that would conceal his misery at a distance, as a mirage conceals hot, dry sand. His jokes were a shield, a last line of defense against the grim world outside and the sadness within, a brave face to put on his numerous troubles.

Six understood now. He had been doing the same thing. These days, when people asked how he was, he said, "Good, thanks, how are you?" Kyntak had been doing it for much longer. He'd been forcing his smiles for so long that they seemed completely genuine — perhaps even to himself.

Kyntak hadn't bounced back from the despair he'd felt two floors below. He'd simply re-created the illusion of contentment.

"You know what?" Six said.

Kyntak looked at him.

Six grinned. "That *was* pretty cool."

Kyntak laughed and slapped a hand against Six's shoulder. Six smiled.

But they'd wasted enough time. The next part of their escape was going to be the most dangerous. "We have to get out of the tank now," Six said, stepping towards the hatch.

Kyntak raised an eyebrow. "Why?"

Six pointed through the dark window. "The doorway isn't wide enough," he said.

Kyntak stared at Six. "We're driving a tank, Six, not a golf cart. If the doorway isn't wide enough, we'll make it wide enough." He reached over to the levers and threw them both forward.

Six grabbed the handles on the periscope as the tank powered across the landing. The cabin shook, and Six was wrenched forward as the nose smashed into the doorway. Through the glass he saw concrete shatter outward as chunks of the wall were crunched into dust under the treads.

The tank rolled out of the stairwell into the barracks. But the room didn't look at all like when Six had seen it last — it was a war zone.

Most of the bunks in the middle of the room still stood, although the mattresses had been shredded by gunfire. But the ones near the stairs had all been overturned to make cover; Vanish's soldiers were crouched behind them, firing single shots from their Owls over the top. Their Eagles lay discarded on the floor. Six's earlier sabotage had made them useless.

The soldiers weren't firing at the tank, although they scrambled away from its path as it thundered out of the stairwell. They were firing in the opposite direction, towards the armory. And as Six swung the periscope around and put his eyes to the viewer, he saw why.

The ChaoSonic troops had arrived. Cockroaches had toppled bunks to make their own barricade at the opposite end of the barracks. They were blasting bullets right back at Vanish's soldiers.

There were only two dozen troops there, fighting more than fifty Vanish soldiers. But as Six watched, another eight cockroaches ran through the armory to join the ranks, having taken the elevator down. There was an explosion up above, and Six tilted the periscope, watching as a square chunk of the ceiling fell, crushing three bunks into twisted metal debris, and crashed to the floor. More ChaoSonic troopers emerged through the hole in the ceiling, abseiling rapidly towards the floor and firing as they came. Within seconds another five troops were on the ground, knocking over more bunks to make firing positions, and plenty more were raining down from the ceiling.

Six looked at the scene with horror. The concrete floor was already littered with fallen soldiers from both sides, some writhing in agony as they pressed their hands against their wounds, some slumped lifelessly on the floor. Six hoped that they were merely unconscious rather than dead. He watched as a Vanish soldier clamped one hand around a gunshot wound on his arm to stop the bleeding and used the other to repeatedly press the MORPHINE button on his remote. It was useless.

We caused this, Six thought, guilt squeezing his stomach painfully. *I caused this. This is my fault.*

"Six," Kyntak yelled. "We have to go, and I don't know how to drive this thing."

Six nodded grimly. If nothing else, the presence of a tank in their midst would distract the soldiers from killing one another for a while. He shoved the levers.

The treads spun to life again, and Vanish soldiers ran aside as the tank plowed through their ranks, grinding their makeshift barriers into the floor. The ChaoSonic troops opened fire with their Crow KOT45s, and Six flinched instinctively as the bullets slammed into the hull of the tank, sparking harmlessly off it and the glass. He kept the pressure on the levers. Row after row of bunks toppled over as the tank slammed through them.

Vanish's side had been panicked by the loss of their nanomachines and radios. The cockroaches had no such hindrance. Instead of scampering aside, they retreated slowly, facing the tank, concentrating their fire on the windows. Six doubted that they would have much luck. If the windows could be broken by bullets he would have seen signs by now.

The tank kept rolling forward, and the soldiers kept retreating backward towards the armory. Now the tank had passed the halfway mark — the troops abseiling down from the ceiling were behind it. But they weren't retreating, Six saw as he stared through the back window. They were following the tank, step after smooth, swift step, Crows raised.

"Hit the deck!" Kyntak roared. Six looked through the front windows long enough to see a PGC387 grenade spinning through the air towards the tank. He ducked and dived, hitting the floor of the cabin with a graceless thump that was lost beneath the sound of the treads pounding the floor.

The throw had been accurate and well timed. Six heard the tap of the grenade clipping the window only a split second before it detonated, smashing the thick glass into thousands of deadly slivers. The light burst through the cabin, which rocked as the explosion pushed the tank backward. Six wrapped his arms over his head and kept his eyes shut, face pressed against the floor. The sound of the treads squealing as they scraped backward over the concrete was almost masked by the shrieking din of the explosion.

Six scrambled up from the floor, ears ringing. He checked himself for injuries — he was clean. The control panel had shielded him from most of the blast and the flying glass. "Kyntak! Are you all right?"

Kyntak was at the far end of the cabin, apparently having been blown back by the force of the blast. He climbed to his feet, and Six saw that his hands were bleeding. "I'm fine," he yelled. "Just cuts and bruises. Keep going!"

Six pushed the levers, wincing as the still-hot metal singed his palms. The ChaoSonic troops kept retreating, but now they were all aiming at the windows. Six tried to draw one of his AM-92s, but it was caught in his belt and he was too slow. "Incoming," he yelled back to Kyntak as he ducked down, keeping his hands on the levers.

A storm of bullets sprayed through the window into the cabin, most hitting the roof and ricocheting down. Kyntak crawled forward across the floor towards Six, who was shielded by the control panel.

The firing stopped for a moment, and Six had a pretty good idea why. He rose to his feet, drawing the AM-92 in one smooth motion and pointing it out the window. He was right. There was a soldier about to throw a second grenade. Six pulled the trigger. The dart hit the soldier in the shoulder, and his throwing arm flopped as he lost consciousness. The grenade bounced half the distance between him and the tank. The other cockroaches dived for cover as the grenade hit the floor.

Boom! Concrete dust spurted up towards the ceiling and the blast carved a deep trench into the floor. The explosion only slowed the tank down this time, and it rolled forward slowly before toppling into the blast crater. Six jammed the levers forward, but the nose was stuck against the other side of the trench, and so the treads ground uselessly against the rubble.

Six heard the thunk of boots on the roof and turned to see soldiers clambering up across the rear window. The cockroaches who had abseiled down from the ceiling and followed the tank were making their move now that it was stuck. They were boarding.

Six swung the gun alignment wheel, and the turret on top of the tank spun wildly. One soldier lost his balance and tumbled off the top. The other howled with pain as the half-finished gun stump slammed into his hip, knocking him down onto the concrete. Six heard the clumping of footsteps above. More were coming.

"Kyntak!" he yelled, but Kyntak moved too slowly. The hatch was torn open from above, and a grenade fell through.

It bounced on the floor of the cabin. The stomping across the roof indicated the hasty retreat of the soldiers. Six scanned the cabin for possible exits. If they were still inside when the grenade went off, they'd be vaporized.

The grenade bounced a second time. The only exits were the hatch and the smashed window. The hatch would take too long — they had perhaps two seconds before detonation. He turned to the window — and recoiled in horror. The last explosion had not only deepened the trench — it had breached right through the floor! There was a gaping chasm through which Six could see the shattered remains of the glass cube, the hollowed-out bus, and the unconscious soldiers on the floor below. They were lucky the tank hadn't already fallen through the hole. And if they tried to climb out that way, they would both fall to their deaths.

The grenade drifted downward through the air, ready to bounce a third and final time — and Kyntak caught it. Six watched him throw it back up into the air, through the hatch, and then reach up and pull the hatch closed behind it.

He only had to pull it halfway — the explosion slammed it closed with a metallic *clank*. The muffled boom was like a thunderclap, and the cabin shook wildly, stirring up the dust from the floor.

Kyntak grinned smugly. *Why didn't you think of that?* his expression asked.

Six turned to the controls again. There was still no way to cross the hole in the floor. He doubted the tank could drive at a fast enough speed to jump the gap, and if he tried, it would either get stuck or fall right through. And suddenly he realized that this had been the reason the last few grenades had been thrown — to trap the tank on the other side of the gorge, forcing him and Kyntak either to retreat or to get out of the tank and continue on foot.

He pulled both the levers back and the tank rolled out of the trench. He drove it backward about twenty meters and stopped. He looked at the hole, at the soldiers behind them, and at the controls.

Then things suddenly got a whole lot worse. Two ChaoSonic soldiers marched forward out of the armory carrying a giant square cannon — an EMU D-38. Six gaped. He'd only seen an EMU once before in his life, in a secret ChaoSonic weapons bunker — and he'd never seen one in action. But he knew of its destructive capabilities — it fired thirty-millimeter depleted uranium bullets at a rate of ninety per minute.

The tank could shrug off rounds from Crow KOT45s as if they were spitballs. An EMU would tear it to pieces.

"Six," Kyntak said, moving away from the window.

"I know!" He pulled the levers back, and the tank rolled back towards the barricade Vanish's soldiers had made. They were by far the lesser threat now.

"Six!" There was an urgency in Kyntak's voice.

"I know!" There was no cover. Nothing for them to hide behind. The hull of the tank was thick steel, reinforced with tungsten, and therefore the toughest surface in the room by far, but the EMU bullets would tear through it as if it were paper. Their best chance was to either back up to the stairwell they had just emerged from and hope the gunners weren't expert marksmen — or to get out and run . . .

"No, behind us!" Kyntak insisted. Six turned, and his jaw dropped. Silver eyes stared impassively at him through the back window.

"Harry?" Six said, although he doubted that the robot could hear him.

The cabin lurched up at a crazy angle, and suddenly the front window was facing the ceiling. Looking out the back, Six found himself staring at Harry's torso and upper arms.

"He's lifting the tank!" Kyntak shouted.

"I can see that!" Six yelled as he grabbed the control panel for support. "Why?"

Harry staggered forward, one slow step at a time — Six heard the synthetic legs groan under the strain. Earle Shuji had told Six that the bot could lift weights of up to one ton — surely the tank must weigh more than that? Then Six saw the smoke from Harry's exhaust valve. His jet pack was on. He wasn't flying, but he was removing some of the strain from his legs — probably at least a hundred kilograms' worth, Six thought.

The floor shook with each step Harry took. For a moment Six thought it couldn't be Harry after all. Harry was instructed to protect his owner, and moving Six closer to the EMU didn't seem to fit with that.

Thump. Six's second thought was that Harry didn't know he was inside the tank — but he had seen Six through the window. So why would . . .

"Grab hold of something," Six called to Kyntak suddenly. "He's going to throw us over the gap!"

Kyntak immediately gripped the periscope handles. Six grabbed the wheel that controlled the half-made gun. The cockroaches had apparently worked out what was happening before he had — bullets were already pinging off the tank's underbelly in thousands. Harry's footsteps kept a steady pace. Through the window Six saw a few rounds hit Harry's torso — they chipped away the plastic skin to reveal the steel abdomen.

Six heard an electronic bleep — the EMU was loaded and ready to go.

"Kyntak!" he roared. "Take cov —"

The rest of the warning was lost as the EMU opened fire. Bullets punched through the underside of the tank and kept enough momentum to rip through the ceiling. Six held on to the wheel with one arm and curled the rest of his body into a ball. Kyntak did the same with the periscope.

Most of the EMU bullets hit the rear end of the tank, which was closer to the ground — Six suspected that this was no accident. The gunners expected him and Kyntak to have tumbled down to that end as Harry lifted the tank. They didn't know that they were hanging from objects closer to the front.

The storm of bullets stopped. Six heard another bleep — presumably the EMU was out of ammo. This was only a minute's reprieve — if they were prepared to expend an entire magazine that quickly, they probably had plenty to spare.

Thump. Thump. Harry kept walking. Six guessed that they had almost reached the hole in the ground, but it was hard to tell with one window at the ceiling and the other at the floor.

Thump. Thump. He was willing to bet that when the EMU fired next, it would be at the middle of the tank's hull — right about where Kyntak was dangling from the periscope. The same thing had obviously occurred to Kyntak — Six could see the panic dancing in his eyes.

Six stretched a hand down and hung as low as he could from the wheel. Kyntak executed a one-armed chin-up on the periscope handle and grabbed Six's outstretched arm with his free hand. Six dragged him up to the wheel.

Harry's footsteps stopped. *We're about to get thrown*, Six thought. He hugged the wheel tightly.

A mechanical howl boomed out from Harry's speaker as the robot heaved the tank over the hole. Six was suddenly weightless, and he bumped into Kyntak as they flew through the air. He guessed that they probably wouldn't be going very high — Harry had struggled to lift the tank, let alone throw it. He watched the warehouse spin by through the shattered window.

The crash of the treads smacking down onto the concrete floor was deafening. Six was dragged off the wheel by the impact as if he had been kicked in the chest, and his body smacked down painfully onto the floor. His vision sparked and crackled as if he were watching an old movie. The ringing in his ears disoriented him until it was replaced by the sound of the EMU firing.

Six reflexively took cover — but the tank didn't seem to be the target. He looked out the rear window and saw Harry's arm tear off at the shoulder as the depleted uranium bullets shredded it. Another volley stripped the synthetic flesh off his leg — and a single round thudded into the center of his chest, where the heart would be if he were human.

Harry beeped, the same as the robot Six fought earlier had done when its exoskeleton had been pierced. Then the C-4 inside Harry detonated, blasting pieces of circuitry out of the exhaust valve. The electric luster drained from the silver eyes, and Harry hit the ground face-first with a lifeless *clank*.

ESCAPE

"Six," Kyntak said.

Six didn't respond. He stared out the window at Harry's broken body, waiting for him to move. He didn't.

"Six!" Kyntak shouted. "We have to keep moving!"

Six slid to the floor. He heard Kyntak's words, but he wasn't sure how to respond to them. He kept watching Harry, his roommate of eight months, his rescuer a dozen times over, the last of his kind.

Kyntak swore and grabbed the controls of the tank. Six heard him shove the levers forward, but the sound seemed to come from a distance. The left treads spun much faster than the right ones, which had been crippled by the fire from the EMU, and the tank plowed crazily through the bunks of the barracks.

Harry's dead, Six thought. *Two is dead. Methryn Crexe is dead. All the soldiers killed by the sniper in the Timeout are dead. Half the soldiers in this room could be dead by now. Everyone was alive this morning, and now everybody's dead. And we'll be joining them any second . . .*

Overbalanced by the mismatched speeds of the treads, the tank slipped over sideways. Six was thrown backward against the wall; he barely felt the impact. Kyntak screamed as the side of the tank scraped across the concrete floor. The shouts of soldiers could be heard as they were knocked out of the way, and Six made out the noise of a few more shots spitting out of the EMU before it was crushed beneath the sliding tank.

Thump! The cabin shook as the tank collided with something, and then everything was still. Six sat on the wall. Crow and Eagle bullets were still pinging off the hull, but all seemed to be focused on the underbelly of the tank; Six could see the soldiers taking aim through the holes left by the EMU.

Kyntak was opening the hatch. "Get up," he said. "We're nearly out."

Six didn't move. There was no way out. He'd be beaten up and shot at, blown up and thrown off things until the day he died. The upside was that today was probably the day.

"Six," Kyntak said. "The tank has blocked off the entrance to the armory. We have a clear run to the elevator. We can be on the surface in minutes."

Six looked up at him. Kyntak was covered in grit, blood, and broken glass.

"I know you're tired," Kyntak said urgently. "But, *please*, Six, trust me. Do what I tell you and you'll be glad you did later."

Six nodded. He did trust Kyntak. He hadn't always, but he did now. He got to his feet.

"Good," Kyntak said, and he grabbed Six's arm and dragged him through the hatch. The noise of bullets hitting the tank faded as they stepped into the darkness of the armory.

Kyntak was right. The tank had completely blocked the doorway between the armory and the barracks. There was no way for the ChaoSonic or Vanish soldiers to get inside, unless there were more coming down in the elevator at the other end.

Kyntak pulled him through the armory and pushed the button to call the elevator. He handed Six into the shadows beside the racks of helmets. Six slid to the floor again — Kyntak didn't stop him; he just stood on the other side of the corridor. Six sat staring at his hands.

The doors slid open. The elevator was empty.

Kyntak ran towards it. "Come on!"

Six climbed to his feet and followed Kyntak to the elevator. The doors closed behind them. "Is there a button I have to push?" asked Kyntak, scouting around.

Six shook his head. The elevator started moving a second or two later. He glanced up at the surveillance camera — the lens had been smashed, probably by a gun butt. The ChaoSonic soldiers presumably didn't want Vanish to know how many troops were being transported down into the facility.

"Six," Kyntak said. Six turned to face him. "Are you all here?"

"Who?"

"You," Kyntak said. "Do you remember who I am?"

"You're Kyntak," Six said. He remembered Kyntak.

"I'm scared, Six. I've never seen you like this."

The doors slid open. Kyntak peered out into the warehouse; it looked empty to Six. Some corner of his mind told him that the soldiers must all be going in through the abseiling hole now.

They stepped out. "Almost there," Kyntak reassured him. "The Deck agents will —"

"Freeze!"

Six did. Kyntak turned his head quickly from side to side.

"Cockroaches," he hissed. "One on either side, three meters away, one Crow each."

"Put your hands on your head," said a voice on Six's left. He did, and Kyntak followed suit.

"If we duck, will they shoot each other?" Six asked. The question was automatic. The part of his brain used for situational analysis had taken over.

"No," Kyntak replied. "They're not quite parallel."

"Turn to face the elevator," said the soldier on the other side of Kyntak. Six turned, and heard Kyntak do the same.

"On your knees," the soldier said. They both complied.

"I didn't come this far to be shot by a couple of grunts," Kyntak whispered.

"*You* didn't come this far?" Six muttered. "I did all the work."

"Shut up," one of the soldiers said. There was a long silence.

They're deciding whether to execute us or take us prisoner, Six thought. Presumably mouthing the words, or doing one-handed sign language. He breathed deeply, and the City air filled his lungs. Someone had opened the giant warehouse door, so air from the outside was blowing in gently. The polluted fog in it was overpowered by the sweetness of the predawn chill. Six couldn't look at his watch, but he guessed it was probably around 6:00 AM.

It wasn't perfect, as far as last breaths went. But nothing ever was — and maybe it would do.

Six took a moment to remember all the good things in his life. Making King proud of the work he had done. Saving lives in the City, be they good or evil. Watching Nai rise from a crawl to a walk for the first time. Seeing Earle Shuji's remorse, and realizing that people could change. Cheating death a thousand times, because he still had work to do — but maybe now he'd done enough.

That was more or less all of them — Six hadn't often been happy in his life. But those few things were rewards for his suffering, and perhaps now he could finally rest.

He turned his head slightly to meet Kyntak's gaze. Kyntak's eyes were narrow, and his mouth was a hard line. *At last,* Six thought. *My brother has finally grown up.*

Two shots echoed through the night. Six and Kyntak dropped to the floor and lay still.

FLOWN
THE COOP

For a moment, the world was completely still.

"Are you hit?" Kyntak whispered.

"No," Six replied. "What happened?"

They scrambled to their feet. The two cockroaches were lying facedown on the floor. Each had a single bullet wound to the head.

Six stared around the warehouse. It was deserted. The cars sat around the jet, dark and empty. The giant door was open. There was no movement in the night outside.

"The shots were separate," Kyntak said, confused. "They can't have shot each other."

"No," Six agreed. He started searching the bodies of the cockroaches. "It was a sniper."

"Deck agents on the perimeter?" Kyntak said skeptically. "That's a long way."

"No." Six thought about the girl who'd been at the apartment building and followed him to Insomnia. "I think it's my guardian angel."

Kyntak frowned. "What are you talking about?"

"There's a girl who's been following me all day," Six said. "I don't know who she is, or why she's doing it. But she's saved my life a few times."

He pulled a phone out of one of the soldiers' pockets and dialed.

"Who are you calling?" Kyntak asked.

"Queen of Hearts. I need someone to get the clone out before ChaoSonic finds him. The Spades must be almost here, but I can't let them see him or they'll find out about Project Falcon. Queen was outside when they initiated the lockdown, so she can do it."

"How's she going to get to him?"

"Through Vanish's escape tunnel," Six said. "It must come out on the surface, or there would be no point building it."

"Then why don't we go back for the clone?"

"Vanish has got to be here still," Six said. "After escaping from the cell, he wouldn't have left the facility altogether — he figured his soldiers would be able to trap us. And by the time the cockroaches arrived, there would have been no way out. Even if he could get past them somehow, there will still be a line of Spades between him and freedom." He continued searching the warehouse with his eyes. "Queen can get the clone. We have to find Vanish."

Queen answered immediately. "Who is this?"

"It's Six."

"I figured I'd be hearing from you," Queen said. "I just called King. He said Kyntak was kidnapped eight hours ago, you've been missing since seven PM yesterday, the Spades called lockdown and then left, and the Deck's funds have been almost completely depleted somehow. Something about a beacon being used to track ransom money piercing the firewall. Why didn't you tell me what's going on?"

Six's jaw dropped. He remembered Grysat explaining that he had put an irremovable time-activated beacon on the ransom money for Kyntak, which would broadcast the name and password of the account it was in at 6:00 AM — ten minutes ago, he saw, looking at his watch. When Vanish hadn't delivered Kyntak to the Timeout, they had put the money back in the Deck account — and its details had been broadcast instead.

Vanish had been a step ahead of them the whole way. He had known they would bug the money, and he'd used it against them. Now the Deck was broke.

"I'm fine, and Kyntak's fine. I'll explain it all later," Six said. "Right now, all you need to know is everything will be okay if you do what I say."

"I'm listening," she said. Technically she shouldn't have been taking orders from Six. But apparently she had decided to sidestep that rule.

Six told her the coordinates. "It's a warehouse by an airfield. There's a war raging underground, and the Spades will establish a hidden perimeter, which you'll need to avoid. But that shouldn't be too hard — they'll be looking for people trying to get out, not in."

"How do I get inside?"

Six was remembering something. When he'd first arrived at the warehouse, the construction vehicle he'd used as a ramp for his motorcycle had seemed to be in mint condition — but the lights on the dash hadn't worked, implying that the battery was dead.

A car, never used, hand brake on, no battery. Obviously not intended for driving. And the area was otherwise completely featureless and empty.

"I think there's a secret entrance under a vehicle parked outside near the warehouse wall. It should lead you down to a cellblock three levels below the surface. I think it'll be deserted, but be careful."

"Got it," Queen said. Her voice was as calm as ever. "What do I do once I'm in there?"

"There's a clone of me, probably in the sixth cell from the south end. I need you to get him out."

There was a pause. *The one time I've managed to surprise Queen*, Six thought, *and I don't even get to see her face.*

"Okay," she said. "How will I know him? Will he look just like you?"

An image of the clone's frightened face appeared before Six. "No," he said. "He only has one arm and one eye. He doesn't speak English and he might not want to follow you. But you'll be able to overpower him."

"Anything else?"

"Come quickly," Six said. He hung up.

"Six," Kyntak said. "Vanish had a sample of my blood with him when he left."

Six rubbed his hand over his eyes. "So he'll be able to get your DNA from it?"

"Best-case scenario, he uses it to grow another clone," Kyntak said. "Then he uses the clone for whatever he wanted from us. Worst-case scenario, he sells the DNA to ChaoSonic afterward."

"Then finding him is even more important than I thought," Six said. "But there's no way out past the Deck agents on the perimeter, and the airfield is crawling with cockroaches. If I'm right, and the tunnels do lead to an exit under the vehicle outside, he's probably hiding somewhere in this room."

They started moving through the warehouse, peering under the cars and in the tinted windows. *There aren't many places he could be*, Six thought. *If we can't find him in here, we'll have to check outside. But if he's not there either, then we'll have to go down into the tunnels ourselves to search.*

The warehouse suddenly blazed with light, and Six squinted against the reflections from the walls. The headlights of the jet plane had clicked on, and the blades in the engines were starting to turn.

He's in the plane, Six thought. He forced his tired legs into a run, his boots slapping against the concrete. Kyntak was in front, apparently not as exhausted. But the plane was already accelerating at a reckless pace towards the door. They were losing ground.

The plane shot through the door and its left wing almost scraped the asphalt as it wheeled around to face the runway. Six and Kyntak gained on it as it turned — Six could see Kyntak racing towards the left wing as though he intended to jump onto it and run along it until he reached the body of the plane. He remembered seeing Kyntak run across the top of the wall and jump into the helicopter less than eighteen hours ago, and had a sudden horrible feeling that if Kyntak got onto the plane, he would never see him again.

The plane was facing the runway now, and the pilot had turned the engines on full blast. The wheels thundered across the tarmac and the air behind the plane melted into a dark haze.

Kyntak and Six stopped running. Kyntak hung his head and rested his hands on his knees. Six stared as the plane lifted off the ground farther down the runway.

"What do we do now?" Kyntak asked him.

"There's nothing we can do," Six said. "He's gone."

"We can call the Deck," Kyntak said, walking towards him. "They can track the plane on radar."

"Neither the Deck nor ChaoSonic has noticed Vanish using

this airfield before," Six replied. "He must always fly under the radar and have some way of shielding the thermal signals."

They watched the plane. It was now curving around back the way it had come. Six thought for a moment that it was going to attack them, but he knew that made no sense — the plane didn't have weapons. It was just changing course to get to where Vanish wanted to go.

"But he's right there!" Kyntak roared. "Right there!"

"There's nothing we can do, Kyntak," Six said. "He's gone." He stared down at the tarmac under his boots.

Kyntak was rapping his knuckles against his bald skull. "We can follow him. There must be something we can do!"

Six shook his head. "No. He won."

Kyntak stared at Six for a long moment. "What happened to 'there's always a way'?"

"Not this time," Six insisted. "He's gone. It's too late to change that."

"But what about the vial of my blood — our blood — in his pocket? What about when he sells it to ChaoSonic and the City is flooded with super-soldiers? Is it too late to change *that*?"

"What am I supposed to do?" Six was shouting now. "I tried my best and it wasn't good enough. Okay?"

"Think harder!" Kyntak shoved him in the chest. "We can't always win, but we can't just give up! There must be some way we can follow that plane."

Six shoved him back, with force that would have knocked a normal human flat. "Like how? It has a top speed of more than nine hundred kilometers per hour — about nineteen times as fast as I can run."

"Six!" Kyntak bellowed. "We're following that plane, even if I have to pick you up and throw you after it!"

There was a long silence. Six stared at the jet as it finished its curve and started heading back towards the opposite side of the warehouse, flying low, under the radar.

Hope was dawning in Kyntak's eyes. *Yes*, Six thought. *This could actually work!*

"Hammer throw?" he asked.

"Hammer throw," Kyntak confirmed.

We have to hurry, Six thought. *The plane will pass the warehouse in less than a minute.* They both sprinted to the cadmium ladder welded to the side of the building. Six reached it first. He started climbing, slamming his hands and feet against the rungs at a blistering pace. Kyntak jumped on after him as soon as there was room, and the ladder started shaking under their combined weight.

Within seconds they had reached the top. The plane was coming closer; the whining of the engines was already painful. Six ran to the corner of the warehouse roof closest to where the plane would pass if it continued on its current trajectory. He dropped into a push-up position, and Kyntak grabbed his ankles.

"Where did Vanish put the blood sample?" Six yelled over the screaming of the approaching jet.

"In the left front pocket of his trousers," Kyntak shouted. "Are you ready?"

"Ready." Six hoped that Kyntak knew what he was doing; Six weighed sixty-nine kilograms more than the average throwing hammer. And the timing was important. If Kyntak let go too early, Six would be hit head-on by the approaching jet, which would kill him as surely as free-falling a kilometer and landing on concrete. But if Kyntak let go too late, Six would fall short of the plane's tail and plummet to his death on the tarmac. He hoped Vanish didn't pull up. The plane was only about fifteen meters higher than them, but that was about as high as Kyntak would be able to throw him.

Kyntak must have known what was going through Six's mind, but there was no time to stop and reassure him. The air was already vibrating with energy as the plane approached, and the warehouse was illuminated in the headlights.

Kyntak started to pull, and Six pushed himself up into the air with his hands. He watched the warehouse roof zoom past his face as Kyntak completed the first rotation. The blood was already pounding in his ears, having rushed to his head with the centrifugal force. Six's venous valves were excellent at preventing reverse blood flow, but the current pressure on his brain was equivalent to doing a handstand for four hours.

The roof rushed sideways past Six's face again — Kyntak had completed the second rotation. The aluminum surface was farther away now — Six estimated that he was being spun at around Kyntak's shoulder height.

The dizziness was unbearable. Six choked down the bile rising in his throat — vomiting mid-flight would make this already unlikely attempt impossible.

Whoosh. The roof was almost two meters away as Kyntak completed the third spin. Six heard the howling of the approaching engines, and was blinded by the lights . . .

. . . then Kyntak let go.

Six spun out into the void, heart pounding, ears aching, and braced himself for impact. The light from the plane swept out across the tarmac far below; he twisted his head around to get his bearings. He could see Kyntak, distant now, standing on the roof of the warehouse. His legs twisted around in front of him again, and he tried to keep his muscles as limp as possible — too much struggling in midair would change his trajectory, and his best bet was to trust Kyntak's aim.

The roar of the engines seemed to be right in his ear. He spread his arms out to their full span, then bent his legs to absorb the shock of the impact. His body swung smoothly around as the plane rushed up to meet him; its nose swept past his face, seeming to miss him by mere centimeters.

He had microseconds to find a handhold, something on the plane to grab. The jet was forty meters long, and traveling at about seven hundred kilometers per hour, which meant there would be less than 0.3 second between when the nose rushed past Six and when the tail did.

Six shoved an arm out against the body of the plane, hoping to snag an emergency exit. The metal was speeding by so fast that it burned his fingers, and he missed the exit closest to the cockpit. *There should be another one over the wing*, he thought.

Suddenly he was pulled away from the body of the plane. His eyes widened as he realized what was happening. The sheer amount of air being dragged into the engines created a vacuum, and it seemed that he had just been caught in it. He was being sucked into the engine.

Instinct directed Six to put his hands and knees out in front of him to protect his torso — but he knew that that would be no use against the spinning blades. Instead, he stretched his arms and legs out sideways to their full span, spinning through the air like a throwing star.

The engine loomed up in front of him, roaring with deadly energy, dragging him towards the center like a black hole drawing cosmic debris into its event horizon. Six opened his mouth to scream and felt the engine suck the air out of his lungs.

Wham! His wrists and ankles slammed into the curved rim of the engine, jarring every bone in Six's body. He found himself face-to-face with the whirling blades in the engine, sweeping by only centimeters from his eyeballs.

But he wasn't dead. He'd managed to catch the edge of the engine with all four limbs, and so now, in a sense, he was on the plane. Craning his neck back, tilting his head to the side and peering down, Six saw the warehouse and the airfield disappear, replaced by the lights of the City, muffled by the omnipresent fog.

Six had no idea where the plane was headed, but he knew he wouldn't last the whole journey in his current position. Sooner or later his muscles would become fatigued and he'd be dragged into the thrumming blades of the engine. It was taking all his strength to pull away from the suction.

Pushing as hard as he could, he managed to throw his whole body over to one side of the engine, keeping his hands on the rim but leaving his legs flapping in the relative safety of the outside wall. He clung tightly to the edge as the blasting wind tried to tear him off.

Don't look down, he told himself. The plane was flying low to stay under the radar, but if he fell, the height and speed of the plane would still be enough to dash him to pieces.

He shifted his hands up across the rim of the engine, higher and higher, until he was holding the corner where it met the lip of the wing. He could hear faint thuds as the ailerons at the rear of the wing lifted up and down, keeping the plane at a constant altitude and direction.

He dragged his torso over the lip, the wind crushing him against the wing. For a moment he was flying backward without handholds, with only the g-force to keep him against the plane. Then he swung his legs up, grabbed the lip again, and suddenly he was stretched out flat across the wing, with his hands gripping the front edge. *If I had a cape*, he thought, *I'd look like Superman.*

The wind pushing against his face was freezing; it stung his nose and his lips. He started to work his way closer to the body of the airplane, hand over hand. There was an emergency exit above the wing, as he had expected, with a bright red handle on the outside. He hoped that because the plane was flying so low, when he opened the door there wouldn't be a significant drop in cabin pressure and the instruments in the cockpit wouldn't register it.

He had reached the spot where the wing met the body. He couldn't stand up to open the door — the wind would blast him off the plane. Instead, he rose into a crouch, with one palm gripping the wing, and reached out to grab the handle with the other.

He expected it to be stiffer than it was. It turned smoothly, and the door popped open with a hydraulic hiss. The hinge was at the back, so Six had to duck aside as the door swung outward, caught by the wind. He slipped into the plane, pausing just long enough to grab the inner handle on the door and heave it closed.

The inside of the plane was luxuriously furnished. There were hardwood cupboards to one side, with a minibar built in to the paneling underneath them. A soft, synthetic leather sofa stood opposite a giant LCD television screen on the other side. The floor around the sofa and the exit was covered by a soft white carpet; the rest was gleaming dark floorboards. Six heard music wafting out from hidden speakers above his head and was surprised that after a few bars he recognized it — one of Samuel Barber's cello concertos. A painting that hung on the wall was familiar to him too, although he didn't know the artist.

Six knew better than to think that his knowledge of art and music was broad, or to think that Vanish had intentionally filled the plane with things Six would recognize. *It still has its original furnishings*, Six realized. This model of plane was marketed to rich customers, and would have been purchased with this classical MP3 disk in the player and that painting on the wall. Vanish hadn't decorated it with items he liked — it was an emergency escape vehicle, and today might well be the first time he had set foot in it.

There were square seams stretching across some of the uncarpeted floor, and there were four small silver plates next to the corners. Escape hatches, Six guessed. *You open the plate, there'll be some controls, and then you can open the door to a pod that will fall out the bottom of the plane.*

He considered trying to lift one of the plates to test his hypothesis, but decided against it. They could easily be alarmed, and it wasn't relevant right now. He could safely assume that Vanish thought he had escaped, and he was probably in the cockpit rather than one of the escape pods.

Six made his way to the rear of the cabin, where there was a narrow cupboard next to the bathroom. He opened it and discovered dozens of firearms, mostly pistols. Six grabbed an Owl, checked that it was loaded, and shut the cupboard. He turned away to head for the cockpit . . .

. . . and saw Vanish standing in the middle of the cabin, eyes wide.

They both raised their weapons and stood still, guns trained on each other's skulls for a tense moment. Six noticed that Vanish had a remote control in his other hand, but it looked bigger than the ones the soldiers had had.

"How did you get in here?" Vanish demanded, after a stunned silence.

"There's nothing we can't do," Six said. "Drop the gun."

Vanish smiled. "Do you know how dangerous it is to fire a gun on an airplane?"

"When there's no pressure difference outside and inside the cabin?" Six said. "No more dangerous than firing a gun anywhere else. Besides, I never miss." He held the pistol steady. "Drop the gun and you get to live."

Vanish pointed the remote at him, as well as the gun. "Not a chance."

"Sorry," Six said, "but your nanomachines don't work anymore. We fried them with an EMP."

"That's a shame," Vanish said. "They were expensive. But this remote doesn't control nanomachines. It controls the plane."

He pushed a button and Six fell sideways as the cabin lurched around him. He tried to keep his gun trained on Vanish, but it was hard enough just keeping his eyes on him.

He rose into a crouch as the plane righted itself, and steadied the gun on Vanish's head once more. "You haven't thought this through. If you crash the plane, we both die."

"Who said anything about crashing the plane?" Vanish asked. He pushed another button on the remote.

Nothing happened. Six expected Vanish to hit the button again, but instead he advanced slowly towards Six, gun first. Six didn't know what Vanish thought he could achieve once he was within arm's reach, but he wasn't keen on finding out. He backed away at an equal pace.

As his foot reached for floor that wasn't there, Six realized that this was just what Vanish had wanted him to do. He had used the remote control to open the escape hatch behind Six's feet. He tumbled backward into the pit, but reacted quickly, springing off the padded seat in the pod as if it were a miniature trampoline. He whooshed back up through the air and landed on the other side of the hatch, leaving the hole between him and Vanish. He steadied the gun on Vanish's head.

"I'm not going to ask again," Six said grimly.

Vanish pushed a button and the escape hatch closed itself. "If you shoot me, you'll never find the vial of Kyntak's blood."

Six aimed at the left pocket of Vanish's jeans and pulled the trigger. The gunshot was sudden and loud in the enclosed space, but it didn't echo — most of the sound was absorbed by the carpet and the sofa. Vanish hissed through his teeth and stumbled backward, the wounds in his thigh already starting to bleed. Six

could see shards of the broken vial poking through the shredded denim. "I think I just did," he said.

Vanish was half doubled over now, grey-green eyes blazing with malice. "You've damaged my body," he grunted, keeping his pistol trained on Six. "I'll make you pay for that."

"You were lucky," Six said. "Anyone other than me would have shot you in the head. Now drop the gun."

Vanish stared at Six for a long moment. His hands shook with the pain from his leg. *What's he thinking?* Six wondered. *He's wounded now, he can't possibly expect to fight me and win; he's got no leverage, nothing to bargain with.*

Vanish dropped his gun on the floorboards with a clunk. He fell forward onto his hands and knees.

"Slide it over," Six said. He wasn't going to risk approaching while the gun was that close to Vanish's hands.

Vanish put his hands on top of the gun and held it there. Then he slid the gun across the floor. Six put his foot on it, then picked it up and hooked it into his belt.

He stepped forward. Vanish's head was hung low; Six couldn't see his face.

Vanish's hand was inching towards the remote control.

"Hold it right there," Six shouted. But it was too late.

Vanish pushed the button and the plane lurched; Vanish had thrown it into a steep upward climb. Six fell back as the floor tilted beneath him, rolling towards the weapons cupboard and the bathroom. He smacked into the wall and immediately spun aside, dodging the barrage of glasses from the minibar, which exploded against the wall like tiny fireworks.

Six rose to a crouch, one foot on the floor and one on the wall, and jumped out of the way as the couch slid down the cabin towards him. It hit the wall behind Six with a thump, and Six heard the crunch as a beam in its fiberglass skeleton snapped.

He had managed to hold on to the gun, and he pointed it back at where he had last seen Vanish. But Vanish wasn't there any longer. Six started to half walk, half climb across the shuddering dark floorboards. *Where is he?* he thought. Either Vanish had made it into the cockpit, or . . .

As Six got closer, he saw the hatch covering one of the escape pods smoothly folding closed. He dived forward, trying to get to it before it swung completely shut, but he had no chance. The hatch became an impenetrable wall of hardwood-covered steel before his eyes.

The plane leveled out, resuming a constant altitude.

No, Six thought. *No! I've come too far to let him get away now.* He knew better than to try to force the hatch open; escape pods were always airtight and reinforced, much like the black box in a plane. Instead, he tried to pry open the silver panel next to the hatch. No luck. The seam was too fine to get his fingers into.

"For the record, you've done well," Vanish's voice said. Six looked up — Vanish had appeared on the giant television. The proximity of the camera made his looming face swell to fill most of the screen, but Six could just make out the interior of the escape pod surrounding him. In the corner, he could see a keyboard and a monitor — the display read 27 SECONDS TO DISPATCH.

"You shouldn't be disheartened by your failure — I have ninety years more life experience than you."

"Don't celebrate yet," Six said grimly. He put the gun against the floorboards next to the silver panel and pulled the trigger. The bullet punched a hole through the wood. Six dropped the gun and immediately slipped his finger into the hole. It burned his skin. He tugged and the panel cover came free, revealing a narrow screen and a polished black keyboard with a series of commands.

Twenty-four seconds until the pod ejects, Six thought. *Twenty-three.* He searched for the right key, skipping past LOCK, UNLOCK, LAUNCH, CLOSE, and ALARM. The button marked OPEN was on the left. He tapped it twice.

The CPU beneath the keyboard emitted a beep — the text POD LOCKED blinked on the screen. Six hit UNLOCK. The text changed to REMOTE OVERRIDE ACTIVE. He growled, reached down into the panel, grabbed the keyboard, and started pulling.

"I'll have to change bodies soon, thanks to you," continued Vanish. "I'll keep doing it until I can find an immortal one. If you don't want that on your conscience, I have a proposition for you."

The keyboard came free, exposing a tangle of wires. Six checked quickly which colors led to which buttons. Blue led to

UNLOCK. He traced them back to the wall of the pod. *Nineteen seconds*, he counted. *Eighteen.*

"Give me Kyntak," Vanish said. "I'll take his body, and you can work for me. I'm impressed by your ingenuity and range of skills. I could use you on my team."

"Every psychopath I meet offers me a job," Six said as he pulled the wall panel free, exposing a switch marked MANUAL OVERRIDE. *Eleven, ten.* He pulled it, and the CPU beeped again. MANUAL OVERRIDE ACTIVE, the screen said. *Eight, seven.*

He pushed UNLOCK on the keyboard. "I'll tell you the same thing I tell all of them." The screen blinked: POD UNLOCKED.

Five, four. "No way," he said, pushing the OPEN key.

The floorboards folded down as the hatch opened. Six swung his gun up, training it on the interior of the pod.

It was empty.

LOST AND FOUND

Six stared up at the screen and saw that Vanish was still holding the remote control. He must have climbed into a different escape pod and used the remote to open and close the hatch of this one. And Six had taken the bait.

"Think about it, Six," Vanish said. "I'll be watching you." And then the feed cut out as his pod was ejected from the underbelly of the jet. The floor shook a little as the plane's mass was altered.

With a howl of rage, Six smacked his fist down onto the floorboards concealing the hatch. The steel didn't budge beneath the impact. He ran through the options in his mind. He could leave via one of the other escape pods, but they had no sensory apparatus and no controls — it wouldn't help him follow Vanish. And the plane would crash, killing anyone who had the misfortune to be nearby. He could call the Deck instead and ask them to search for the escape pod on the ground nearby, but Six was sure that by the time they found it Vanish would be long gone.

He was beaten, and he knew it.

He punched the floor again. The pain in his knuckles momentarily distracted him from the agony of failure.

"I doubt that will help, Agent Six."

Six whirled around, gun first. He found himself facing the sniper from the Timeout, the girl who'd asked him to dance in Insomnia. There was a gun in a holster at her hip, but she made no move to draw it.

"How did you get on board?" he demanded.

"With less dramatic effect than you," she replied. She looked around the cabin as she spoke, constantly scanning for threats, Six realized. "I stowed away in the bathroom before takeoff."

Now Six was thoroughly confused. "Why?"

"I knew Vanish would get on the plane when he saw he couldn't get past the Deck, and I knew you'd try to follow him."

"Why have you been trailing me?"

"My father's orders," the girl said. "My mission is to protect you."

"Why does he care? Who is he? And who are you?"

"Put the gun away, Six. I could easily kill you before you had the time to pull the trigger."

She looked him in the eye and, in a flash, all the pieces snapped together in Six's head. *Retuni Lerke disappears off the face of the earth. Armed men break in to Kyntak's home and steal the baby. The aging drugs left behind in the Lab go missing. Then a few months later, a superhuman teenage girl surfaces.*

"Nai?" he breathed. "Is that you?"

She ignored the question. "Can you fly a plane?"

Six's brain fought the truth, and he slowly lowered the gun. "Why does Lerke want me protected?"

She pushed past him, walking towards the cockpit. "You're not making my job any easier, Six."

Six followed her through the door as she sat down in the pilot's seat. Hundreds of questions bubbled in his brain, and the least important one surfaced first. "How'd you learn to fly a plane?"

Nai was tapping keys on the NavSearch. "I read the manual while I was hiding in the bathroom. I like to be prepared."

Six almost asked her how she had learned to read, but stopped himself. Various feelings grappled inside him — relief at finding her safe, but confusion at the circumstances, sadness that he'd missed her growing up, and dawning horror that she appeared to be the kind of soldier he himself had narrowly avoided becoming.

"How did you escape from ChaoSonic after they took you from us?" he asked.

"Escape?" She shot him a withering glance. "Those soldiers *rescued* me, under orders from my father. I wasn't safe with you; that event proved it. My father warned me that I have enemies out there. You weren't even training me. If I had grown up with you, I would never have been prepared." The NavSearch bleeped and Nai shifted the thrust levers on the control panel, banking the plane to the right. They were turning around.

"Training you?" Six demanded. "You were two months old!"

"I'm sorry, Six," she said. She sounded sincere. "If Crexe had let our father raise you instead of setting you free, you'd be stronger and smarter. As it is, I doubt you'll live much longer. There are too many people who want you dead."

"Nai," Six said, "Lerke is a madman. He's not your protector. He's the one you need protection from!"

"He said you'd say that," Nai said. She straightened the levers and pushed the thrust up to full blast, sending the plane back the way it had come at more than two hundred kilometers per hour faster than it had originally been traveling. "It hurts him that you're so misguided."

"Listen to me," Six said urgently. "He doesn't see us as people. We're like . . . pets to him."

"He's looked after me," Nai said coldly. "Better than you could. He wants me to be strong."

"He's crazy!"

"He's my father." Anger was creeping into her voice.

"Come back to the Deck with me," Six said. "You'll find you have more friends than you think."

"There's no such thing as a friend," Nai said. "Just people who treat you well because they want something."

"Why do you think Kyntak and I rescued you?"

"Perhaps you thought I could be useful later," Nai said.

The spires of the buildings piercing the fog were thinning; Six realized that they were already approaching the airfield near the warehouse. The dim glow of the sun began to paint the grey-streaked air as it rose above the distant Seawall.

"Why do you think Lerke looked after you?" Six demanded. "Is everyone in the City selfish except him?"

"He's my father," Nai said again. "He loves me."

Six shivered. Lerke had brainwashed her thoroughly, and she clearly wasn't going to be disillusioned quickly. But maybe Six could get her thinking.

"Nai," he said. "There are people out there who will help you not because they want something, but just because they can. I know plenty of those people. I'll be glad to introduce you. I understand if you're not ready for that yet, but please listen to what I have to say."

Nai pushed a lever forward, and the plane began its descent. There was no indication that she was listening. He took a deep breath and continued.

"Just because someone says they know what's best for you doesn't mean they do. And just because you think you can make it on your own doesn't mean you can. And just because you're born a soldier, and raised a soldier, that doesn't mean you have to die as one."

Six sat down in the copilot's seat. "Those three things won't always agree," he admitted. "Sometimes you won't be sure whether to trust someone or question them and, sometimes, it'll be hard to tell whether it's better to fight or walk away. But now you have enough information to make your own choices."

There was a long silence. Nai extended the landing gear and lowered the flaps on the wings.

"That's it," Six said finally. "I'm not going to force you to come with me. But if you ever decide you need a friend, you'll be welcome."

"You couldn't force me to do anything," Nai said, as the wheels touched the runway.

Six sighed. "I know." His words were lost in the roaring of the plane's reverse thrust as it shed its velocity against the tarmac.

Nai taxied the plane back into the warehouse and applied the brakes harder than necessary. Like a flash she was out of her seat, ducking back into the cabin. Six stood up slowly and watched her pull the handle on the emergency exit. It popped open and she stepped out onto the wing. She jumped down to the floor of the warehouse, catlike, as Six climbed out behind her.

"Don't come looking for me," she said, walking away. "This time my orders were to protect you. Next time you might not be so lucky."

"Hey," he said. "Do you know why we named you Nai?"

She stopped and half turned, her dark eyes roaming the warehouse. "No," she said.

"I'll make you a deal," Six said. "Call me sometime, and I'll tell you."

He thought he heard a scuffle behind the plane, but he couldn't see anything. When he turned back, Nai had gone, with no evidence that she had ever been there. For a moment he even thought that perhaps he had dreamed the encounter, and she was still just a baby waiting to be found. But he didn't know how to fly a plane, so she had to have been there, saving his life again.

He jumped down off the wing, landing on the cement with barely a sound. He heard the scuffling noise again, and turned around to see Kyntak emerging from behind one of the cars.

"Who was that?" Kyntak said. "You managed to get yourself a girlfriend while I was kidnapped and out of the picture?"

Six grimaced as he turned around. "She's a murderer," he said. "And she's only eight months old. And she's our sister."

Kyntak stared. "That was Nai?" he demanded.

Six nodded silently.

"But what's happened? She must be — what, fifteen? Sixteen?"

"Retuni Lerke took her, not ChaoSonic," Six said. "I think he loaded her up with Chelsea Tridya's aging formula — I'm not sure why, exactly. Maybe because he needed a new operative or an assassin. She seems to work for him now."

"That's terrible," Kyntak said after a long pause.

"It could be worse," Six said. "She's alive, I guess. And who are we to decide her path?"

"We're the good guys," Kyntak said. "He's a bad guy."

"I almost left you behind," Six said. It came out suddenly, unexpectedly. "So many times today, I thought about giving up. About running."

"But you didn't do it," Kyntak said firmly. "You came through."

"You don't understand," Six whispered. "When you were kidnapped, I thought about running, finding a faraway corner of the City, and hiding there. When the Spades were coming after me, I wanted to give myself up and let them put me in a cell just so I could rest. And when Vanish's plane was taking off, I wanted to let him go so he could be someone else's problem." Six shut his eyes. "I'm not one of the good guys," he finished. "I just do good things."

Kyntak put a hand on his shoulder. "What's the difference?" he asked.

Six didn't reply — he wasn't sure how to. His confession and Kyntak's forgiveness had relieved the weight on his soul. His feelings of guilt were slipping away faster than he could work out how to express them.

"So Vanish got away," Kyntak said. It didn't sound like a question.

Six sighed. "Got into an escape pod, ejected it from the plane. He's wounded, but he could be anywhere by now."

"No," Kyntak said. "He's got no vehicle and no troops, and probably no accommodation. He needs medical treatment, right?"

Six nodded. "Gunshot wound to the thigh. But he's got money. Almost all the Deck's funds plus whatever he accumulated over his century of stolen life."

"Could be a lot if his interest rate is good," Kyntak conceded, "but we know more about him than anyone ever has before, and so does ChaoSonic. The City isn't big enough for him to hide in anymore, not after what he's done to us."

"I'll chip in to replenish the Deck's account," Six said. "I have at least sixty million across a few of my own —"

"Sixty million?" Kyntak gaped. "How did you get that much money?"

"My job pays well, I walk most places, I grow my own food, and I don't buy gifts." Six shrugged. "Look after the pennies and the dollars look after themselves. How much of this facility will ChaoSonic leave intact?"

"They'll probably strip it bare," Kyntak said. "But they won't know about the tunnels underneath it, and with all the weaponry, medical supplies, clothes, electronics, and surveillance equipment down there, we should be able to make another few million, easy."

Six stared into the grey air, watching the fog slowly acquire a crisp whiteness as the early-morning sun touched it. "It doesn't feel right," he said. "We're not supposed to lose."

"We didn't." They started walking out onto the tarmac, heading for the Deck extraction team. "Vanish wanted to do his brain-swap operation and we didn't let him. We just wanted to stay alive, and we have. He lost, not us. We haven't caught him yet, but in a way that's just a formality."

"He offered me a job," Six said. "Why do they always do that?"

"Did you say, 'No, thanks, I know you only want me for my body'?" Kyntak laughed. "I would've said that."

"Did Queen find the clone?" Six asked.

"No," Kyntak said. "The whole cell block was empty. He decided to run after all."

"Good for him," Six said. "I guess. I hope he's okay."

Six could see the Deck extraction team on the other side of the fence now. They were supposed to be hidden, but he knew their training and the likely hiding places. The QS must have lifted the lockdown. He couldn't see her anywhere, but there were numbered Hearts agents lurking in the darkness. He could see King casually walking a dog around the perimeter.

"So we're immortal?" Kyntak said as they walked. "The telomeres . . ."

"No, we can still die," Six said. "We just don't age."

Kyntak grinned. "So I could be the best-looking guy in the City forever."

Six raised an eyebrow. "You wish."

"Oh, you think you're competition? The dark, mysterious look isn't as cool as you think it is."

"Shut up," Six said gruffly.

"I could have you demoted, Agent Six of Hearts."

"Shut up!"

EPILOGUE

Vanish leaned against a concrete pillar in the underground parking lot. He touched his fingers to his thumb one at a time on his right hand, getting used to the feel of the new body. It was always hard, the first couple of days. Hard to use his hands properly, hard to walk gracefully. And talking was difficult enough anyway, without the added complication of having to impersonate his host's voice.

He'd had to move quickly this time. It had been less than a week since the failed plan, and the Project Falcon kids were already drawing closer. He couldn't shake his paranoia that they would find his old body soon. With no employees other than Niskev Pacye, he had been unable to dispose of it as well as he usually would. The former music teacher was floating facedown somewhere in the sewers underneath the City, eyes glazed and skull hollowed out.

It was risky, impersonating a woman so soon after stealing her body. But Vanish had watched video footage of her, listened to phone messages she'd left, read her e-mails, seen pictures of her friends — and tortured her to find out her darkest secrets. It had been rushed, but he was ready.

A dark silhouette appeared at the other end of the parking lot and started walking towards him. Retuni Lerke was wearing a dark grey coat with the collar turned up, a hat tilted forward on his head, and a pair of glasses Vanish knew he didn't need.

"I don't like meeting here," Lerke said as he approached.

"You'll do as I say," Vanish replied. "You tricked me."

"I did no such thing," Lerke protested. "I was —"

"Save it. I gave you a month to prove the abilities of the girl, and you couldn't make the deadline. I know she ruined my plans a few days ago, and I know she did it under your instructions. But your betrayal was also your saving grace."

Lerke met his gaze evenly, but he was terrified. Vanish could hear the faint quivering of his breaths, see the thin film of sweat on his brow. He could smell Lerke's fear.

He leaned in close. "I'm impressed," he said. "I wanted Six of Hearts or Kyntak. But Six saved Kyntak and Nai saved Six. It seems she is the strongest of your creations. So I'm prepared to revisit the old deal. You deliver her to me, along with Tridya's original formula. The one that keeps age at a standstill. Do that, and your sons live."

Lerke nodded. He opened his mouth to speak, but seemed to think better of it. Then apparently his scientific curiosity got the better of him. "Have you ever inhabited a female host before?"

Vanish raised an eyebrow. "No," he said. "But my surgeon said the transplant wasn't much harder." He grabbed Lerke's arm at the bicep and squeezed, enough to cause pain. "You have one month," he said. "And I am deadly serious. One month to deliver the girl to me, or I take Six's body instead. Are we clear?"

"Yes," Lerke grunted, his other arm paralyzed at his side.

Vanish looked at his watch. He had an appointment to keep. He released Lerke and stepped back. "Go," he said.

Lerke turned and walked quickly into the darkness, coat billowing behind him. Vanish watched him leave, making sure that he had disappeared up the ramp and out of the parking lot before turning around himself. It could ruin everything if Lerke was caught hanging around.

Vanish didn't like meeting here any more than Lerke did. But ironically, it was the least suspicious place for him to be.

He turned and headed for the elevator in the corner of the parking lot. His polished shoes scraped the dusty cement floor.

He reached the elevator and pushed the button. It came quickly, and was empty. No one was heading for their car at this time of day. He stepped inside and pushed the button for Floor 6.

The elevator hummed smoothly upward. Vanish watched the light on the display above the doors.

Floor 1, Floor 2, Floor 3 . . .

The elevator stopped at the fourth floor, and three more people got in. They all nodded to Vanish, and one said "Morning" before pushing the button for his floor. Vanish nodded politely back, and looked up at the lights once again. The light representing Floor 5 blinked.

The elevator stopped at Floor 6, and Vanish stepped past the three other passengers. He held up a hand, open-palmed, by way of good-bye — he had seen his host do this in the footage he had studied. The passengers smiled as the doors slid shut.

Vanish's shoes clicked against the linoleum. He reached the office door, opened it with a silver key, and stepped inside, shutting the door behind him. He looked at his watch. Just in time.

He sat down behind the desk and switched on the computer. It requested a password, which he had hacked ahead of time. He should reprogram it so it asked for a fingerprint or DNA sample instead. They were harder to fake, and the owner's fingerprints and DNA were his now.

The buzzer rang; someone was at the door. Vanish smiled.

He knew who it would be. He pushed the button under his desk that unlocked the door.

· It swung open, and Agent Six of Hearts stepped inside. Six forced a smile, showing perfect teeth. *It wouldn't be so bad if Lerke fails*, Vanish thought. *Those teeth would look good on me.*

"Queen of Spades," Six acknowledged with a nod. "Am I under arrest or not?"

"No," Vanish said. "The investigation has concluded that you are innocent of all charges. You're free to go." He smiled. "But I'll be watching you."

ACKNOWLEDGMENTS

Thank you to the Griffiths/Robin family, who read drafts, sent copies of *The Lab* all over the world, and showed up to the launch in Jack Heath T-shirts. Where would I be without you?

Thank you to Caitlin Sherring, who lent her appearance to Earle Shuji; Alex Schinzinger, who inspired Ace; and Brendan Magee, who became the model for the villain of this book. Thanks again to my ever-supportive brother Tom Heath, for giving Agent Six his face and body. All of you, remember that only the good bits are based on you. Honest.

Thank you to my brilliant medical consults, Jessi Thomson and Hansel Goh, and my maths advisor, Tom Heath. Mistakes are mine, not theirs.

Thank you to the following people and their families for lending me a bed, a couch, or a floor while I was traveling: Meg Dale, Toby Holm, Hannah Selmes, Caitlin Sherring (again), Chantelle Suttor, Lara Willis, and Gab Worthington.

Thanks again to the incredible team at Pan Macmillan. They've shown a lot of faith in me, so I'll work hard to earn it. Special thanks to Claire Craig, who encouraged me when my ideas were good and stood up to me when they weren't, and Sue Bobbermein, who held my hand while putting me on millions of screens and radios and pages.

Thank you to the following people who didn't let me become a recluse while working on this book: Sophie Chapman, Alex Detott, Mitchell Goodfellow, Reuben Ingall, Sam McGregor, Laura Pharaoh, Jeremy Quay, Paddy Quiggan, Alex Schinzinger (again), and Seon Williams. Special thanks to Trephina Mackay, who called me every single week to check up on me, and Paul Kopetko, who still makes me laugh after ten years of friendship.

Lastly, a huge thanks to the thousands of people who made *The Lab* a success. Thank you to everyone who bought it, everyone who took the time to tell me how much they enjoyed it, and everyone who recommended it to their friends. Consider this book your reward.